CW00840356

NOMADS

NOMADS

CHARLES BROBST

Copyright © 2019 by Charles Brobst.

Library of Congress Control Number: 2019908005
ISBN: Hardcover   978-1-7960-4141-5
               Softcover   978-1-7960-4140-8
               eBook   978-1-7960-4139-2

All rights reserved. No part of this book may be reproduced or transmitted in any form or by any means, electronic or mechanical, including photocopying, recording, or by any information storage and retrieval system, without permission in writing from the copyright owner.

This is a work of fiction. Names, characters, places and incidents either are the product of the author's imagination or are used fictitiously, and any resemblance to any actual persons, living or dead, events, or locales is entirely coincidental.

Any people depicted in stock imagery provided by Getty Images are models, and such images are being used for illustrative purposes only.
Certain stock imagery © Getty Images.

Print information available on the last page.

Rev. date: 06/18/2019

To order additional copies of this book, contact:
Xlibris
1-888-795-4274
www.Xlibris.com
Orders@Xlibris.com
797370

As Ken came walking across the small grassy area toward the RV trailer that he and his wife, Betty, used as their home, a horned toad scurried back under a flat rock behind the trailer where it lived. Ken had been out walking around on a pretext of hunting. He did this often as a way to keep busy so the dreams wouldn't come back. Sometimes he even shot a rabbit or a sage hen.

Before Ken and Betty Bachman had come here, this was just a hardpan area, just like most of the area around them. The sun was at its zenith, with not a cloud in the blue sky, and it was hot for him compared to the past forty years living in Fairbanks, Alaska, and working as a heavy equipment/diesel engine mechanic on a "two weeks on, two weeks off" shift on the North Slope oil fields in Alaska and the mines in the area. The seventy-five-degree temperature was like an oven to Ken and his wife, and this was winter. What would summer bring? They had retired two years ago and were traveling around the lower forty-eight states with a Dodge 3500 diesel pickup truck that Ken had restored by rebuilding its diesel engine and a thirty-eight-foot fifth-wheel toy-hauler camping trailer. It was unusual since it had four tip-outs instead of the usual three and was as roomy as most small apartments.

In anticipation of his retirement several years ago, Ken signed up for emails from websites called Workcamper and Workers on Wheels. He received weekly emails of businesses that were looking for temporary workers. Most of the jobs were with campgrounds for office workers or groundskeepers who worked twenty hours a week, and for that, they were paid minimum wages, but they were also provided a free camping spot, and some also provided electricity and propane with it. This job was different. It was a guard position at a remote oil well pad where you were required to protect the well and storage tanks from vandalism and pilferage of the crude oil and to notify the company if a problem developed with the operation of the well. This required a guard's license from the state of Texas to do this. A tank truck came by every three or four days and drained the crude oil tank. The well was an old well, but it was still producing enough crude to keep it pumping.

It was Ken's job to make sure the truck was from the company he was working for. The company provided him with a satellite phone since cell phone service was spotty at best. He would receive a call on the satellite phone on the day the truck was to do a pickup with a series of challenge words and reply words from the driver. To keep up with the news and current events, there was a big satellite-dish TV antenna. A large diesel generator provided power for the site and trailer. A fuel truck came by once a week and filled a five-hundred-gallon fuel tank for the generator and, at that time, performed any maintenance needed, but mostly, it was just oil and filter changes that were performed on the generator.

This was the kind of job both Ken and Betty needed for different reasons. For Betty, it was after the past fifteen years working as a welfare case manager in an office being understaffed and overworked. The pressure of trying to balance the needs and wants of people who really needed the help with what was available and managing those who, for the most part, were able to work but who had grown up in the system, they knew how to scam the system, and were ungrateful for the service provided and, at times, rather caustic in their demands. This position in a remote area with limited public contact allowed her to basically unwind from the stress she had in the past years.

Ken was a former army paratrooper who, in April 1968, when he was just eighteen years of age, was deployed with the Eighty-Second Airborne Division to Washington, D.C., to help quell the race riots that had erupted there because of the assassination of Martin Luther King Jr. They were issued live ammunition and tasked with providing security coverage for firemen who were being shot at while trying to extinguish the fires set by the rioters and looters. When tasked with this, their orders were to protect the firemen with deadly force if necessary. His unit also patrolled the streets, helping the police keep the order. On one occasion, his platoon was sent to help quell a riot, rocks and bottles were thrown at them from the windows and roofs of buildings. Several of the bottles were filled with urine, and one was a Molotov cocktail. Fortunately, that one landed harmlessly behind him. This was a very tense time in his unit. Some of the black soldiers didn't like what they were doing and were very vocal about it. Their reasoning was they had un-sheathed fixed bayonets on the end of their rifles when they were breaking up the crowds doing the rioting. There were also rumors that the Black Panther movement was sending young black men into the military to learn combat tactics for later riots. These rumors didn't help with trust in the smaller squad units.

Several months after that, when he turned nineteen years of age, he was sent to Vietnam as a rifleman in an infantry company. Since he was a paratrooper, he was assigned to the 173rd Airborne Brigade. It wasn't long after Ken had gotten to his unit that he was asked to join a long-range reconnaissance patrol team. Upon his return to the States after his required one-year tour, while he was headed home on leave in his class A uniform, he was attacked in the Sea–Tac Airport in Seattle, Washington, by peaceful protesters of the Vietnam War. At home, there were people who went out of their way in support of what he did, but there were also many who let him know that they thought that he was a baby killer and gave him a hard time. It was these, especially the ones he had gone to high school with and thought of as his friends, who had hurt him the most.

After two weeks of this, he went to the recruitment office in a town close by to see if he could cut his leave short, which they told him he could. He then went back to the Eighty-Second Airborne Division at Fort Bragg, North Carolina. He felt more comfortable there with other veterans, and soon after being assigned to his new unit, he learned of a levy for troops to go to Vietnam. At that time, the Eighty-Second was basically a replacement division, with the men either coming from or going back to Vietnam. He went to his personal officer and volunteered to go back to Vietnam. When he got off the Flying Tiger DC-8 at Tan Son Nhut Airfield, the hot fetid air assailed his body and nose it felt like he was putting on an old comfortable coat. He served several more tours in Vietnam because every six months, when he was to rotate home, he would extend his tour to keep from being sent back to the States. He reenlisted for six years while he was in Vietnam. With each extension, it progressively got harder to do his best because of the ungrateful liberal public and the restrictions the liberal American government had placed on the troops when they were fired upon by the Viet Cong. He eventually went over to the army special forces, as many other Vietnam veterans had done, where he completed the ranger course and got his tab.

His screams or cries from the nightmares of what he had seen and done would wake Betty during the night. It seemed that the job at this remote site helped him at times to sleep untroubled through the night, and on those other nights, he could sit outside under the stars and just stare into the night sky and doze off.

At first, Betty had asked Ken about the dreams, but all he would say was "You don't want to know" or "You wouldn't understand," so Betty stopped asking and supported Ken as best she could.

Ken would take his scoped Mossberg 10/22 rifle three or four times a week and go rabbit hunting to supplement the food stock they had. The feel of a rifle in his hands was familiar and almost therapeutic for him. He would go out early in the morning as if he were on patrol once again, looking for sign of a rabbit or a sage hen to shoot for a change in their diet. Sometimes he would try to stalk up as close to them as he possibly could before shooting them, and other times, he would lie in wait with a spotting scope and the scoped 10/22 and shoot them from a distance. They really didn't need this for food since the company they worked for would supply them on a weekly basis with almost anything they wanted. They were given a food budget and a book, more like a catalog, to order from. At first, it took Betty some adjustments and getting used to since if something was forgotten to be ordered, it would take two weeks to get that forgotten item delivered. There was no going to the corner 7-Eleven for a loaf of bread or quart of milk. Betty soon realized if she was frugal and careful with her meals, there were items other than food in the shopping book—as she liked to call it—that she could purchase. As a result of this, Betty had acquired quite a stock of items they were storing in and under the trailer, pressure cookers, canning jars, and lids. One month there was a section on flower and vegetable seeds that she had stocked up with. There even was a section on sporting goods with firearms and ammo.

Ken quickly became friends with one of the fuel truck drivers who came by on a regular weekly schedule. One time, when the fuel truck came by, he asked the driver if he was able to acquire some baby chickens and the necessary supplies for a chicken coop if he provided a list of materials and a check up front for the estimated expenses. A few weeks later, a pickup truck came to their trailer. It was Hulio, the fuel truck driver. His pickup was loaded with two-by-fours, chicken wire, nails, wire staples, chick feed, and all the supplies needed for the one hundred straight-run chicks sitting in boxes on the front seat of the truck plus a book on how to raise chickens. Ken could see there were more supplies than what the check had covered. He asked Hulio about the added expense and offered to pay him the extra expense, but Hulio said he would split the cost for fresh eggs and, when the time came, half the roosters that they would have to cull from the chicks. Ken readily agreed to this arrangement since he figured that half of the one hundred chicks, if they all survived, would be hens, and that meant twenty to thirty eggs a day, more than they could eat.

As the chicks grew into chickens, Ken lost a few to local predators. Hawks got two until he put wire across the top of the pen, and coyotes got three more. Ken would spend the night hidden with his 10/22, and he managed to kill several of the coyotes. He skinned them, and Hulio took the pelts to a person he knew who tanned them. It was a constant job, but he finally got the coyotes under control. It was during this time that Betty ordered some grass seeds, and Ken mixed some of the manure from the chickens in with the hardpan dirt and was able to grow a nice grass patch, which Ken now had to mow, but the grass clippings went into the chicken run, and the chickens would eat and scratch around in the clippings with much gusto. Ken liked to sit and watch the antics of the chickens before he put them into the coop for the night for their protection.

***

Shirley looked like a little gnome as she scurried around the booths and stalls at the flea market. Her quest was canning jars, rings, unused lids, pressure cookers, and other items useful for home canning, such as cast-iron pans and Dutch ovens, plus sewing supplies like buttons, thread, cloth, and needles. She also looked for any items that would make life easier on a remote ranch or homestead. When she found anything she thought she could resell, she was sharper than a tack, dickering with prices, more so than anyone else around the flea market, as she hovered around the booths of vendors while towing a red radio-flyer wagon behind her, piled high with her finds, and while doing so, she would pick up on any gossip from the vendors and pass on what she had heard to the other vendors.

There was a joke among the regulars at the market: "Telephone, telegraph, and tell Shirley." While the other vendors joked about Shirley, they knew that she would check out any strange stories before she passed it on and could be relied on, telling the straight poop. Shirley usually ignored the antique and collectable dealers and only gave a courteous glance at the vendors of new cheap made-in-China merchandise bought at trade shows or on the docks of Long Beach, California. The exception was cast-iron bells with a horse or cattle motif she knew these would be popular with farmers and ranchers, as she zeroed in on the vendors who bought at defaulted storage auctions. These were where she got her best finds and where newly retired seniors were selling items that they had brought with them from the colder Northern states, items that they thought they would need but realized they no longer needed or wanted. These were the ones who usually had what she was looking for—good pressure cookers, canning jars, cabbage shredders, cooking utensils, wine- or beer-making equipment, occasionally a good older cast-iron food mill or grinder, cast-iron pans, and Dutch ovens or sauerkraut crocks—the items that she and her husband could readily sell at the summer markets in Eastern Washington State, Idaho, and Montana.

Since they had retired three years ago, they fell into this by accident. Soon after they had retired, they found a campground in Arizona, and when summer came along with the heat, they would go North, stopping at a few flea markets or auctions along the way, buying and selling their wares. Shirley kept overhearing people asking for certain items when she was at other vendor booths, and she was now buying these items for resale locally. Many of these vendors went back in the summer to their homes in Michigan, Ohio, and the other Northern states, and while there, they went to estate auctions, and knowing what Shirley wanted, they bought items at estate auctions and flea markets to bring South to sell in the winter. Some of these snowbirds made a good side income from this, and since it was all cash, the government and IRS didn't get any of it to waste on its failing, feel-good, social giveaway programs, which many of the retired seniors didn't agree with anyway. Ever since the second immigration amnesty bill and the failure to secure the border with a fence between Mexico and the United States, more and more illegals came into the country, and if you were to believe some of the internet blog sites, not all of them were Mexicans but people from Muslim countries bent on carrying out terroristic acts in the hope of disrupting life in the United States or, with luck, toppling the United States.

Sam, Shirley's husband, came quietly up behind her and kicked the back of her wagon. As she turned around, he started to berate her as a woman driver.

"Where did you get your license from? Walmart?" As a crowd of strangers gathered, expecting a fight, Sam would say, "If you come with me to my camper and cook me a dinner and spend the night with me, I'll forgive you this time."

"But what about my husband?" Shirley would say.

"Don't worry about him. He's busy trying to impress that cute girl lifeguard at the campground pool."

The regulars knew his spiel by now and would get a chuckle out of the shocked faces of the unwitting audience as the drama unfolded, as Sam tried to seduce her.

Shirley was semiretired from being a real-estate agent, and for a long while, she had held a broker's license in Seattle, Washington. During this time, Shirley had many opportunities to be the first person to see the new property listings in the MLS catalog as they came in and soon realized that the real money was not in selling real estate but in buying distressed properties that were multifamily and were in default with the banks, doing any repairs they may need and then renting them out. At first, Sam wasn't very happy with this, but he went along with it since it was mostly Shirley's money from her commissions and didn't affect the family budget too much, and since Sam liked to go hunting, fishing, and camping, Sam had a few firearms and other things around the house. This was something that Shirley tolerated.

Then one day Sam was with Shirley at the local Barnes & Noble bookstore. Besides selling books, they had a Starbucks that also sold snacks. Starbucks was gaining in popularity in Seattle, and almost everywhere you looked, there was a Starbucks kiosk selling coffee and lattes. It was common for people at the bookstore to pick up a book, get a latte, and read the book while they drank their latte to see if they wanted to buy the book. There were signs posted that people were supposed to pay for their books before entering this part of the store, but management didn't enforce it because they knew that most of the time, the people would get hooked on the storyline and then purchase the book.

As Sam came out of the restroom, he passed a shelf of books under the description of modern fiction. One of the books caught Sam's eye, titled *Patriots*. He picked it up and quickly read the inside front and back jacket flaps. He was running late to meet Shirley at the latte stand—she was supposed to get him a latte—so he tucked the book under his arm and went and sat down at a table just as Shirley came with a tray holding two lattes and a toasted onion bagel cut in half with cream cheese to share with him. Sam started to leaf through the book in his hand as Shirley asked him about it. He replied that the title had caught his attention and that he was thinking about buying it. As he read bits and pieces of the book, he also carried a conversation with Shirley. It annoyed her that he could do both. As they were finishing their lattes, Shirley said she had seen some real-estate magazines that she would like to read, so they went back to the bookstore section, and Shirley got them. She paid for those and Sam's book. They then drove aimlessly around Seattle and wound up at a food stand on Lake Union that sold Ivar's clam chowder. They each had a bowl of it and watched the boats going by on the lake.

That night, Sam started reading his book in earnest and was soon hooked on the storyline. It took him less than three days to finish the book. Then he read it again, this time more slowly. Shirley asked him if he hadn't read the book already.

Sam said, "Yes, but now I want to read it closer."

This would drive Shirley nuts as she would read a book only once and be done. Sam went on the computer and did some web searches and went onto some websites. Soon, it was almost like an epiphany for him when he had realized what was happening in the country and how Shirley was unwittingly getting things set up with her rental units so they would be able to comfortably retire in a few years.

After Sam had gotten out of the army, he went to work as a machinist for Boeing aircraft and was sent to several schools and courses that included sheet metal and riveting, welding, a short course in drafting, and, of course, in his machinist field. Boeing had a good 401(k) plan, and Sam put 10 percent of his wages into it, and Boeing matched the first 5 percent, so about 15 percent of his wages was put away every paycheck. While in the break room about twenty years back, Sam had overheard two of his coworkers talking about their Schwab accounts and how they had set up an IRA and were buying stock and managing their accounts so they would have more retirement income. Sam looked into this, read some articles on investing, and he did the same thing, slowly at first, and then when the government allowed Roth IRAs, he got one of them also. Sam learned about dividend stocks and widow-and-orphan stocks and purchased a mix of both. With dividend stocks, while slightly risky, they paid a dividend in the 10-to-12-percent range, and widow-and-orphan stocks were more secure and paid a steady 3 percent dividend. He was averaging about a 6-to-8-percent return a year on his stocks and built his accounts up to six figures, not including his company 401(k) plan, which was a high six-figure account.

About five years before they planned on retiring, they had thought about buying a big class A motor home, but what changed their minds was when they had vacationed with some retired friends who were living in Arizona. They had a large fifth-wheel trailer with several tip-outs that gave them almost as much living area as a small apartment, but instead of being completely finished as and plush as many travel trailers were, this one was a toy hauler. The back third of the trailer was unfinished. It had a durable floor with tie-downs to secure off-road vehicles like four-wheelers or sand buggies, and the back wall dropped down to form a ramp for these vehicles to drive into the trailer. There also was a thirty-gallon fuel tank to carry extra fuel for the Onan 5 kilowatt generator and to refuel the off-road buggies. This intrigued the mechanic in Sam. He would be able to outfit the back of the trailer to do what he wanted, almost like a garage to work in or a small office.

As it came closer to retirement, Sam and Shirley needed to make a decision on whether they wanted to go with a big class A motor home or a fifth-wheel toy hauler. He and Shirley went over the pros and cons of both and even rented a class A motor home for two weeks. They finally realized that if they went the class A route, they would need a second vehicle and pay the added expense of the insurance and registration of a second motorized vehicle to drive when they came to an area where they wanted to stay awhile and explore the area they were in. So they decided to go with a one-ton pickup and a thirty-eight-foot fifth-wheel toy hauler.

Also, Sam needed to make a decision, since he was an avid sportsman who liked to hunt and fish, on what he was going to do with all his firearms. He didn't want to sell them, partially because of what he had read in the book *Patriots*, and he knew from reading *Shotgun News* and other outdoor and shooting magazines that there were states where his firearms would not be permitted. All it would take was for some overzealous deputy sheriff or police officer to stop them because they would have out-of-state license plates, knowing that since they were senior citizens and out-of-state vacationers, it would be a soft stop and an easy arrest or traffic ticket for some minor traffic infraction.

It was while Sam was under the trailer, checking the condition of the flooring, that an idea had come to him on how to hide his firearms that were not allowed into other states. The stringers from the frame of the trailer reminded him of the stringers on an airplane, and they would provide perfect pockets for his firearms. All he had to do was rivet some aluminum across the stringers, thus enclosing the bottom of the trailer. This would also streamline the bottom of the trailer and increase fuel economy, and if stopped by police and questioned, he would tell them that it was for streamlining for fuel economy. Then all he had to do was cut some hatches in the floor in the trailer and cover the hatches with indoor–outdoor carpet.

One day, while coming home from work on Interstate 5 in Seattle, he saw an improperly loaded trailer start to fishtail and eventually roll over, so he knew that weight and balance and the center of gravity would be important, especially if he were to carry a lot of ammunition for his firearms. He went about with his modifications with meticulous planning. He bought some sheet aluminum and two-part epoxy, knowing that although it was messy to work with, it would waterproof the compartments, and if done professionally, it would look like it had come from the factory this way. He eventually sheeted the entire bottom of the trailer with cutouts for the holding tank discharge line. When he was finished, it looked like it had come off the assembly line, with the underside covered. He even made data plates with the manufacturer's name and "Elkhorn, Indiana" on them and the trailer's VIN. He riveted these at areas easy to see if any official was to inspect the underside.

***

Eric was sitting on a lawn chair while on his sundeck at his home, staring toward the southwest and the Kenai Peninsula. It was a raised deck since the house was what was called a "raised ranch," with the kitchen, dining room, living room, bathroom, and two bedrooms on the upper floor and a family room, laundry room, a second bathroom, and a third bedroom on the lower floor. He had a bottle of Alaskan Amber beer on the floor of the deck by him as Susan or "Sue," his wife, came out of the house.

"What are you looking at?" she asked him.

"Oh, nothing. I'm sitting here, remembering how I felt when Mount Spur erupted."

"Yes, I remember that time. It was a scary time."

"I know, as we watched the ash cloud approach us, with lightning flashing inside of it, how strong the feeling of dread and foreboding disaster was and then the smell of sulfur that burned your nose and skin. It was like the end of the world was approaching. I have that feeling now, like something ominous is about to happen again."

"That's because all you read is those gloom and doom books and news articles."

"No, I read other news, but you cannot be a Suzie Sunshine all the time and not realize what is happening in our country and the world around us. It will be the people who aren't prepared who will suffer the most. People who see the signs and are prepared for a disaster will be the ones who will survive. Do you think for a moment that the government gives a crap about us? Well, they don't, and if we cannot fend for ourselves and aren't ready to defend what we have, we will be like the millions of other people who will starve if they cannot get their groceries on a daily or weekly basis. You see those people when we go to Costco, Carr's, or Fred Meyer. They start coming in around four thirty, when they get off from work, running around, buying the items for their evening meal. These people don't even have three days' worth of food in their house. Some will die within three or four weeks, and then there will be the people who band together to take by force what they think you have, and within a month or maybe less, it won't be a pretty picture, what will be happening."

"You're just a doom-and-gloomer," Sue replied.

"No," Erik replied. "I'm a realist. It's just that we should get at least some food and water stockpiled, at least in case of another volcano eruption or another big earthquake. We have insurance on our house and cars in case of a problem but hope we never have to use it. Well, extra supplies would be just like that—an insurance policy so we can survive and eat."

Erik didn't tell her that he was secretly buying food, guns, and ammunition with money he had saved from some side-business transactions he had done over the past few years. He had quite a small arsenal of firearms and ammunition and a large stash of long-date food hidden in the garage of the house they were living in.

"Well, anyway, we should talk about our retirement. In two years, we will be sixty-six and will be able to start drawing social security. Have you thought of what you wanted to do? I have thought about it, and I really don't want to sell our little side business, not just yet. Maybe we can get someone to manage it, and we could still draw a small salary as consultants to the business and then sell it three or four years later. We could also keep it and move to a piece of property out in the Mat-Su Valley. With our arthritis, we would build a ranch house so we don't have to climb steps and come into town once or twice a week, or we can get an RV and travel around the lower forty-eight for a year or two, just looking around for a place to live, and visit the places we saw on those TV travel shows. These are just some things to think about."

***

On the ride from the flea market back to their camper at the campground, Sam and Shirley were discussing their finds.

"It seemed there were less people selling today than last week."

"Yes," Shirley replied, "and I didn't find much that I could resell up North. It seems like it slowed down much earlier this year. Maybe we should plan on moving soon."

"I'll check the website Auction Flex on the computer when we get back and see what estate auctions are on our route back. Who knows? Maybe we'll find something good along the way."

As Shirley was pulling some chicken breasts out of the refrigerator that she had marinating while they were gone, Sam was on the computer in the little office area he had made in the rear part of their trailer. He came out as Shirley was finishing making a salad.

"Boy, I'm going to miss fresh vegetables for a while. We're going to have to do something about the garden here."

"I'll talk to Peter, the campground owner, after dinner and see what he wants us to do with it, but in the meantime, we'll just harvest what we can, and if there is too much, we will can some of it—that is, if you will part with some of your precious Mason jars."

"Here," Shirley said. "Take these chicken breasts and grill them outside while I finish up in here."

As Sam fired up the small propane tabletop grill sitting on the park bench next to the trailer, Peter White came walking up.

"Hi, Sam. What's cooking?"

"Hi, Pete. Some chicken breasts Shirley had marinating. There's an extra one if you're hungry. I was going to come by the office later after we finished dinner. I have to discuss something with you."

A frown came on Peter's face. "Nothing serious, I hope?"

"No, it's just that we will be pulling up stakes in a day or two, and what do you want us to do with our garden?"

"You know, when I gave you two permission to plant a 'little' garden, I didn't know how big 'little' meant to you guys. You could, if it was managed right, feed a family year round from this little garden."

"Yes," Sam said. "If you plan right, you can grow a lot on a small space. If you want, I'll dig it up and replant grass for you, or we can let it as is, and you can put someone in here who will take care of it."

"Well, Sam, truth be known, in the summer, after you snowbirds leave, we don't get many people in here. So I tell you what—I'll take care of it, water and weed it while you are gone, and harvest any items as they ripen for my efforts and in the fall when you come back. You guys are coming back, aren't you?" he asked, cocking his head and looking out of one eye at Sam. "And then I'll put you back in this spot."

"That sounds fair and means one less thing I have to do before leaving."

"When will you be pulling out?"

"Well, we were planning in a day or two. How about April 15?" Sam said.

"You mean you are going to bail just before your taxes are due?"

"Taxes? What taxes? All my money goes to the government, and they give me what they think we need to survive."

"I know how you feel," Peter said. "It seems like they take more and more each year."

"We should be back here, if all goes right, around middle to late October as the snows and cold weather push us South."

***

Pres. Warron Jefferson Calloway was the product of a well-monied Southern Democrat family. His political career started right after he had left college. He worked in Washington, D.C., as an intern in his uncle's office. His uncle was a senator from Arkansas and was a fixture in the Senate. He had been there for forty years and carried much sway in the Senate. After a two-year intern position with his uncle, he ran for a seat in his district's legislature and spent six years in that position. He then ran for U.S. Congress, was elected, and spent another six years as a congressman. When his uncle decided to retire, he was paraded around as the best choice for his replacement. President Calloway spent thirty years as the senator from Arkansas before he had run for president. In all his years in politics, he had made a lot of friends and helped many people, but most of all, whenever any news media wanted a story, he was able to provide information for them. As a result, the news media published only good news about him and only negative news about his opponent. Even with all this, he had narrowly won the election as president.

Now he was seated at the head of the conference table, his advisors were sitting with him around the table. The topic now was how he could get the country to go along with the flood of illegal aliens since the last two mostly ignored amnesty programs for all the illegal immigrants who crossed the Southern border. The general population of the country was up in arms with the latest flood of illegal immigrants. He had the border patrol cut back in funding as far as he could, and that was causing problems for him with the farmers and ranchers along the border states because there was a steady stream of people crossing the border that were destroying crops and killing cattle. The Republicans were starting to claim that more than just Hispanics were coming into the United States by this route. They now had pictures of people who were stopped by the local border militias who were Oriental in facial features, and some even looked like Muslims. The situation along the southwest border was becoming a tinderbox, and the Mexicans in the United States weren't helping any with their demands of returning Texas, Arizona, New Mexico, and Southern California back to Mexico. There were agents for this movement going around to colleges and universities, pushing for the annexation by Mexico of these lands that they felt were taken from them illegally at the end of the Spanish–American War. It had gotten so bad that fifty miles into U.S. territory, they had to put up signs in state and national park campgrounds warning people that it wasn't safe to camp at night with their families anymore in these locations. This action basically seceded the southwestern fifty miles of the United States to a foreign power.

The second item on the agenda was how to get the public to accept his desire to bring in a large group of Syrian Muslims, especially with all the problems Great Britain and Europe were having with their Muslim refugees. The last item on the agenda had to do with the budget—what they would do with the debt owed to China and other foreign countries. The social programs he had instituted were eating up the GDP, and soon, it would exceed the amount of money collected from the income taxes and tariffs. They were now looking at the looming shortfall and the resulting inflation of printing more money to cover the national debt or cutting social security and military disability payments. The Republicans and the Teabaggers wanted the inner-city social programs cut, but all the free programs to these people were what was getting Democrats elected. If any of the social programs were cut, even just a little, there would be riots in the streets, and his party would lose their votes in the upcoming election. *Well, we will have to get our spin people on it and make it look like the conservatives are behind it.*

As the president was leaving the meeting, an aide came to him to inform him of a visitor. The president told him to give him ten minutes, have the visitor meet him in his office, and bring a tray of coffee, tea, and pastries to the office. The president liked Danish-style pastries with his coffee. The president used a key to open an unmarked door and went into one of the many private toilets just for the president.

Warron Calloway knew that this day would be coming. When he first ran for the presidency, he had met many people who were power brokers, but this one was the one he feared the most. It was like there was an endless supply of money and volunteers to help his campaign, and now it was time to pay the piper. He had meetings before, and it was usually a suggestion here or to do this there, but now there was a strategic plan that involved the whole country.

***

As Sam made sure the boxes of items that he and Shirley had bought were secure and the weight evenly distributed in the fifth-wheel camp trailer, Shirley got the kitchen and the rest of the trailer ready for travel so that in the morning, all Sam had to do was unhook the electric, water the sewer hoses were already disconnected. They both were methodical in their work. They had done this many times before, and each knew what jobs they had to do as they listened to the radio. Both Shirley and Sam liked to listen to country music, and when the news came on at 4:00 p.m., the announcer covered the growing unrest in the southern part of Arizona and how the stock market just had another "off" day, with stocks lower than they had been five years ago. As Sam came up front from the storage area in their toy hauler, he had a list of auctions along their route North in his hand. He had used the website auctionzip. com. This was a site many auctioneers used to list their auctions.

Shirley looked up from making the salad and said, "There are some steaks for the grill in the fridge, and did you hear the news?"

"Yeah," Sam replied. "It looks like the illegals are acting up again, and Wall Street is crashing, so what else is new?"

"Do we still have any stock in our IRAs?" Shirley asked.

"Only a few. I sold most of our stocks, luckily, just before the last bubble burst," Sam replied, "and there is now around $450,000 sitting there in cash, but we still have a few DRIP stocks, with a few shares in each one. It's about $1,000 for all of them."

"Well, what did you do with the rest of the money?" Shirley asked.

"Well," Sam said, "most of it is in the brokerage account as cash ready to pull out, Some of it is in a REIT that pays a dividend each month and like I told you, I bought pre-1964 silver coins with some of it, mostly dimes and quarters but some half dollars."

"Did you buy any silver dollars?" Shirley asked.

"Not many since it was discovered that China was counterfeiting Morgan dollars by punching them out of sheet steel and then electroplating them with a thin layer of silver. I stayed mostly with dimes, quarters, and some halves and one-ounce silver bars. I also bought one-ounce gold Canadian maple leaves and one-tenth-of-an-ounce American gold eagles."

"How much did you put into silver and gold?" Shirley asked.

"I slowly bought from several different dealers so as to not draw attention to ourselves and whenever silver was down below $14 an ounce. We have about $5,000 face value, and at today's price, it's worth $28 an ounce, so we have somewhere around $140,000 in silver. Plus, we have thirty one-ounce maple leaves. That's around another $75,000, give or take. And we have 120 one-tenth-of-an-ounce gold eagles— that's about another $30,000—and what we have in our bank accounts and, of course, our investment properties, pension funds from our jobs, and social security."

Sam didn't tell Shirley about the guns and ammunition he had bought with some of that money. Sam always carried a large quantity of money with him because, as he would say, "you never know when you meet someone who needed some quick money and they were willing to sell a rifle, pistol, or something else real cheap." This was happening more frequently since inflation was inching up and the wages for the working people were stagnant. The sad thing was the news media was not saying anything about this and the talking heads were just parroting the government's news releases about how good things were and how the recession had turned around. What many people failed to realize was that there was hidden inflation, and all you had to do was look at ice cream. You used to be able to buy ice cream by the half-gallon. Now the containers are one and a half quarts for the same price as what that half-gallon used to cost. Cereal boxes are half as thick as they used to be, and the price had increased. This was hidden inflation. Sam was able to pick up four AR-style rifles that used 5.56/.223 ammo and six pistols—of which two were 1911-style .45s and the other four were 9 mm—while they were living in Arizona. He had also managed to acquire a large quantity of ammunition for various guns, but Shirley didn't know this as Sam used money, he had made by buying and selling items, and he kept this money secret.

"We should be okay for several years, and we should start pulling the cash from our bank accounts. We should continue buying silver coins from the other snowbirds when they winter down here, and by doing this, we should be in an even better shape."

"Why should we start draining our bank accounts?" Shirley asked.

"Well," Sam said, "the government has changed the rules on banking again, and the government might do what has happened in other countries and raid the bank accounts to help bolster the economy. But I don't know how stealing working people's money is a good idea. Also, with the new banking rules, we are no longer depositors with our money in savings accounts in the bank, but now these accounts are classified investor accounts."

"What does that mean?" Shirley asked.

"Well, if the bank where you have your money—and for most people, that is their life savings, however meager it is—has financial problems from making bad decisions in the derivatives market, the bank can use your money because you are now considered an investor and not a depositor to bail the bank out and not pay you. The first people who would get their money will be the stockholders and other creditors. The investors and depositors will be the last to get any money. So in short, if a banker makes a bad investment decision and goes bankrupt, it can take your money to bail them out. As for the FDIC, if enough banks go under, there isn't enough money in the FDIC account to cover all the depositors, and the country is over $20 trillion in debt, so it won't be able to put more money into the FDIC account. The money people put into the banks is there on good faith that the bankers won't screw things up again. If this happens, it will make the Great Depression of the thirties look like a picnic. Millions of everyday working people will be left high and dry. The resulting chaos will be horrific. I think we should have a small cache of five or ten thousand in small bills for an emergency in case the banks do close, and we should pull all our money but a small operating fund out of the banks and put it into precious metals like gold and silver. We can pay our bills from our social security payments, which are being directly deposited to our bank account, for as long as that program will last. Then we will have our backup money."

"How soon will or would this happen?" Shirley asked.

"I don't know," replied Sam. "It would be like trying to trap the wind. You just don't know. But I feel we might have two or three years, but with an election coming next year, who knows what the stock market and the economy will do? Not to change the subject, but I have a list of auctions for our trip North if we pull out tonight or very early in the morning. There is a storage auction at 10:00 a.m. one hundred miles north of here. They are advertising sixteen units. If we leave early, we would be able to get to it. It seems more and more storage units are being defaulted on lately. I guess it's a sign of the times and coming economic crash."

"Yes, it's sad," Shirley said. "Here. Go grill these while I finish in here. There is no telling how long we will be able to afford to eat steak."

***

Ken was on one of his regular hunting missions. Several months ago, when he had come upon an area where grass was growing and the ground was slightly damp, he made a mental note of the location and came back with an old surplus army entrenching tool, one that had a blade on one side and a spike pick on the other side like the ones he used when he was in Vietnam. It was quick work, and he had excavated an area about two yards in diameter and about three feet deep and was gratified when he saw water start to seep into the hole. When Ken made his hunting trips, he would either check the waterhole he had made with the scope on his rifle to see if there was any animal activity or, after checking the area go, down to look for tracks. It wasn't long before he had begun to see antelope in the area. Today he decided to check out his creation to see how much water was accumulating in case they needed to come this way if for any reason they had to leave their trailer. As he made a wide circle around the waterhole, he was looking for animal tracks to see just what was using the seep.

As he came downwind of the hole, he smelled smoke. This got his curiosity up, and at the same time, his warning hairs on the back of his neck stood up. This would happen to him while he was in the army while on patrol in Vietnam just before contact was made with the enemy. Ken went down on one knee and was assessing the situation. His instincts told him to back off and circle back to the trailer to his wife, Betty, but he reasoned that no one knew he was there, and the waterhole was in a slight depression. So what he did was to carefully back off to find a slight hill from where he could monitor the waterhole with his spotting scope in his pack.

Ken was settling in on his observation area, with the sun behind him just in time, when he saw a head pop up and look around. Then the person walked a brief distance from the camp and squatted to relieve himself and then go back to where he had come from. Ken was nervous. The person was carrying an AK-47 rifle with him, and he seemed relaxed, as if he didn't have to be security conscious. Ken spent most of the rest of the day observing the area, and as best as he could tell, there were no guards posted, and he watched as three more men left the area to relieve themselves.

It was getting late, and Ken knew Betty, his wife, would start to get worried, so he slowly and quietly backed away from the slight rise he was on, circled wide around the camp, and headed back to the trailer. While doing so, he passed up several easy shots at game, but he didn't want to risk the noise of a shot. Ken got back to the trailer at around 4:00 p.m. as the sun was getting low on the horizon.

"What took so long? I was getting worried," Betty said as Ken came walking into their makeshift yard.

"We have to talk," Ken said as he took off his pack and drank deeply of the sweet mint tea Betty had made and handed to him.

They had planted seeds from the catalog, and some of these were peppermint, which made an excellent tea. Whenever Ken left the trailer area on his hunts, he always had his pack with him. In it were a couple of MREs, extra water, about a hundred feet of 550 parachute cord, a small block and tackle, good for a thousand pounds, a small tarp, a first aid kit, two of those compressed silver survival blankets, some unbleached muslin game bags, and a few other items that he thought would be handy. Ken liked this tea and thought it was more refreshing than any of the tea mixes that could be bought in the stores.

"What's wrong?" Betty asked.

"While I was out, I swung by the waterhole I had made, and there were people camped there. I don't know who they were or why they were there, but I don't like it. I think we should get our signal devices out, and I'll show you how they work. The main one is the boat air horn. It operates from cans of compressed air and is very loud. The sound will carry out here for a long way. I'll clean and oil the Mossberg 500 shotgun and have you do some dry firing with it with the practice plug in it. We are well off the beaten track. Heck, the closest road is over two miles away, and you cannot see anything of what is back here from it, and there is just a dirt track back here, so you should be relatively safe here while I go out hunting, but I will stay closer just in case."

"Well," Betty replied, "the fresh meat is much better than the frozen crap they send us, and there is no telling what is in the mystery hamburger meat they send us in those plastic tubes. I'll be fine. Just come running if I ever blow that horn."

"Don't worry, babe. I'll be here as fast as I can, and I'll start carrying my M1A along with the 10/22 and my Beretta 92FS. It will be a big shock if anyone messes with us. We will be able to get them in a crossfire. But the thing is if anyone does attack us, we will have to make sure no one escapes to bring back any friends."

"What do you mean?" Betty asked.

"Just what I said. If anyone comes to harm us and shooting starts, we will have to make sure we kill all of them so they don't come back with a larger force and kill us. I'm going to stick around tomorrow and plant some booby traps around here, and when I'm finished, I'll show you where they are so you don't trip them."

"What are you going to do?" Betty asked.

"Well," Ken replied, "there are some things the gooks did to us in Vietnam. I guess they will work here. Do we have an empty five-gallon bucket around here?"

"Yeah, I put one behind the trailer this afternoon. I used it to carry some water to the flowers I planted. Why?"

"Well, I guess I should unhook the sewer hose, drain some shit into it, let it ripen overnight, sharpen some sixteen-penny nails, and find some thin boards for them in the morning."

Ken did not sleep fitfully that night. The nightmares returned, and every little noise, it seemed, woke him up. He was up, it seemed, every hour, and he had to look out all of the windows. At around three fifteen in the morning, Ken had enough. He quietly got out of bed and went into the kitchen area and turned the coffee pot on. He did this in the dark, as he often did, and this always drove Betty crazy. She didn't know how he was able to do this because when it got dark, she needed lights to see to get around. Ken tried to teach her by blindfolding her and then let her move around the trailer while he would ask her for things, but she never could get the hang of it. Ken quietly went outside with a thermos of coffee in one hand and an old M16 in the other hand. When he was in Vietnam, he had had a chance to acquire the M16 on the black market. He broke it down into small parts and mailed it home to his parents to hold for him if he came back. He quietly sat on a lawn chair and slowly drank his coffee.

Just like the old days, he said to no one but the ghosts in his head and reflected on what Sergeant Addams would do. He was the squad sergeant whom Ken was assigned to when he had first gone to Vietnam after a brief tour stateside with the Eighty-Second Airborne Division. Boy, he reflected, he was green. The other members of his squad called him a cherry because he was the FNG in the squad, and no one wanted to be near the FNG for at least two months. Sergeant Addams told him it wasn't anything personal, just that they didn't want to know him too well in case he got killed. After two months, the rest of the squad started to warm up to him. That was when he had found out that many of them were on their second or third year in the country and that Sergeant Addams had been in the country for four years. Ken thought that as soon as he got his year in, he was going to leave the shithole that Vietnam was and head back to the Land of the Big PX. He later learned that Sergeant Addams's brother was in Vietnam and was killed in an ambush. He was told by a member in his squad that Sergeant Addams's goal was to kill as many Viet Cong as he could to avenge his brother's death.

When his year was up, he went home, but many of the people he had gone to high school with, while some supported what he did, were antiwar protesters. He went back to Fort Bragg and volunteered to go back to Vietnam when the next levy came down. He spent his year and extended for another six months and then another, and he reenlisted for six years. When he reenlisted, they made him go home on a thirty-day leave. It was the worst time he had ever had. He was accosted in the Seattle Airport by a young mother with a daughter of around five years old. She pointed at him and told her daughter to kick him, and then she threw a cup of urine on him, calling him a baby killer. It wasn't much better at home. Two of his classmates who had been his friends in high school bragged about their avoidance of the draft and called him a fool for being in the army. While on leave, visiting an aunt and uncle, he was told by his uncle, who had served during World War II, that many of the guys in his platoon shipped weapons home from the war that they had captured from German soldiers, and if he had a chance, he should do the same thing. At the end of three weeks, he had had enough and called the airline to see if he could get an early flight to California and found out he could. He checked into the transit company early and soon found himself on his way back to his old unit. When he got back, it was like being home again.

The sun started to rise and interrupted Ken's musings of what he called "things past." He slowly got up from the lawn chair, stretched his muscles, and went into the trailer to make breakfast and a fresh pot of coffee. The aroma of frying bacon and fresh coffee brought Betty out from the forward-raised bedroom, and sniffing, she asked Ken how long he had been awake.

"Only a few hours. I was thinking of things past and what I saw yesterday. We're going to have to change how we do things around here starting today."

***

The night before, Sam had the fifth-wheel camp trailer hooked onto the pickup truck so that all he had to do was disconnect the electricity and water hooked to the trailer, and by 6:00 a.m., he and Shirley were on the road to the storage auction in Phoenix. Sam had a map to the location that he had printed, and with the help of an onboard GPS, he found the location without too many problems. Now his biggest problem was finding a place to park the truck and camper. As he circled around, he found a church parking lot only a block away and pulled into it, parking at the closest end of the parking lot to the storage yard.

"Well, this is the best we can find, so it's just a short hike to the auction. It should start in about an hour. Are you ready to see the competition?"

"I have to go potty," Shirley replied. "Then we can go."

"I guess I better go potty also. You never know if these storage places have public restrooms."

As Sam and Shirley walked hand in hand to the storage site, Shirley remarked on how run-down the area looked and if the truck and trailer would be safe while it was left unattended. Sam said that he was sure it would be all right there during the day but that he wouldn't want to be here overnight. When Sam and Shirley got to the storage lot, it was fifteen minutes before the auction, and there were people already there, milling around as Sam went into the office to sign in for the auction. Sam came out and found Shirley off to one side with no one around her, and being strangers to this locale, they were left alone.

With his back to the milling group, he asked, "Well, what did you learn?"

"There are two slightly overweight guys with short haircuts and Vietnam veteran hats. They look like they are here for the show. There is one loudmouth trying to intimidate some of the bidders and is really talking trash about the auctioneer, saying how incompetent he is and that the storage company should be using him. I guess he is a competing auctioneer. He may cause trouble. The auctioneer the storage company is using looks like a nice fellow, but we will see."

At 10:00 a.m. sharp, the young auctioneer called the people together and started his announcements as the people gathered around. It was cash or credit card only, and there were no dumpster privileges. They had to take all but the personal papers that they might find in the unit with them, and there was a $50 cash-only refundable cleaning deposit. They all went to the first unit, a small five-by-five-foot unit, and the manager cut the lock and rolled the door up. They all filed by, looking inside the unit. All that was in it were about a dozen garbage bags full of what looked like clothing and some particleboard furniture. Sam thought, *A small apartment of someone on welfare.* The unit went for a surprising $30.

Sam happened to be standing next to the two veterans and overheard one say to the other, "Yeah, Tom always buys these for his thrift store."

He looked to see who Tom was and filed this little nugget of information away for use later if he needed it.

The next unit opened was another five-by-five. It had a little better furniture and some hand tools. Tom and the loudmouth auctioneer got into a bidding war, and the loudmouth dropped it on Tom at $500 and started to laugh about how he had run the bid on Tom. His kind of attitude and arrogance angered Sam, but he knew he must not let his emotions affect his bidding. The next two units were much of the same. One was a five-by-five and the other a five-by-ten, packed full with boxes and furniture. Loudmouth won the bid on this one for $950 and was strutting around like a bandy rooster, crowing about how good he was and that no one had pockets as deep as his.

After another average unit, Sam was starting to worry that this was a wasted trip, coming to this storage auction. Then they stopped in front of a ten-by-ten-foot unit. It was unusual in that instead of a roll-up door, it had a regular door to it. Sam was standing at the front of the line as they cut the lock. It was one of those circle or disk locks and wasn't easy to open. The manager had a DeWalt eighteen-volt angle grinder and, after several tries, finally got it cut and opened the door. There in front of them was the dirtiest mattress Sam had ever seen. It was covered in dirt, oil, and unknown stains.

Loudmouth started yelling that he would empty the trash unit if he was paid fifty bucks. Then he said, "Pull the mattress away from the door."

Sam loudly replied, "I would open the bid at $100 if you keep the mattress there and sell it as a mystery unit."

He don't know if it was his opening bid or his standing up to Loudmouth, but the crowd started chanting, "Mystery unit!" while some looked at Loudmouth.

"Let's see who the gamblers are," Sam called out.

Loudmouth, looking at Sam, said he would go for $105. Sam knew it was a dare, so he said $150, and Loudmouth looked at him with eyes that could kill. He was trying to intimidate Sam. He said $175. Without pause, Sam said $200. Loudmouth's face got red. He came over to Sam and asked him who he was.

Sam replied, "Just a citizen and a bidder."

This really pissed him off, and Loudmouth said $300, staring at Sam and daring him to bid. Sam said $400, and Loudmouth spun around, yelling that Sam was an outsider running the bid on him. He was so agitated that spit was coming from his mouth as he yelled at Sam. He then yelled $450 and looked at Sam, daring him to bid.

Sam calmly said $500, at which point Loudmouth said, "Give him the dirty mattress!"

As Sam was walking up to the unit to put his padlock on it, Loudmouth came up and tried to grab the mattress, yelling, "Let's see what's behind it!"

Sam grabbed his arm with a vise like grip and said, "It's now my unit. Keep your hands off it. If you wanted to see what was in it, you should have bought it."

Loudmouth gave Sam a dirty look and then took a swing at him with a fist that Sam easily ducked, and with Loudmouth being off balance, Sam easily tripped him. Loudmouth fell onto the ground as Sam quickly locked his unit with a padlock he had hidden in his pants pocket. Loudmouth got up and said he was going to call the police and have Sam arrested because he had assaulted him.

Sam looked him in the eye and started walking toward him, saying, "You are an ass and have been causing a disturbance the whole auction, and I will call the police on you if you don't shut up and behave."

The rest of the auction, Loudmouth stayed away from Sam. As Shirley and Sam were walking to the storage office to pay for the unit he had bought, they were holding hands, not saying anything, when the two veterans came up from behind them.

They said, "You sure made an enemy today."

Sam replied, "Yes, but de oppresso liber."

They looked at each other, and one said, "To free the oppressed." He put his hand out to shake Sam's and said, "Seventh Group."

Sam replied, "Fifth Group."

"Welcome home, brother," Sam replied.

Shirley and Sam hung back until Loudmouth and the other winning bidders paid, and then they went into the office.

The storage manager was there and came over to Sam, looking at the registration sheet. "Sam, is it?"

"Yes," Sam replied, expecting to get chewed out for the incident he had had with Loudmouth.

Instead, the manager said, "You're not from around here, are you?"

"No," he replied. "We're just passing through."

"Well, usually, we don't allow anyone to use our dumpsters, but you put the jerk, Gary Archer, in his place. It was about time someone did. He intimidates the people at his auctions, and if anyone stands up to him, he bans them from his auctions. He deserved what he got, and if you want to, you have free access to our dumpsters for any trash and that mattress."

Sam thanked him, paid the auctioneer, and said, "We'll be back a little later after we get a little lunch."

The manager said, "No problem. You have twenty-four hours to remove the items from the unit, and if you're interested, Gary won't be back until tomorrow to pick up his unit."

Sam looked at the young auctioneer and told him he did a good job and not to let Gary intimidate him. He could see from the auctioneer's body language that he had appreciated the comment. Shirley and Sam were holding hands as they walked back to where they had parked their pickup truck and trailer.

She said, "Five hundred on a dirty mattress? What did you see in there?"

He said, "All I saw was a dirty mattress, just like everyone else."

"Then why did you buy it? To prove a point with the loudmouth?"

"No. I was standing there when they opened the door, and I was able to smell what was in there before it had a chance to air out. You know how you would complain when I would come back from the range and clean my firearms in the house and how it would stink up the house and now the trailer? Well, that odor is Hoppe's No. 9 solvent. I got a brief whiff of that odor when they opened the door, and then it was gone. I thought if I had any firearms in a storage locker that I would put the nastiest mattress in the door to deter any thieves. I'm betting there is at least one firearm and hopefully more in there. It's twelve thirty. Let's eat a sandwich, and hopefully, the other buyers will be gone. Then we can load up without anybody rubbernecking on what was in the unit that we bought."

Shirley agreed. She didn't like rubberneckers either. She felt the same as Sam, if you want to see what is in a unit then buy it.

As they sat in the camper, eating tuna-fish-with-tomato sandwiches and listening to the radio, the news came on, and it wasn't good. There was more talk of illegals crossing the border, and some were saying there were not just Mexicans but also Arabs, Al-Qaeda, and ISIS crossing into the country also.

Sam looked at Shirley and said, "It won't be long before something happens here in this country. I just hope the president can stop it before it gets out of hand."

Sam pulled the truck and trailer into the storage yard. It was a really tight fit, and for a while, he thought he couldn't get close to the unit he had bought. He hated the thought of having to carry whatever was in the unit to the trailer, but finally, after much backing and pulling forward and maneuvering, with Shirley spotting him, he was able to jackknife the trailer blocking the aisle and get the back door of the trailer next to the unit's door. He parked close, and he jackknifed the trailer so people couldn't easily snoop while they unloaded the unit.

Sam hated when people were able to watch him unload a unit. He felt that if you wanted to see what was in the unit, then you had to buy it. He unlocked the padlock and opened the door up, and there it was, in all of its glory—the mattress. He put gloves on, carefully pulling it out, and set it three doors away from their unit. As he did this, he thought the mattress wasn't as smelly as everyone had thought. Upon closer examination it looked almost new and the oil, dirt and stains were placed on it intentionally to make it look dirty.

As he was doing this, he heard Shirley gasp and say, "Oh my."

Sam came back and just stared into the unit. He couldn't believe it. It looked like a military arms room. There were two-gun racks down the left side of the unit holding two SKSs, two AK-47s, and four AR-15s. He saw at least two Springfield M1As. They looked like the old military M14s, but Sam knew they were new civilian models, and there were three Mossberg 500 twelve-gauge pump shotguns with their spare barrels and other rifles. Some were bolt actions with scopes, and where the gun racks ended, a wooden shelf was nailed to the wall with eight boxes of new Beretta 92FS 9 mm pistols and four boxes with new Colt 1911 .45 pistols. There were other pistols in boxes also. Some were Taurus, Glock, SIG Sauer, Smith & Wesson, and Ruger revolvers and others.

There was a shelf down the other wall with ammo stacked in both old military ammo cans and twenty-round boxes marked for the guns in the rack and the pistols and revolvers in boxes on the shelf. On the floor in the back was a pallet with nine large OD green wooden military-style footlockers stacked on top of one another with a hinge lid. When they opened the top two of them, they saw that they held woolen military blankets and military style down mummy sleeping bags. There were two brand-new Stihl Farm Boss chainsaws and two Diamond Copperhead crossbows, with two dozen hunting bolts with broad heads and two dozen target bolts for the crossbows. On another pallet were cases of canned dehydrated food from Mountain House and Augason Farms and five-five-gallon buckets each of wheat, pinto beans, and rice.

Sam looked at Shirley, and she looked at him. They couldn't believe what they had.

"Pinch me," Sam said. "I must be dreaming."

"No," Shirley said. "I need to be pinched. What are we going to do with all this? Is there room in the camper? There must be a thousand pounds or more here."

Sam said, "More like two thousand or more pounds. It will be tight, but we can do it. We must watch our weight and balance, but first, I must pull the area rug off the floor in the back."

"Yes," she said. "We must open all the compartments."

When Sam had first bought the fifth-wheel trailer, he knew they might be going through some states that were not gun friendly, so he had welded and riveted some compartments under the trailer using the framework of the trailer. Then he had made hatches in the floor to access these compartments. He had also made several false walls throughout the trailer for the guns that were in the gray area. The most guns he had ever had in there besides his own were ten, and he had picked up five more this time while they were in Arizona during the winter. This would really test the capacity of the hidden compartments. He arranged the firearms that were already in there, and coming out of the trailer, he remarked that he wanted to use some blankets to keep these guns from rubbing since most of them looked new and never fired. Shirley said she would get the blankets from the wooden footlockers.

"That'll do," Sam said. "Let's get to work."

As they emptied the storage unit, Sam recorded the make, type, caliber, and serial number of each weapon into a notebook he had kept with him all the time. They worked fast, but it still took almost an hour to move the firearms. Then he opened one of the three wooden unmarked boxes sitting on a pallet in the back behind the footlockers and just stared.

What the heck is Kenna Stick? Sam wondered. Then he found an instructional pamphlet. After a quick scan, he quickly put it into one of the boxes and quickly closed it. He had Shirley help him carry them into the trailer and wishing he still had room in the hidden compartments, but the newly found firearms took all the space, so he did the next best thing and stacked them in the middle of the floor next to the items they had bought over the winter and then stacked the ammo and the food and everything else around them. There were cases of reloading gun powder, lead bullets, bullet molds for various calibers, and thousands of primers for both small- and large-caliber pistols and rifles. Books on reloading and reloading tools.

Shirley opened a large ammo box, asking Sam, "Why would anyone put wash line rope into a box?"

Looking in, Sam said, "Who knows?"

"Well," she said, "we can use it to tie things down."

Sam looked at her and, when she wasn't looking, buried it deep into the growing stockpile in the trailer. *Wash line rope, my butt.* It had been years—no, decades—but he knew det cord when he saw it. They had used it in Nam to blow trees for LZs. With what was here, Sam thought there would probably be a box or two of blasting caps somewhere, and as luck would have it, he found them before Shirley did, and he hid these also. Besides things that went *bang*, there were two come-a-longs, two high-lift jacks, three rolls of barbwire, two Honda EU2000i gas generators with synchronizing panels, which, at first, he thought was odd, and first-aid kits—and not the Band-Aid kind but serious ones. One even had operating gear, Israeli bandages, and a blood expander in it.

The manager came by at around 6:00 p.m. to tell them he was closing the office for the day but that he lived in an apartment on the premises behind the office and, when they were ready to leave, to give him a call, and he would refund their $50 cleaning deposit. Sam asked him if he could leave the shelves in the unit since they were nailed to the wall. The manager said that was fine with him. Sam looked at his watch. *Wow! We started at 2:00 p.m., and it's now six.* He figured they had another half hour or more of work, and then they had to tie it all down so the load wouldn't shift while they drove. They finished unloading the unit at seven thirty, and then Sam tied everything down with some camouflage netting they had found in the unit. He then grabbed the mattress to put it into the dumpster.

Sam said to Shirley, "Boy, I must be tired or getting weak in my old age. This mattress seems heavier than when I moved it the first time."

He tripped over something that had fallen out of the mattress going to the dumpster and fell face-first on the mattress. Shirley, laughing, said it was a good thing he had something soft to land on, and Sam said it wasn't too soft. It felt like rocks were in it, and he wondered what it was he had tripped on. They looked and saw a blue Crown Royal bag on the ground. Sam picked it up and looked at Shirley, saying it had some weight to it, probably a bag of pennies. He opened the bag, and it had silver dimes in it. They went over to the mattress and looked it over and found where the stitching in the back was not to factory standards. Sam took out his Buck knife and cut the stitching. There were five Crown Royal bags with drawstring tops that were knotted in it, but they didn't have the Crown Royal liquor in them. He now knew why the mattress was heavy. They were packed with pre-1964 dimes, quarters, and half dollars, and one had Morgan silver dollars and a Ziploc bag with one-ounce gold Canadian maple leaves, Krugerrands, and other gold coins. They hurriedly checked the mattress for more but found nothing else. They looked at each other and then hurriedly looked around to see if anyone had seen this. They quickly went back to the truck and put them under the back seat of their extended cab pickup. Shirley spotted Sam as he maneuvered the truck and trailer out of the area where they were parked, and as they were leaving, the manager came out of his apartment next to the office. Sam saw he had a Colt 1911 pistol on his hip.

"Well? Did you find anything good?" he asked.

Sam gave him his stock answer to this question. "Just some odds and ends, but it was fun," he replied.

"Well, here is your cleaning deposit back," he said.

Sam looked at his hip, and he looked down, and then there were two gunshots close by.

"That's why I have this," the manager said. "It seems to be that gunshots are getting more frequent in this area."

Sam thanked him, and he wished them well on their trip.

As Sam pulled out onto the street, Shirley asked, "How does the trailer feel? We put a lot of weight back there."

Stepping on the gas pedal, Sam lied. "It seems fine. Should be no problem. I know we are tired and hungry, but let's get out of this neighborhood and put some miles between here. You know, I'm kind of hungry for some pickled garlic. Do you want to swing by Gilroy and get some?"

"What about going into California with what we have?" Shirley asked.

"Unless they make us unload the trailer, we should be okay. After all, we are just a couple of retired old people who are no problem," Sam said. "If they do stop us, we will say we are headed to Gilroy for garlic to sell at the flea markets up North and the stuff in the back of the trailer is merchandise for the flea markets. We'll try to get to the port of entry for California around noon, and all they will be thinking of is their lunch."

As they headed for Interstate 10, they heard two more gunshots from a different area. This only made Sam want to hurry and get out of the area. They spent the night in the parking lot at a Walmart superstore in Sundance.

***

The president woke up later than he normally did. He usually awoke around 5:00 a.m. so he could read his morning briefs, but today it was around 7:00 a.m. Usually, his trips to Camp David were relaxing, but last night, he had had a very long private conversation with his most trusted advisor during a walk around the grounds, and then he and his most trusted advisors worked late into the night, discussing the upcoming midterm elections. He and his party enjoyed having a super majority in the Senate, but it looked like they might lose it with the midterms. Even though the Democratic Party pumped over $5 million into the primary election in Alaska, the results were still too close to call, and in the other states where Democratic senators were up for reelection, the polls showed the same results. He was a lame duck president with only two years left as the president, and there was more left to do with the agenda. The Republicans, especially the Tea Party Republicans, were getting stronger, and the candidates for the upcoming presidential election were gaining ground with the voters. There was one Republican candidate many thought was a joke and a buffoon—who would ever think a reality TV host would be president?

Polls were showing that a large segment of the population were fed up with all the illegal immigrants and wanted the border between Mexico and the United States closed to stem the flow of people and drugs coming from Mexico and Central America. There were plans to get them registered at the last minute to vote for the Democratic Party, but now it seemed even this would not be enough. The people were also angry over the loss of jobs, inflation, and the recession they were in. The spin masters were working hard, getting the news media to blame the Republicans for this, but there were cracks starting to show.

The plan laid out during his walk was a very dangerous one, and if it failed, there would be problems for the Democratic Party for decades. What they needed was a patsy to take the blame for what was proposed. After all, the Kennedy assassination had gone off almost perfectly, and if this worked, he would be able to get the gun control legislation that many of his party wanted, the NRA be damned, but it would be very risky. This plan was still running through his mind as he sat down for breakfast and the morning briefing sheet about what had happened overnight.

***

Eric's cell phone rang, and he debated if he wanted to answer it.

Sue looked at him and said, "Well? Aren't you going to answer it?"

"I don't know. What if it's work and I have to go in?"

The phone warbled again.

"Hello?" Eric said.

"How many beers have you had?" the voice on the other end said.

Eric immediately recognized the voice on the other end. It was the foreman from work. He thought of lying and saying five, but he didn't as he said, "Just one. Why?"

"Well, we have a broken airplane, and we need your help. Gargle some mouthwash and come in."

"It's work, isn't it?" Sue said.

"Yeah. There is a broken airplane, and they want me in."

"It's your day off. Why can't they leave you to rest for two days?"

"It goes with the job. They have the station staffed with minimal mechanics, and if something big happens, they must call us in. Besides, the overtime will be nice."

"Did they say what was wrong?"

"No, but usually, it will be two or three days of work."

Eric got up off the chaise lounge he was sitting on and went to the bathroom to rinse his mouth and put on his mechanics uniform. Sue had a freshly laundered stack of pants and shirts for him, but he knew it would do no good. No matter how clean his uniforms were, the foreman would write him up at the end of the shift for having a dirty uniform. He thought, *Show me a mechanic with a clean uniform, and I'll show you a paycheck, thief.*

The foreman must have gotten orders from the general foreman to set him up for termination because anything he said or done was used for a disciplinary action. It was ironic. Here he was, one of the most skilled and reliable mechanics the company had at the station, and he was being targeted for dismissal. Maybe it was because he could still spell U-N-I-O-N and the bigwigs back east didn't want a mechanics union on the property. *Well, there is always the ground-handling companies. The pay and benefits won't be as good, but at least I would still be working on aircraft.*

These were the thoughts going through Eric's mind as he got dressed and headed out the door for work. He kept this from Sue because if he confided his suspicions with her, she would freak out with worry. She didn't know that he was putting away 10 percent of his pay in a 401(k) plan, but the company stopped matching half of it with cash but was matching it with worthless stock that they said would never go below $72 a share. *Bullshit.* It was worthless stock, so he had to take care of his family. He had a Schwab Stock account that he was building, and with his 401(k) and the Roth IRA that he had, they would be okay at retirement.

As Eric pulled into the north employee parking lot, he saw an MD-11 airplane with the cowling on the number one engine open. *Well,* he thought, *at least it's not number two and we would be working on the "patio" fifty feet in the air.* He swiped his employee ID badge in the badge reader. This was done because of the 9/11 attacks. Before that, you just walked through the employee door into the baggage-handling area and then onto the ramp. Now everyone was security conscious— as if this would do any good. If terrorists wanted to use an airplane to attack the United States again, it would take some time, but time was on their side, and the baggage handlers were low-paid workers. Most of them were in it for the flight benefits that were constantly being cut, and the background checks on them were a joke. If you had a friend or relative working for the airline, then it was almost an automatic hire as a baggage handler.

He walked into the bottom of the terminal, passing the door of one of the ground-handling companies, and as he did so, he stuck his head in to see who was there. He thought it was in his best interests to be on good terms with some of the mechanics there because he knew there would be a day he would be going to them or one like them for a job. The room was empty, so he kept going to his company's maintenance room. He went to his wall locker, unlocking the padlock on it, and put on his steel-toed work shoes and then went to see what the problem was.

"What's up?" he said to no one in particular.

"Well, it took you long enough to get here," the foreman said.

"Well, I had to put on a *clean* uniform," Eric replied, "but when this is all over, you will still write me up for a dirty uniform, won't you?"

The foreman just gave him a scowl and said, "Number one engine on 1012 was written up by the pilots for having a compressor stall upon landing and going into reverse. I called maintenance control, and they want us to look at it and send it on its way South."

"No way," Eric said. "A compressor stall on these big engines is serious, and the backlash could be serious to the compressor blades. Has anyone done a borescope on it yet?"

"No. Maintenance control wants us to send it South."

"You mean without checking the blades for damage?" Eric said. "Well, I won't sign it off, and anyone who does will be a fool. Let's get the borescope and the book out and open some inspection plugs and look inside before anyone puts their license or the lives of passengers on the line."

"Well, that's not what maintenance control wants," the foreman replied.

"Well, I don't care about maintenance control. They just want to move iron, and to hell with the consequences. If the plane crashes, the people at maintenance control will lie through their teeth, and the mechanic who signed off the book will be left hanging in the wind. When the FAA comes after his license, the company won't back him and will let him be the scapegoat. Let's get the equipment and have a look," Eric said to another mechanic.

The hex-head bolts on some of the inspection plates came off easily, but there was always one that didn't get enough anti-seize put on it or was over-torqued and was difficult to remove. As Eric worked on this, he had another mechanic remove a gearbox cover so they could put a ratchet in there to turn the engine slowly while they looked at the blades.

"You have to be careful," Eric told the two mechanics who were watching him. They had never done this on an MD-11 engine and were curious as to the procedure of a borescope. "You don't want to get the tip of the wand too close to the blades as they turn. Otherwise, the blade could cut the tip off. Then we would have a real mess on our hands. Slowly turn the gearbox." He looked through the eyepiece and rotated the wand. "Okay, stop. One of you guys take a look and tell me what you see."

The two other mechanics took turns to have a look.

"What are we looking for?" one said.

"On these big engines, the blades have a lot of backlash on them, and with a compressor stall the air flow in the engine tries to go backwards and the blades can hit one another, so look for a smiley mark on the back side of the blades. If you see one, that means the blades struck one another during the stall. This damages the blades, and the book calls for their replacement, which we cannot do here on the ramp. The engine must be disassembled in a shop to do this, and this is why maintenance control wants us to sign it off and ship it South as a revenue flight. The alternative is a two-engine ferry or an engine change here on the ramp, and that is expensive and time-consuming to do here in the field. At best, it's a hangar job, but we can do it if needed."

Eric went into the maintenance office and told the foreman what he had seen and showed him what the book said to do. He told him to recommend to maintenance control either a two-engine ferry or an engine replacement. Eric saw from his body language that he didn't like this message, but he thought, *You are the foreman. You call them and give them the bad news.* He left his office and headed to the maintenance room to the computer and pulled up the section on the engine inspection, and as he was printing it off, Jack, the foreman, came from his office. Eric could see he wasn't happy. As long as there were no problems, Jack was all right. He was a paper pusher, not a decision maker, and liked it when other people made his decisions for him, and many times, that was what he had Eric do.

"Eric!" he yelled. "Maintenance control wants to talk to you on the phone!"

Eric knew what was coming. Jack didn't have the stones to stand up to the techs at maintenance control and wanted him to be the bad guy.

"Eric here," he said as he picked up the extension in the mechanics area."

"Eric, this is Robert at tech support. The engine problem you have up there—can we fly it down to Seattle as a revenue flight and change the engine there?" he asked.

Eric knew if it left, they would continue to push it, and with the blade backlash, it could have damaged or weakened other blades or the blades' mounting roots and possibly come off with a catastrophic failure in flight. "Listen, I said the book shows pictures of what damage to look for and what actions must be taken. Either it's a two-engine ferry or an engine change here in Anchorage," he replied.

After a pause, Robert said, "Are there any MD-11 run-up people at the station?"

"Yes," Eric replied. "I'm qualified."

"Well, then can you take it to a run-up area and run the engine to see if it will stall again?"

"Sure," Eric replied, "but it won't change what we saw on the borescope. I'll give you to the foreman and tell him what you want me to do, and I'll get it ready." He handed the phone to the foreman and waited for the conversation to end.

"Well," the foreman said as he hung up the phone, "it looks like maintenance control wants you to do a run-up on the engine to see if it will stall again. Call the tower and get clearance from them and then take another mechanic with you. Do you have an engine run check sheet?"

"Yes," Eric replied. "I pulled it off the computer while you were talking to maintenance control."

"You're a bit cocky, aren't you?" the foreman asked.

"No," Eric replied. "Just being a professional at my job."

He headed out the door to the ramp with two mechanics. "We'll need wing walkers," he said to one of the mechanics. "Go into the bag busters' break room and get two of them. Then hook the tug to the MD-11 to push us out. Eric climbed into the pilots seat while another younger mechanic climbed into the right co-pilots seat. They started going through the engine start checklist and got the APU running and switched over from ground power to AC power."

Eric tuned the radios to Anchorage ground frequency. Then he called the tug driver on the ground intercom. "You ready?" he asked.

"Yep," the reply came over the cockpit speaker. "You really pissed off the foreman."

"Yeah, well, I have nothing to lose. They are setting me up to fire me, so I'll play their games and do everything by the book. At least they won't be able to fire me for my job performance."

"Well," the driver said, "you're one of the most experienced mechanics here at the station. Why do you think they are going to fire you?"

"To make an example of me so the rest of you will toe the company line, my comrade. Anchorage Ground, Aircraft Maintenance MD-11 at Gate Alpha 2 engine start and push back to north engine run area.

"Aircraft Maintenance, engine start and push your discretion taxi Kilo to Romeo to the north engine run area. Winds at five from 160. Thank you. Ground pushing."

"Okay," Eric said to the tug driver. "Let's get this show on the road." He broke off.

***

The sign said, "All trucks—including rental trucks, U-Hauls, cars and vehicles pulling trailers, motor homes, and RVs—exit at the California port of entry inspection station."

Sam looked at Shirley and said, "This reminds me of the book *The Grapes of Wrath*. I wonder what the official would say when he asks me my name and if I say Tom Joad."

"Don't be a wiseass," Shirley said. "With what we have back there, it could get very nasty if they do an in-depth inspection of our trailer. Besides, all they are looking for is fresh fruits, drug runners, and illegal aliens."

Sam followed the arrows and directions for campers and motor homes and stopped in line with another camper in front of them. A woman inspector came toward them as he thought, *Great. Someone with more testosterone than estrogen who will have to prove her ability to have her position.* He rolled down his driver's window and turned off the truck engine as she approached.

"Good day," she said.

Sam replied, "Yes, it is a good day. How can I help you?"

"Where did you come from?" she asked.

"We were wintering in Arizona," Sam replied.

"Where are you headed?"

"To Gilroy."

She looked at Sam with a quizzical look and asked, "What will you be doing in Gilroy?"

"Well, we stopped there several years ago, and they had this place to buy pickled garlic, and it was very tasty, so we thought we would go there again and get a case or two to take with us as we head North."

"How far North are you going?" she asked as she jotted notes on the sheet of paper that looked like a list of questions on her clipboard.

"Well, we thought of going to Alaska and doing some salmon fishing this summer," Sam said.

"Uh-huh . . . and do you have any fresh fruits in your truck or trailer?" she asked.

"No," Sam replied, "but if the navel oranges are in season, we thought of getting a small bag of them if we could find any available."

"If I were to look into your refrigerator, what would I find?"

"Well some eggs, half of a pack of bacon, about three pounds of potatoes, some lunch meat, bread, mayonnaise, mustard, ketchup, relish, a half-gallon of milk, and half a can of coffee grounds."

"You're traveling light on groceries, aren't you?"

"Yes. When we travel, we normally dine out, and we were planning on stocking up when we hit Gilroy."

"Okay. You can go have a nice stay in California. Oh, one more thing—do you have any firearms in your trailer?"

All kinds of thoughts immediately came to mind, but Sam tried to keep his best poker face on as he turned to face her and replied, "No. Since we started to travel two years ago, we found that we do not need them anymore, and I sold them."

"Thank you," she said. "You can go now."

Sam looked at her and said, "Thank you. Have a nice day." He started the truck and pulled forward to Interstate 10 as his heart started to beat normally again. "That went better than I expected," he said to Shirley.

"Yes, and for a change, you weren't a wiseass, and what's this bit about Alaska?"

"Hey, I know when to toe the line, and I figured if I said Alaska instead of Idaho or Montana, she would go easier on us. You know there are a lot of conservative, antigovernment people in Idaho and Montana, so I didn't want to alarm her liberal instincts."

The trip to Gilroy went without much of a problem. Sam kept his speed slightly under the posted speed limit. He didn't want any overzealous state trooper to pull him over for speeding or changing lanes without using his turn signal, knowing with out-of-state tags, it would be a soft and easy stop with a couple of old retired people. Getting through LA with a large travel trailer was a royal pain in the ass, but they got onto Interstate 5 and, at the Kettleman exit, pulled off for the night.

The next day at Gilroy, they had a discussion among themselves on what kind of garlic and how many cases of each they should get. They then found a manager to see if they could get a discount for buying in quantity. The manager said it was company policy and wanted a business license for this, and Sam just happened to have one he had made up on the computer for Alaska. They loaded up and headed for I-5. They drove up Interstate 5 until they came to I-205, which went around Portland. Then they took I-84, the Columbia River Highway, to I-82. The drive along the Columbia River was a nice scenic drive. At Kennewick, Washington, they then took U.S. Route 395 to I-90 to Spokane, Washington. This took them through some nice farmlands and forested areas.

While they wanted to get to Coeur d'Alene, Idaho, as fast as they could, they stopped at campgrounds along the way, and whenever they could, they would attend any auctions they came across. They were attending one every day or two all the way. At these auctions, Sam and Shirley would split up, she going toward the groups of women and he wearing his Vietnam veteran hat, trying to get any of the men to talk with him. They would then, after the auction was over, compare notes in the trailer. One recurring item was how the people didn't trust the government anymore and how they felt on the illegal alien issue on their Southern border and taxes. They both agreed that the mood of the people at every location where they stopped was one of mistrust of the federal government and, surprisingly, their local governments, whether it be state or the town they lived in. This held true with both the women and especially the men. At one location, they even had a picture of the president and their governor hanging upside down.

While at these auctions, Sam and Shirley picked up a few more items that they felt they could sell at a profit once they got to where they were going, and that was the Palouse area of Idaho, Montana, and Eastern Washington. But mostly their attendance at these auctions was for entertainment and to talk to people.

***

Eric always sat with awe as to how high above the tarmac they were sitting in an MD-11 airplane. It was the equivalent of sitting on the peak of a roof on a two-story house. They had gotten the request to set the breaks, and the headset walker removed the hydraulic bypass pin from the nose gear, held it up for them to see, and walked away following the pushback tug.

"Anchorage Ground," Eric called. "Aircraft Maintenance taxiing to the north run-up area."

"Aircraft Maintenance, you're clear. Kilo to November. Call us when you want to come back."

"Roger that," Eric replied.

Sitting that high up, you had to watch your speed closely since your driving perception changed. They turned into the wind at the north run-up area and set the breaks. Eric made sure there was enough room so that if the brakes failed, he would have enough room to either reset the brakes or maneuver the aircraft so they wouldn't run off the taxiway.

"All right, let's get the checklist out and do this by the book so they won't have another item to use against me when they fire me," Eric said to the mechanic in the right seat. "OAT 17C, EGT 465. Winds five knots at 160 heading 160. All right, let's increase the throttle on number one. You watch the EGT, and I'll watch N1 and N2 and EPR if it stalls again. We need the readings when it stalls."

Eric slowly came up, and around 88 percent N2, there was a rapid series of bangs that shook the airplane. "You get the EGT?" he asked the other mechanic.

He looked at Eric sheepishly and said, "No, the compressor stall startled me."

"This is your first run-up on one of these things?" Eric asked.

"Yes."

"Well, it's kind of impressive, isn't it?"

"Yeah. It felt as if the engine was going to fly off the wing."

"Well, yes. That's why compressor stalls are so critical on these big engines. There is a lot of metal spinning out there, and when it stalls, the blades try to stop turning one way and try to go backward. The engine tries to twist off the wing, mounts get cracked, bolts fail. You weren't here when an Evergreen 747 lost a number two engine on the climb out to the east and the engine dropped on Anchorage?"

"No. What happened?"

"Well, on takeoff to the east, it's believed that the number two compressor stalled. The engine left the wing, ripping out the fuel and air lines and a bunch of other stuff. The engine landed in what was then a wooded area behind the now school district admin building on Northern Lights, but back then, it was a shopping mall. Parts also hit the roofs of the apartments at Checkmate Plaza on Boniface. A few years later, I was talking to an Evergreen maintenance instructor who was here to train Evergreen mechanics, and he said the plane had almost crashed on Anchorage. Okay, let's do this again, and trust me, it stalled before. It will again."

Eric called the tower, telling them he was finished and wanted to head back to the alpha 2 gate. They headed back to the terminal and called on the company radio for guidance into the alpha 2 gate. After parking the plane, they secured the airplane and headed to the line maintenance office. Eric looked around and didn't see the foreman anywhere, so he got a cup of coffee. Just as he had started writing their run-up report and the results of the run-up, the foreman came into the room.

"Eric, can you come into my office?"

As he got up, he looked around. None of the other mechanics were there, and an airport rent-a-cop came into their break room. *This isn't good*, he thought as he entered the foreman's office.

"Close the door and sit down," the foreman said. "Maintenance control is concerned that you intentionally caused the engine to hit the compressor stall when you did your run-up to sabotage the engine and prove your point."

"That's bullshit," Eric replied. "I'm the most conscientious mechanic you have here at the station. They can check the ACARS readings if they want to. Just because I won't roll over for maintenance control, they think I sabotaged the run-up? Their job is to get dumb or willing schmucks to push iron for the company. When something happens, it's not their license or reputation on the line. Nor are they in front of an FAA investigation. I go by the book, and on instances like this, people's lives are on the line. What if it was your wife riding on that flight? Oh yeah, that's right. You're divorced."

"Well, Eric, you are on two weeks' suspension, and an airport security officer will walk you out of the terminal. You will be contacted within two weeks on the status of your suspension or employment."

***

"What are you getting at?" Betty said to Ken.

"A few months ago, while I was out hunting, I came upon some green grass, so I went back later with an entrenching tool and dug down and hit wet sand. So I dug some more, and soon, the hole started to seep water. I enlarged it, and I soon had a small watering hole. I would swing by there from time to time to see what animals were using it. Over the past month, I saw tracks of mule deer, coyotes, and other small animals.

Well, yesterday I saw some Mexican coyotes shepherding what looked like five Muslims. It was obvious that the Mexicans didn't think much of the Muslims and the Muslims didn't think much of the Mexicans. I think it's just a matter of time when things get hot here, and I don't mean the temperature. When do you put in our next food and supply order?"

"It's due next week, but we can put it in a few days early."

"Well, see if you can get as much freeze-dried food as you can, along with bags of pinto beans and rice, and then if you can get two thousand rounds of .223, two hundred rounds of twelve-gauge .00 buckshot, one hundred rounds of slugs, one thousand rounds of .308, and five hundred rounds of 7.62×39."

"Why 7.62? We don't have any guns that shoot that round."

"Trust me, honey. We soon will. Also, see if they have canning jars and lids, no quarts but two cases of half pints, ten cases of pints, regular mouth, and fifteen cases of wide-mouth pints and get a bunch of lids. Use up all our allotment for the next two months. I have a feeling it's going to get interesting here very soon. I'm going to stay around here for the next few days and do camp chores."

Ken went outside. He didn't like lying, but he didn't want to scare Betty yet. *Better to get things set up first, and then, well, then I will have a heart-to-heart talk with her.* He got a garden rake and walked a perimeter around the trailer first at 100 feet, raking a three-foot-wide swath smooth, and then at 150 feet, 300 feet, and 400 feet. It wasn't hard work but hot work. When he finished, he now had a tattletale perimeter around the trailer and drill pad at different distances. If anyone came by, he would know how many there were and how close they came to the trailer.

The day was almost over, so Ken went back to the trailer, got the outside shower hose from the side of the trailer, stripped down, and took a shower outside. Even though there was no one for miles, he couldn't get Betty to shower outside without a privacy curtain put up for her. He walked around the trailer, carrying his clothes, just as Betty came out of the trailer, carrying a plate of steaks.

She looked at him and asked, "Did it hurt?"

He asked, "Did what hurt?"

"Those."

"What? These tattoos?"

"No. Those," she said, pointing at the pockmarks and scars on his body.

She had asked Ken this question before, but he always joked about them or brushed her off, not answering her, but today, with what was brewing, he figured to level with her.

"Not at first," he said. "The first time, I was scared, so when I was in the hospital, I talked to the medics and doctors. They said that for some people, during a firefight, with the adrenaline flowing in their blood and with their training, they reacted differently. Well, for me, I didn't know I was hit until afterward. Then it was gradual. I guess the adrenaline was wearing off. At this point, some guys would go into shock when they realized what happened. For me, it was more of, I don't know, a clinical thing. I saw the blood and the entrance and exit wounds and what my body looked like under my skin. I guess all my hunting prepared me for some of what I saw. I watched men with little more than a grazing wound or a minor wound go into shock and die, and I saw men who should be dead live.

"I think it's all in your frame of mind. If you think that if you get shot, you will die, then you will die no matter how minor the wound is. But if you believe that you can survive, then the chances bearing an infection are you most likely will survive a bullet wound. The thing you must get into your head now—right now, right this minute—and believe is you will not die from a simple bullet wound. It might hurt like hell, but if you suck the pain in and use it to your advantage, you will survive more than you ever thought you could. You see this?" Ken lifted his right arm up. "This hurt like hell. It really burned, and it bled a lot, but I knew the bleeding was from subsurface blood vessels and they would soon clot by themselves or with a compress. If you get hit, don't panic. It will get you into trouble. Keep your head and do the mission or what you have to do. After the shooting and all the enemies are dead, you can break down, but not before then. Your buddies or I will need your help. Now give me those steaks, and I'll grill them."

"Aren't you going to get dressed?" Betty asked.

"Why? There's no one around, and the sun, while it lasts, feels good on my body. Now go make a salad while I grill these."

"We'll make sure you are dressed tomorrow. I got a phone call. A truck is coming tomorrow to pick up some oil, and Jerry is also coming. Jerry was our regional supervisor."

"What does he want?" Ken asked.

"Maybe to question us on our last supply order," she said.

***

"I got on the computer," Sam said, coming front from his little office in the back of the trailer. With all of the stuff they had it was really tight back there and Sam even considered moving his computer and printer forward but knew Shirley wouldn't like it so he just made do. "and I printed up a list of farmers' market and flea market locations."

"Good," Shirley said. "I want to start getting rid of some of what we have and find out what the people in the area are wanting for next year. We can hit a farmers' market in Coeur d'Alene in two days and then go on U.S. Route 95 through several small towns like Pullman, Potlatch, Moscow, and Lewistown and a bunch of other small towns that are nothing more than a wide spot on the road."

***

"You're home already?" Sue asked Eric.

"Yes. Things were like I thought and didn't go too good."

"What do you mean?" Sue asked.

"Well, it was an MD-11 that had a compressor stall on landing and thrust reversal when that happens it screws up the compressor blades in the engine, but the assholes in maintenance control, even though they know it, tried to get someone to sign it off for another flight. It's their job to push the iron—and to hell with the mechanics and their license. If things go bad, they just claim ignorance and that they were not given all the facts. The mechanic gets a reprimand, the FAA jerks his license, and the company then fires him. With no union to back you, you are then hanging out in the wind."

"So what happened?"

"Well, I held my ground, and now I'm on unpaid leave for two weeks until the head honchos can figure out what to do with me."

"What are we to do now?" Sue asked with panic in her voice. "You will be fired, and how will we pay our bills."

"Don't worry," Eric said. "Something will come up. I'm going to take a shower and get some sleep."

The phone was ringing next to the bed. It was an old habit from Eric's military days to have a phone in the bedroom so he could be contacted if something came up in the middle of the night. He woke and groggily answered it.

"Is this Eric?" the voice asked.

"Yes," Eric replied warily.

"Well, this is Thomas Bellman. I heard what happened."

"Well, good news travels fast," Eric replied.

"Yes," the voice said, "but I'm setting up a line transit maintenance company here in Anchorage. I know your reputation as a mechanic and your reputation of running your mouth. I would like to meet with you and talk about some things."

"Well, my schedule is kind of full, but I guess I can find some time today."

"Always the wiseass, aren't you?"

"Well, there is a coffee shop at King Street and Diamond called Vivace. How does two hours from now sound?"

"Okay. I'll be there."

"How will I know you?"

"Don't worry. I know you."

Then the line went dead.

"Who was on the phone?" Sue asked as she rolled over.

"It seems someone already knows about my suspension and wants to talk to me about working for them." Eric rolled out of bed and headed for a shower.

As he left the house, Sue shouted at him to watch his mouth while he talked to this guy. "Remember, you need a job!"

Eric walked into Vivace and looked around. No one was in there, so he got a latte, grabbed a loose newspaper, sat down, and started to do the crossword puzzle. He soon saw someone come in, look around, and get a latte also. He came over to Eric and sat down.

"Hello, Eric," the man said. "How are you feeling?"

"Well," Eric said, "like someone kicked me in the nuts. You know, I worked faithfully and really didn't complain when I worked on my wedding anniversaries, kids' birthdays, holidays, and such, and now I'm thrown to the side like a used piece of toilet paper."

"Well, I have an offer for you. We are setting up a transit line maintenance company. We will be working mostly foreign transient freighters, MD-11s and 747s mostly. Their planes are in reasonably good condition, in fact better than many that you have been working on in the past few years."

"You're right. I have seen more deferred maintenance items coming through on the books, and parts are harder to get."

"Well, that isn't the case with the foreign aircraft companies. It's almost a badge of honor to keep their airplanes problem free."

"If I come over, what would my position be with you?"

"I would have wanted to use you as a lead mechanic, but I already have two of them, and I don't need any more, so you will be a senior line mechanic and trainer."

"Trainer? I'm not any good as a classroom instructor."

"You won't be. You will have mechanics who don't have much experience assigned to you, and you will be expected to show them the way around line maintenance."

"Well, the big question is what will I be paid to be a babysitter?"

Thomas gave Eric a dirty look but didn't say anything to him. This meant he really wanted Eric on board with him. "Well, it won't be as much as you used to make, but it will be a good wage. You must realize you will be like kryptonite for a while. No one will touch you. Think it over and talk to Susan, your wife."

That got Eric's attention, and Thomas saw it.

"Yes, we checked you out before I called you. Here is my card. Call me tomorrow."

Thomas got up and left his latte untouched, no goodbyes or anything. It didn't matter since Eric wasn't much of a handshake person anyway. He sat there and sipped on his latte and thought about what Thomas had said. He pulled out his pocket notebook. He carried this with him always, a leftover habit from his military days. He flipped the pages to a list of phone numbers. These were the numbers of foremen for the different airlines in Anchorage. Using his cell phone, he called them one by one to see if they were hiring and if they had a position for him. Some were sympathetic, but most brushed him off, but the last one, before he hung up, told Eric to take Thomas's offer. Eric wondered, *How did he know of the offer?*

Eric walked into the house, and Sue yelled down, "What was the meeting about?"

He walked up the stairs and grabbed a beer out of the fridge. "They want me to be a babysitter. I'll have a glorious title of senior line mechanic and trainer. I'll be showing the new mechanics the ropes of line maintenance. I have until tomorrow to call him and accept the offer."

"You will accept it, won't you?" Sue asked with a little panic in her voice."

"Yeah, I'll probably accept it but not too quickly. They need me and my skills and knowledge as much as I need a job."

***

"Well," Shirley said, "I hope the rest of the trip goes better than what we did in Coeur d'Alene."

"I believe it will," Sam said. "Coeur D is just a little too big for what we have, and Spokane is too close. It's easy for the people to get what they want or need. But the next towns are much smaller and are a little more remote. This is a very pretty country" Sam said. "A person could settle here if things went to crap."

"What are you getting at?" Shirley Asked.

"Well, remember the gunshots when we loaded at that storage unit in Phoenix? We cannot continue to live in a trailer and move around forever. We will have to soon settle down at one place, and this area looks just as good as any other, and besides, most of the people here are of a mindset as we are. Seattle is getting like LA, and Washington and Oregon might as well be an extension of California, with all the liberals moving in."

"I guess you're right on that part."

"You were the real-estate agent. Keep your eyes open for some land in this area."

"We could stop at a real-estate office and see what's in the MLS book, or you could check on the computer and see what's available or if there are any estate auctions that include land."

The people in this area were kind of wary of them at first, but Shirley had a way with people. Sam guessed that was why she was a good real-estate agent. They soon warmed up to them. In the towns—if you could call them that—they were little more than a wide spot on the highway with a few houses in close proximity. In Tensed and De Smet, they did much better, and their spirits and expectations rose accordingly. Going through the Mary Minerva McCroskey State Park, they saw signs of farms tucked back, away from the highway, into the trees. This looked like a very remote area, and then it opened up again to rolling hills and open areas.

They came to Potlatch Junction and turned off to Potlatch, a larger town off U.S. 95. There was Potlatch and the town of Onaway. They set up in a vacant area and soon were doing a brisk business. Sam saw Shirley talking to a young woman with a little girl of about three or four years of age while he was talking to an older gentleman about some of the ammunition and tools he had on display. After the man left, Sam went over to Shirley to see how she was doing.

Shirley turned and said, "This is Sally. She has an uncle who is looking to sell his small farmstead. I asked where it was, and she said her uncle was a bit eccentric and his place was at the end of a township road off a small county road with large woods behind it, but the house is little more than a one-room cabin. There were sixty acres in his farmstead, but only forty were tillable."

"Why is he selling it?" Sam asked.

"Well, he is in his seventies and has pancreatic cancer from Agent Orange, so he has less than a year to live."

Sam frowned, knowing her uncle had maybe six months since he had lost a friend a few years ago to the same thing. It was a common cancer with veterans of the Vietnam War. He asked, "When could we go see it?"

"She said she would go talk to her uncle and get back with us later in the day."

Sam thanked her and walked her to her car then went back to his tables of ammunition and outdoor-related items since there was another person there looking at some ATV gun boots that he had on display. Sam knew he was really interested since he had driven up with a Honda Foreman four-wheeler in the back of his pickup. It was just after noon, and things slowed down when Shirley said she was going into the trailer to make lunch for them. Sam was sitting on a folding camp chair they had for sale—it was one of those that was a rocking chair—as Shirley came out with a tray of tomato soup, toasted cheese sandwiches with a slice of onion in it, Sam liked his grilled cheese sandwiches like this, and some iced mint tea. He don't know where she had found it, but the tea was good.

It was slow through the afternoon, but Sam expected it to pick up after shift change, that was around 4:00 p.m. Sure enough, at 4:30 p.m., there were several people at their tables. Several of the men brought their wives, and several of the women who had been there earlier in the day brought their husbands. Sam and Shirley were doing a brisk business. He sold most of the ammunition that he was willing to part with and had a few inquiries if he had any firearms. He always said, "Not now" because he didn't know any of these people, and he didn't want to get into trouble with the BATF for selling firearms for a profit without a license.

Around 7:00 p.m., things quieted down, and they started packing up for the night when Sally, the young lady who had come by earlier, came by and said that she had talked to her uncle and that he would see them tomorrow around 9:00 a.m., and that she would come by at 8:00 a.m. to lead them to his place. They thanked her, finished packing their merchandise for the night, and then got into their pickup truck for a little ride around the area. It took all of ten minutes to view the town, so they went down Route 6 for a while. It more or less paralleled the Palouse River. It was a nice drive, and they turned around at Hampton and headed back to their camper for the night.

The next morning, a few minutes after eight, Sally came for them. They were outside, waiting for her, jumped into their pickup, and followed her down Route 6 for about five or so miles. They crossed a bridge over the Palouse River and went another mile or two on a dirt road, more of a farm lane, and at the end was a wooded area and a turnoff with a cabin—if you could call it that—in the woods. Shirley and Sam got out as Sally honked her horn three times. A man with a neatly trimmed grey beard came out of the cabin, and when he saw Sally, his face lit up in a big smile.

"Uncle Max, these are the folks I talked to you about."

Sam walked up, and Uncle Max looked him up and down.

"You a college boy?" he asked.

"Yeah," Sam replied. "The University of Southeast Asia."

He grinned. "I never heard of it called that. When?"

"March '67 to May '72," Sam replied.

"Did Sally tell you of my situation?" Max asked.

"Yes. It's a bitch. I have seen some of the men from the teams go in the past years. I often wonder when or if it will happen to me and, if not, why not."

He looked at Sam. "The teams?"

"Yes. After my second year, I got tired of the BS and went Special Forces. A lot of us did."

"Well, I don't have much time, and as much as I would like to give this to Sally, her ex is a real jerk and would find a way to get it from her."

"I have a proposition," Shirley said.

Max turned and looked at her. It was an icy stare. It was the first time Sam had ever seen Shirley stop talking.

"Well, spit it out," Max said.

"Well, we could draw up a contract. You can stay in your home until you, uh . . ."

"Until I die," Max said. "We all die. It's a journey we start when we were born."

"Until you pass away," Shirley said. "We set up something like a tenant in common contract with Sally. She has an equal share but no interest in the property. If she wants to, she can live on the property with us as an unpaid tenant whose interest is free rent in lieu of us paying her for the property. This way, she doesn't have any money for the ex to steal, and there is no land for him to steal. In short, basically, she becomes our dependent. Where we own and control the property."

"What are the guarantees that you won't steal the property and kick her out on her ass?" Max asked.

"Her odds are better with us," Sam said, "than going it alone against her ex."

Max turned and went into his cabin.

Sam looked at Sally and Shirley. "Now what?" he asked.

"He does this sometimes when he wants to think about something."

"How long will he be in there?"

Sally said, "As long as it takes. Let's walk around."

The cabin was just inside a tree line, but strangely, it had good fields of fire on all four sides. There was an outhouse, a few solar panels, a well, and a shed with a rabbit hutch and a chicken coop attached to it. There was a garden like Sam had never seen before, and he had seen many of Shirley's gardens over his life. It was compact yet massive. Every inch of ground had a plant, and they were all growing profusely. Sam looked the rest of the property over and decided where to put their house shed and barn and the orientation for the maximum effects for the sun and solar panels and protection.

"This is a nice piece of land here," Sam said.

"Yes," Sally said. "He even has a small orchard behind that finger of trees over there, and he even planted several Colorado spruce trees for Christmas trees."

They were walking back to the vehicles and cabin when Max came out.

"Okay," he said. "Let's do it. How soon can you have the papers drawn up?"

"I can have them done by tonight, and you can sign them in the morning. They'll have to be notarized," Shirley said, "so you will have to come to town to sign them where we can find a notary."

"Sally, when can you pick me up?" Max asked.

"After school lets out, around 4:00 p.m."

Sam looked at Sally. "Do you teach?" he asked.

"I'm a substitute elementary school teacher, and I must fill in tomorrow."

Sam shook hands with Uncle Max and said, "until tomorrow" then turned and joined Shirley at the truck.

Sam and Shirley went back to their trailer and set up their stand. Sam stayed outside and worked the stand, while Shirley was on the computer writing up a tenant-in-common contract. After about two hours, Shirley came out with sandwiches and soup.

"I'm glad," she said, "that I kept all my contracts on a thumb drive. It made it much easier. All I had to do was change a few things like dates and names and locations, and it was done."

"Well, Max," Sam said, "the papers are signed, and Sally will be secure. Do you want to come by our camper for dinner?"

"No," he replied. "I must get back and take care of my animals."

"Okay. I'll swing by in a day or two and talk about the future."

"Fine," he said and turned to Sally's car, and they were gone.

Sam and Shirley went back to their trailer, and Sam got out the grill and started grilling some steaks. While he was doing this, a few people came by, asking when they would be open again. He told them at 9:00 a.m. tomorrow. It looked like they would be busy again all day tomorrow.

The next day, just as he had thought, they were busy all day, and this surprised them until they found out that it was payday for some of the people, and the word got out to the smaller outlying towns and farms. Many of them were little more than a wide spot on a road, with four or more houses in somewhat close proximity of one another, and Sam and Shirley started to see new faces at their tables. Sam looked up from a table after helping someone. It was inevitable to happen since they had been there now for almost a week.

As things started to slow for the evening, the local sheriff's deputy came by. He introduced himself as Sheriff's Deputy Barns and asked them how things were going and then he asked how they had come by all the items they were selling. Sam asked him if he wanted some sweet iced mint tea. This took him back a little. Sam guessed he was expecting a hassle from them. Instead, they were cordial with him. Sam pulled up a rocking camp chair for him as Shirley came out with a pitcher of tea and some glasses.

"Exactly what are your concerns, Deputy?" Sam asked.

"It's rumored that with all the items you are selling, some may be stolen. Can you tell me about the items you are selling and how you came to have these items?"

Shirley sat on a camp chair. "Well," she said, "we winter down in Arizona, and there are a lot of flea markets plus yard sales and auctions. We attend as many as we can and try to buy as cheaply as we can. I know that canning jars and equipment in that area doesn't sell for much, but up here, I can get a fair price on that sort of stuff. Also, down sleeping bags aren't in much demand in Arizona, but up here, they are selling well."

"We also go to defaulted storage auctions," Sam chimed in, "but the problem with them is you sometimes get a lot of junk in those units, but sometimes you hit a gold mine."

"What are your intentions?" the deputy asked. "Are you going to be moving on, or are you going to spend more time here?"

Sam didn't know what the Deputy knew and didn't want to reveal too much about them or their intentions so he said that they were looking for a place to settle since they could not keep traveling and they didn't like the summers in Arizona and so they were looking for a place to settle down while they traveled around.

"Well," the deputy said, "the summers are nice, but the winters can be rough."

"Well," Sam said, "several of my criteria include if I can grow sweet corn and tomatoes in the summer." He already knew he could, but he wanted to throw the deputy off balance a little.

"Well, sweet corn will be no problem, but you will have to start the tomatoes indoors and transplant them in the spring."

"Another of my requirements is if there is a VFW or American Legion in the area."

The deputy looked at Sam with a questioning look.

Sam said, "Vietnam."

The deputy's eyes narrowed, and he said his father and uncle had served over there. "The stories they and other Vietnam veterans tell of how they were treated when they came back to the United States just make me angry. To answer your question, there is a Legion Post in town. Are there any other questions you have for us you want answered?" Sam said.

"It's a shame you came here just to talk to us."

"No," Deputy Barns said. "I come by here about every week to check up on my sister and uncle. My sister has some problems, and my uncle lives out on Route 6 in a cabin."

The hairs on Sam's neck started to stand up.

"He was diagnosed with cancer, and I'm afraid he doesn't have much time."

"Is your sister named Sally?" Sam asked.

The deputy's head snapped up, and he stared at Sam. "How do you know that?" he asked.

"Then your uncle is Max," Sam said.

Deputy Barns looked at Sam—more of a cold stare. Sam then filled him in on what had happened and his intentions. Sam figured it wouldn't hurt to have the local law watching his back. He asked him about what, if anything, he knew of the border crossings down South. The deputy replied that while there were more people crossing, he was told to watch for more than just illegal Mexicans. Sam filled him in on what he had been hearing on his shortwave receiver and what had happened when they left the storage place. The deputy said he wanted to check on his uncle Max before it got dark and got up. Sam stood up and walked him to his car. He told him not to be a stranger, that he was always welcome. They shook hands, and the deputy left.

Sam turned to Shirley. "Well, that was interesting. I wonder how many of these people are intermarried and how many branches are on their family trees."

They finished stacking the tables against the trailer and went inside for the night. Sam listened on the ham receiver that they had for any news, and in the background, he had found Radio Free Redoubt and had that on. Shirley couldn't figure out how he could listen to two radios at once, but it was natural for him to do it.

Sam was just about ready to turn the ham radio off and tune the other radio to a music station when there was a horn blowing outside. He turned the lights off and looked out the door. The deputy sheriff was there. He came walking up to the door.

"Sam," he said, "because of the circumstances and what you told me, I felt you should be in on this."

"What's up?" Sam asked.

"Max has passed away. It seemed now that Sally was to be taken care of, he felt that he could now go."

"Is there anything we can do to help?"

"Yes. I notified the coroner, and he is on his way. Can you come back with me and wait for him so I can go tell Sally?"

"Sure. Let me put shoes on and get a jacket, and I'll be right out." Sam wanted a jacket to cover that he would be armed, but the deputy beat him to it.

"If you have a firearm, bring it," the deputy said.

Sam looked at him. "I have a Beretta 92FS 9 mm and spare magazines. Will that do?" he asked.

The deputy grinned. "Yeah, that'll do."

Sam followed the Deputy back to Max's cabin. It was the first time he was in the cabin, and it was orderly, everything in place and neat, as he would expect from a military person. Uncle Max was lying on his bed with a look of contentment on his face. He had his service medals on a nightstand. Sam saw a silver star and a distinguished service cross.

Among the others awards, there were ribbons. *It looked like Uncle Max back in the day was a badass.*

The deputy turned to Sam, saying, "I haven't told you my name yet. It's Jesse Barns. What I want you to do is make sure no one—and I mean no one—but the coroner comes into this cabin. Use whatever force you need to do this."

Sam looked at him and raised an eyebrow.

"Yes," he said. "Even deadly force if needed. I want you to know that Sally's ex-husband—his name is Randall Gilmore—is a mean SOB especially if he has been drinking which he does a lot, and if he finds out that Max is dead, he may come here. Max was the only person keeping Randall away from Sally. Max told Randall that if he ever hurt Sally again, he would kill him and take the body out into the woods where no one would find it. Randall thinks Max has a stash of money here, and if he finds out that Max is dead, he may come here armed and maybe with a drinking buddy."

Deputy Barns left, and Sam was alone there in the cabin. He resisted the urge to turn on a light, thinking that darkness was his friend. He waited, listening to the night noises, and started to drift off to sleep when he heard a vehicle driving up. He prayed it was the coroner, and the Lord answered his prayer. The coroner backed up to the cabin, and he came into the cabin as his assistant opened the back of the van.

"Who are you, and where is Deputy Barns?" the coroner asked.

Sam replied that Deputy Barns had told him to stay here and not to let anyone but the coroner in and that he had gone to his sister's place to inform her what happened. "And I guess to protect her from her ex," Sam replied.

"Yeah, he is one mean SOB," the coroner replied.

Great, Sam thought. *I'm caught in a family feud—the Hatfield's and McCoy's.*

The coroner and his assistant were just about ready to load Max onto the stretcher when Sam heard another vehicle coming toward the cabin. *Please let it be Deputy Barns*, he prayed, but he guessed the Lord was busy because the man who got out was carrying a rifle and came toward the cabin. Sam stayed inside behind the door but could hear what was being said and could look between the door and the wall.

The coroner stepped out and said, "Randall, this area is a secure area until I'm finished with the investigation."

"So when will you be finished?" Randall asked.

"When I'm good and ready to be finished," the coroner said. "Now get out of here." He turned and came into the cabin, closing the door.

Sam looked at the coroner and said, "You know he will wait down the road until he sees you pass. Then he will come here."

"Yes, I expect that. Jimmy!" he called out. "Can you handle things if I stay here?"

"Sure, boss," Jimmy said.

"Okay. Let's get Max loaded, and you go back to the morgue. I'll get a ride later."

They both loaded Max into the hearse, and the coroner came into the cabin, carrying a Colt 1911 .45. He looked at Sam and asked, "Are you carrying?"

Sam lifted his jacket, showing his Beretta in its holster and extra magazines. "Do you think we will need these?" he asked.

"I hope not, but with Randall, you never know, and with Max dead, he will be even more aggressive. He wants what he thinks is in this cabin," the coroner replied.

"What's in this cabin?"

"As far as I know, nothing worth much. I haven't been out here often, and all I know is Max was living off his military retirement, Social Security and disability checks. It wasn't much, but with his gardens, rabbits, chickens, and an occasional deer or elk, he got by all right."

When Sam had come here, he had parked his truck around the back side of the cabin, out of sight from anyone coming to Max's cabin. They sat in the cabin in the dark, and Sam was asking questions to the coroner. He found out after much prying that his name was Jethro. He asked all kinds of other questions about the area. What was the weather like in the summer and winter? Were there four true seasons or just summer and winter? Was there much rain, or was it dry? What kinds of animals were there? Were there deer and elk? What kinds of predators were here? Were there wolves or mountain lions? What Sam learned was this was a nice place and people, once they knew you, were here to stay, and if you were not a snowbird, they warmed up to you.

"Well," Jethro said, "if you stand watch for a while, I'll get a little sleep," he stretched out on a couch and was sound asleep in seconds.

It wasn't but half an hour later that Sam heard a vehicle coming in the lane to the cabin.

Jethro was instantly awake. "Well, that didn't take too long," he said.

"How do you want to play this?" Sam asked Jethro.

"Well, you stand on one side of the door, and I'll be on the other side, and when he comes in, you turn the lights on, and we will then play it by ear."

The truck lights played across the window as whoever was driving pulled up, and the lights were shining against the door. Sam stepped back a little so the lights wouldn't be in his eyes just as the door opened. He turned on the cabin lights.

"Randall, stop right there," Jethro commanded.

Sam could smell Randall from where he was, and he reeked of liquor.

"You're drunk again," Jethro said.

"Yeah, but not too drunk to get what I want," Randall said.

"I told you once to leave, and I mean it. You're not allowed in here," Jethro said.

"Well, the way I see it, you surprised that stranger there, and he shot you just as I came here, and I had to shoot him," Randall said as he brought his rifle up to point at Sam.

Two shots sounded as one as both Jethro and Sam fired. Between a 9 mm Black Talon hollow point from Sam's pistol and a .45 hollow point from Jethro's pistol, Randall dropped where he was standing.

Jethro looked at Sam and said, "A clear case of self-defense, and if you ask me, I think the county coroner will agree," as he winked at Sam. He pulled out his cell phone and hit a speed dial number. "Jimmy, bring a clean kit and get ahold of Deputy Barns and meet me at Max's place. We have more work to do." Jethro looked at Sam and said, "Well, someone has to move that truck so Jimmy can get in here. I'll throw a blanket over Randall so we don't have to look at his drunk ass until Deputy Barns and Jimmy show up."

Sam went out of the cabin to move the truck when he heard a gunshot inside of the cabin. He went into the cabin and looked around the kitchen area. Jethro looked at him and shrugged. Sam asked what had happened.

Jethro looked at him and said, "Did something happen? It looks like it will be a longer night."

"Yes," Sam said, "and I could use some coffee. How about you?"

"No," Jethro said. "Wake me when they show up." He was sound asleep again in seconds.

How does he do that? Sam wondered. *His adrenaline was still flowing from the shooting, and he just drops off to sleep.* After two hours, Sam thought that maybe he should have followed Jethro's lead and gotten some sleep also. Just as he was settling in on a couch, he heard vehicles coming toward the cabin. Jethro was instantly on his feet as Deputy Barns came in and stepped around Randall's body.

"Well, you guys were busy," Deputy Barns said. "I guess I should split you guys up and question each of you separately, but you already have had ample time to get your story straight. Well, Jethro, why don't you fill me in? Officially, that is."

Sam ducked out for the nearest tree to get rid of some of the coffee he had drunk.

When he came back in, he heard Deputy Barns say, "Well, I guess that will be the official story for the report. Write something up for me, but in a way, you guys did the county a favor." He looked at Sam. "I'm glad that you were able to duck in time to dodge Randall's bullet and that Jethro was able to kill Randall before he could kill you."

Sam looked at Jethro, and Jethro just winked and said, "I'm the coroner, and what goes into my autopsy report will be official."

Deputy Barns looked at Sam. "Sam, I think we are finished with your help here. Why don't you head back to your wife for what's left of the night? If I need anything more, I'll come by your camper tomorrow."

Sam thanked him and shook hands. He looked into his hand, and his empty 9 mm shell casing was in the palm.

Deputy Barns looked at him and said, "The story that Jethro said was that Randall shot at you, and you were able to duck in time as the bullet went harmlessly into the cabin wall. He showed it to me, and the rest of his story holds up. Now go home to your wife."

As Sam headed to his truck, he glanced at his wristwatch and saw it was only 1:00 a.m. He thought it would be later than that. Heading back to the trailer, he knew what was about to happen to him. He had had it happen before. As the adrenaline in his body wore off, he would get a severe headache.

Sam pulled in next to the trailer and was surprised to see a light on. He knocked on the door before opening it. He had made the mistake of not doing that once and was met by Shirley holding a shotgun on him. He walked in and saw Shirley and Sally sitting in chairs, talking.

"Well, what happened out there?" Shirley asked.

"Oh, nothing much," Sam replied as he went to a kitchen cabinet and got two aspirins and a glass of water.

"Well, something happened. Deputy Barns dropped Sally and her daughter here and said he was needed out at Max's place," Shirley said.

"Well, I went out there, and Jethro, the coroner, and his assistant, Jimmy, showed up. Soon after, Randall Sally's ex-husband showed up, but Jethro ran him off. We thought he would be back, so he sent Jimmy his assistant by himself to the morgue with Max. About half an hour later, Randall showed up smelling of liquor. Words were said, and Randall had a gun and was about to shoot me when Jethro shot him. Randall is dead," Sam said.

Shirley looked at Sam and then at Sally and said, "Sally, it's late. Why don't you and your daughter spend the night here? We have room, and in the morning, you can figure out what you want to do."

Sam got up from the kitchen table and climbed the three steps up into the master bedroom of the fifth-wheel trailer as Shirley and Sally got squared away with one of the spare beds in the camper. He brushed his teeth and went to bed.

Sam awoke to the smell of bacon frying and fresh coffee. He looked at the alarm clock on the side of the bed and saw it was 7:00 a.m. *Crap*, he thought, *I overslept*. He got out of bed and went into the bathroom that was above the fifth-wheel hitch where their bedroom was. He hurriedly got dressed and went down to the kitchen, thinking of what had happened last night. He saw Sally at the dining table and went over to her, saying how sorry he was about Randall's death.

She looked up at him and said, "Why? He was an abusive husband and a bully. Whenever he got drunk, which was frequently, he would pick a fight with someone or come home and beat me. I'm relieved he is no longer a threat to me or my child."

Sam went to the kitchen area and got a cup of coffee as Shirley finished frying his normal breakfast of bacon, eggs and toast. He sat at the table across from Sally and took a sip of his coffee.

Looking at her, he said, "Now what?"

Sally looked at him. "What are my options?" Sally asked.

"Well, as I see it, with Randall out of the picture, you no longer have to fear for him trying to coerce you or steal Max's property. So we can let the contract stand as it is, void it, or modify it to where we buy it from you outright at fair market value. This is something not to be taken lightly, and I want you to pray about it and possibly seek counsel from your brother or a lawyer. This will be your decision only, and I want you to feel good about it. Don't worry about Shirley and me. We're just happy to be able to help you for a short time."

Shirley overheard their conversation and set Sam's breakfast in front of him.

He looked up and said, "After I'm finished eating, I want to set up our tables. I don't want the people to know that what happened last night had any effect on us."

Sam was busy placing merchandise from the back of the trailer onto tables when their first customer came up.

"Hi," he said. "Your name is Sam. Is that correct?"

"Yes," Sam said.

Smiling, the man put his hand out to shake Sam's. "I'm Ted," he said. "I guess you could say I'm the unofficial mayor of this small town.

There will be a meeting at the school's gymnasium tonight starting at 7 PM. I expect you and your wife Shirley will be there." It sounded more of a command than a request. "Good luck with your sales today," he said congenially as he left.

Shirley was standing on the back of the trailer's drop gate. "What was that all about?" she asked.

"I guess we are commanded to a town meeting at 7PM tonight," Sam said.

They finished setting up, and all day, people were coming by to say hi to them. Some bought a small item but many just said hi and introduced themselves. Many were regulars who came by before, but some were new to them, and all of them seemed friendlier than they usually were. Their sales were not as robust as the past days, but they were worthwhile. Sam attributed this to the fact that most of their more desirable items had already been sold, with the exception of the firearms that he had. He felt, for some reason, that they should hang on to them.

They closed early and had an early dinner, then they went to the school gym. They found a seat at an out-of-the-way bleacher that was set up. Townspeople started to come in. The ladies were bringing either cakes or pies with them and were placing them on a table that was in front of the bleachers. There was a second table with some chairs behind it and a podium. Soon, two women and two men took seats. Then Ted came into the gym, he came over to Sam and Shirley and shook their hands and a few others, then he sat at the middle chair at the table up front. He looked around, stood up, went behind the podium, and rapped a gavel that was there.

"Good evening, folks," he said. "We'll keep this short as we know many of you want to go home and get to bed to go to work tomorrow. This is a special meeting of the town council. There isn't much of town work to do, but first, let's all stand for an invocation by Pastor Richards."

As everyone stood, Pastor Richards came to the podium, "Heavenly Father, guide us in our work tonight and let us serve you in our words and actions in Jesus's name. Amen."

There was a chorus of Amens'. Then, Ted turned and Everyone faced the U.S. flag and recited the Pledge of Allegiance afterward they all sat down.

Ted was standing behind the podium. "With all of your permission, since this is a special meeting, we will suspend the minutes and treasurer's reports from the last meeting, to be read at the next regular meeting."

There was a chorus of Amens' and seconds from the bleachers.

"For those of you who haven't heard, last night, we had two of our citizens leave us. One naturally and one by aggression."

Sam heard a few snorts and sniggers when Ted said this.

"Max Barns passed away from cancer, caused by Agent Orange that he was exposed to while he served honorably in Vietnam. The other person, well, let's say the crime rate around here will decrease."

A person from the stands yelled out, "Randall finally got what he deserved!"

"Order, order," Ted said. "Yes, Randall finally met his demise last night. Now I don't know all of what happened, but Deputy Barns said there was a clear self-defense issue and enough evidence to back up the claim, and that is all I need. The other thing on the agenda tonight is I would like to introduce all of you to Shirley and Sam Simons. Many of you have purchased items from them over the past two weeks, and from what I have heard, they are about to become residents of our community. I hope all of you welcome them into our community. I also heard that Sam was also at Max's cabin last night and aided our coroner, Dr. Smith, in last night's events. Enough said. Now let's have some fun. Jerry!" he called out.

A woman came out of the stands wearing a black Stetson hat and a beaded buckskin jacket with fringes on the arms. Ted picked up a cake, and Jerry started an auctioneer's chant and, with a lot of ribbing, started selling the cakes and pies. Sam noticed the prices starting to climb from $10 to $100, and it seemed Jerry would push some bidders harder, and on others, she would go easy on them. Also, there was an order in which they were sold, with most of them going to the husbands of the wives who brought them in.

After the auction was over, Ted got behind the podium and said, "I want to thank Jerry for her services." He was handed a sheet of paper and read it and then looked up. "We raised a little over $1,500 tonight. I would like to propose half of it go to the school athletic fund and the rest to Samuel Simmons for his services last night."

There was applause and people agreeing.

Ted looked at Sam. "Sam and Shirley, would you come over here, please? We, the citizens, would like to present the both of you this for what you both did last night. I know you let Sally and her child spend the night with you and that Sam had a minor role at Max's place."

There were a few snickers in the bleachers.

Sam looked at Ted and then turned around and said, "Shirley and I appreciate your gift for our minor services last night, but we just came here and are strangers to many of you, and yes, we hope that under the circumstances, things work out for all of us and that we can stay here as new residents. What we would like to do is donate your gift to us to the school's athletic fund, and we will match that."

Shirley's head snapped up. She looked at Sam and then picked up and said, "After all, it's most of your money," and chuckled.

Everyone laughed, and all of a sudden, they were part of the community.

Ted rapped his gavel and said, "Unless there is any other business related to this matter, this special meeting is closed."

There were seconds and thirds and a bunch of ayes, and Ted banged his gavel.

"Meeting adjourned to the next scheduled time or when we need to get together again, whichever is sooner."

While some people left, many came from the bleachers and shook Sam's and Shirley's hands and welcomed them into the community. After about thirty minutes, the people dispersed, and Shirley and Sam went to their truck and headed back to their trailer. It was 10:00 p.m. when they got to the trailer. They got ready for bed, expecting a busy day tomorrow.

Sam was almost finished setting up the tables—any more this went really quickly since they were almost out of everything they had brought with them—when Sally pulled up in her car. It was an old Ford Focus and looked like it had seen better days.

"Hi, Sally," Sam said as she got out. "How are things going with you?"

"Is Shirley around? I would like to talk to both of you," Sally said.

They went into the trailer as Shirley poured them all a cup of coffee.

"I talked with my brother, Jesse, and he talked to Geraldine. She is the local auctioneer and real-estate agent. She said the going rate for good, clear farmland around here is around $3,000 per acre. There are sixty acres at Uncle Max's place, but some of it is forestland, and then there is the cabin. We feel that $195,000 is a fair price for the property if you are willing to buy it. This way, everything is cut and dried and there are no strings or loose ends this way."

Sam looked at Shirley, who was a real-estate agent in Seattle, and she looked at him.

He nodded, and she said, "It will take a few days for us to come up with the money, but we agree to the price and conditions. Will Geraldine meet us here later with the proper papers for us to sign? We can give you some earnest money at that time."

"Sally, I want to ask you a question about last night. What were the intentions of the cake auction?" Sam asked.

"Well, it was a way to gauge you and Shirley to see what kind of people you are. Giving back the money that was raised showed you were not selfish, and that alone would have made you a member of the community, but by matching it, it showed that you were generous people. You will find out that many obstacles you would have met when you moved here will not happen. It's our way of judging what kind of people are coming into our community."

Sally left, and Sam went outside with a cup of coffee and sat in a camp chair, waiting for customers and reading the *Idaho Statesman*. There were several articles on the illegal immigration problem, the unrest among the blacks, and the speculation that most of the unrest was being pushed by outside interests. It was starting to look as if things were being pushed to create a problem where once, there wasn't one, almost as if there was a purpose for the unrest so that there would be explosive rioting around the country, giving the current president a reason to declare martial law and then suspend the upcoming presidential election until order was restored and to be able to bring UN troops onto American soil to restore order. Sam thought that the setup looked so obvious, it was hard for the rest of the people could not to see what was happening.

Two young people, a boy and a girl—they looked to be brother and sister—rode up on horseback and took Sam from his daydreaming. They got off their horses, walked around, and just looked at what was left, which wasn't a lot. They said hi to Sam, got back onto their horses, and left.

Sam turned, went into the trailer for a fresh cup of coffee, and sat down to talk to Shirley about what they had to do in the next few weeks. He got onto his computer, checked their personal bank account, and was pleased to see there was enough money there to cover the cost of Max's property. Even though they had enough money to cover the purchase, Shirley and Sam discussed that it would be best for the people to think that they had to take out a loan for the purchase. They felt that they should play their money close to the chest and not let the people know how much money they really had.

Shirley and Sam discussed what type of house they should build, and Sam once again went onto the computer and started doing research on fire-resistant construction when he came across an article from a person who had built a house out of eight-inch reinforced poured concrete. It was a ranch-style house, which suited both Shirley and me. Because of the arthritis they were starting to feel in their knees, they didn't want to do steps. There were pictures of it, and looking at them, Sam thought if the roof was metal and extended out about six feet on both sides, the basement of the house would be larger, and the porch area could be concrete with the load-bearing walls set back. Then there would be a wall of washed river rock about thirty-eight inches high around the porch on each side of the house and rock accents against the wall of the house, about thirty-eight inches high under each window. Then siding the rest of the way up, they would have a solid well-insulated house that would be almost bulletproof, and the extra area under the porches would be great for the storage of supplies and act as root cellars. The space between the house and the outer walls of the porch could be used as a greenhouse or defensive shooting areas. Instead of a two-car garage at one end, Sam designed another two bedrooms and increased the length by fifteen feet for a larger pantry and kitchen and dining area. He made some sketches of what he had in mind and found some pictures on the internet similar to what he was thinking of and showed them to Shirley. When she saw what he had in mind for the pantry, kitchen, and dining area, she made a few suggestions. He put them into the plans, and she was sold on the plans.

It was around three in the afternoon when they heard a car pull up to their stand and honk its horn. Sam went out and saw it was Sally and Geraldine. As they got out of the car, he asked them if they wanted a cup of coffee or some iced tea. They both asked for the tea. He went inside the trailer and told Shirley they were here and got a tray with a pitcher of tea and all the fixings for iced tea. Sam poured himself a large cup of coffee and went out to a picnic table they had. Jerry pulled out a stack of papers from her briefcase. It never amazed Sam how much paperwork there was in buying or selling a piece of property. He looked at the stack and then at Jerry.

"Jerry, let's cut to the chase. What's the long and short of this contract?" Sam asked.

Shirley smiled and looked at him. They had been here before, and she knew Sam didn't like mealy mouthed lawyer contracts and property transfers. She was watching Jerry for her reaction to Sam's statement.

Jerry just smiled and said, "A minimum of 10 percent earnest money. Balance due within ninety days, or you forfeit your earnest money."

"What about water and mineral rights if any on the property?" he asked.

"You have all mineral rights within the boundaries of the property and water rights that pertain to the property," Jerry said.

"Okay," Sam said. "Shirley is the realtor in the family. I'll drink my coffee while she goes over the contract."

As Shirley went over the contract, Sam took care of a customer who came to their sale. When he came back to the table, she looked at him and said everything looked good, so they signed the contracts and gave Jerry a check for $20,000.00 as earnest money. She gave them a receipt for it and said the balance was due in ninety days. Sam said no problem, that they would call their bank in Seattle and fly there for a loan in a day or two. He didn't want them to know that they could write a check now for the balance. Shirley and Sam felt they should play it close so as not to be flashing money around. Sam said to Jerry that they would eventually have to go back to Arizona to settle loose ends there, but they wanted to get back here before winter set in. It was obvious they wouldn't be able to live in the cabin. Sam looked at Sally saying, "while we are away could you look after the chickens and rabbits at their place." Sally said that she would for the eggs the chickens laid.

"So do you know any good contractors around here that could build a ranch-style house for us before winter sets in? We will also need a survey of the land with good corner posts installed."

"If you have plans, I know a guy who builds most of the buildings around here, wood and metal or other."

"Well, I do have a good set of plans and specifications. I have a CAD program on my computer, and all I need is a day or two to have a complete set of plans. Then all we need to do is lay out the placement of the buildings and get the required permits, and he can get digging."

"Permits?" Jerry said. "There are no permits needed for construction here unless it's a public facility like a school or town hall."

"So we can start construction as soon as we get a contractor," Sam replied.

Jerry said, "I'll send you a reliable contractor as soon as he can make it. His name is Jesse, and his family has been here for years. His grandfather came here and homesteaded a ranch, and after World War II, his father returned from the Pacific, where he was a Navy Seabee and he set up a construction company."

After Jerry left, Shirley came up to Sam and said, "Wow! Things are moving fast."

"Yes," Sam replied. "I'm wondering if we should use the coins from the storage unit to build the house."

"No," Shirley said. "We could tap some of our retirement money, and I have been thinking that maybe I should sell one or two of our rental properties. If things continue to get as bad as it is now in the city, they soon won't be worth anything. Let's get into the trailer to finish discussing this. I don't want anyone to overhear us."

***

Ken was up early, making sure everything around the oil pad was in order for Jerry's visit. Then he got a cup of coffee and a sidearm and waited. As he sat outside in a folding camp chair, listening to the area waking up to the new day—it was one of his favorite times—he was wondering what Jerry wanted here. Was it their unusual order for supplies? Then he wondered if he should tell him what he had seen on one of his hunting trips in the area. A thought came to his mind. General Patton was fond of saying, "Don't take counsel of your fears." Around 9:00 a.m., a pickup truck followed by a tank truck came up the road.

Ken thought, *Well, here it goes. We will either be fired or at least reprimanded. Oh well. It was good while it lasted.*

Jerry parked his pickup close to their trailer and waited as the tank truck passed and the dust settled. He got out and came to Ken, a smile on his face. Ken tried to read what kind of smile he had, but he couldn't.

Jerry stuck out his hand. "Hi, Ken. How are you and Betty doing?" he asked.

"Fine," Ken replied. "As well as could be expected under the circumstances."

Jerry picked up on this. "What's happening?" he asked.

"Well, let's go sit down. Do you want some iced tea or lemonade?" Ken asked as they walked to their camp chairs and picnic table with an umbrella for shade.

"That was quite an order you put in last week," Jerry said. "What's going on that you need all this ammo for a small arsenal?"

Ken looked at him and then told him of what he had seen in the desert on one of his security patrols. He didn't tell him that he had made the waterhole but let him think it was strangers who made it. Jerry heard him out, and Ken told him of what he had done around the drill pad and trailer.

He asked Ken if he had seen any tracks in the raked areas, and Ken replied, "Only the four-legged kind so far."

Then Jerry told Ken that another pad was hit about twenty miles away from them. The guard and his wife there were able to scare them off, but their nerves were shot, and they were planning on pulling out. He looked at Ken and said the government, by not securing the border, was allowing all kinds of people to cross into the United States. Not only farm workers and laborers but also some real hardcore criminals had been coming into the state. These guard positions, he said, never were meant to be hard-armed camps but just to keep the vandals from doing damage to the equipment or to keep them from stealing it.

"Now," he said, "it looks like we might need a small army and helicopter gunships to protect them. I know you are on a contract and it will end in six months. We cannot provide much support, but we can give a little more support in that we will have a helicopter and six . . . uh, let's say specialists on one-hour dispatch, available twenty-four hours a day, seven days a week if you need any special help. I'll go for a short walk over to the tank truck and see how things are going. You and Betty talk it over. I'll need a decision before I leave. I'm sorry. I wish I could give you more time, but things are happening fast and decisions must be made." With that, he left Betty and Ken alone to talk.

About an hour later, Jerry came back to the trailer, and Betty asked him, "If they attack us, how long before we can expect support from the specialists that the company has hired?"

"About three hours, maybe a little less," Jerry replied.

"If we get attacked, what will happen to us?" Betty asked.

"Well, the company wants to keep these wells pumping as long as they can, but if you are attacked, the security force will stay here as long as they can, and the company will secure the well until things calm down. If the company secures the well, you will be bought out of your contract with three months' extra pay and all the supplies you have accrued while here. If you stay, we will install a panic button. You just hit it, and an alarm sounds at the support force base, or if they are airborne, it will be transmitted to them in the air, and they will head directly here. It's your decision to make."

Betty looked at Ken and He at her, and Ken said, "Betty, it's your call."

She said, "We'll stick it out for a while until things get hairy."

"Good," Jerry said. "Tomorrow someone will come by and install your panic button, and in a day or two, the security force will come by to look the place over and give you any suggestions. I have a few items in the pickup truck to drop off with you before I leave."

They all walked out to Jerry's truck, and he dropped the tailgate.

"Here is the ammo you ordered," he said, "and some things that use it. This is on the company's account and not on yours and this is yours to keep. When the security force comes, they may have more for you. It will be at their discretion." Jerry shook their hands and left.

Ken looked at his watch. It was two in the afternoon. He looked at Betty and said, "I'll put this away, and then I want to take a short walk. I'll be back for an early supper."

He grabbed one of his AR rifles and went a circuitous route to the waterhole. He watched it for a while through his binoculars and was satisfied that there was no one around. He cautiously went up to it and saw that there had been several groups that had used the area since he was there last week. There was litter all over the area, but at least they had enough sense to confine their human waste in an out-of-the-way area. Ken looked around some more and then took another roundabout way back to the trailer. When he got there, Betty had some chicken breasts for him to grill. After eating, he made a sweep around the pad security and then went to the trailer for the night.

Two days later, they got a call that the security force was headed their way and to watch out for them. Ken was expecting a helicopter, but two vans pulled up to the pad. They both had company markings on them, and Jerry was driving one of them.

Jerry got out of the van. "Ken, these are the other guards. For security, they don't want to use their real names, but they are very competent."

Ken looked at them, and their outfits said SEALs, Rangers, Delta, or Special Forces. The expressions on their faces didn't change, but they knew that he knew. The team leader came up and said he was Mr. Grey—Ken thought, *Yeah, right*—and that he and his team would look around. Ken asked if they wanted him to accompany any of them.

He said, "Later. One of them would want a briefing of what you know and have done for defense."

Ken said okay, turned, and went to his camp chair to drink some iced tea while they looked around.

About two hours later, one of the security men came toward Ken. He said his name was Mr. Green and asked if Ken could brief him on his situation.

Ken said, "Give me a minute. I had a lot of iced tea while you were gone, and I want to get a few things. I'll be right out," and went into the trailer.

He came out with a day pack and utility belt with two ammo pouches, a first-aid kit, two canteens of water, and his AR rifle, chambered in 5.56.

"I thought that it would be easier to show you the situation—that is, if you can keep up," Ken said, grinning, and took off at a trot with his weapon at port arms. After about one hundred feet, Ken stopped on a small hill crest and said, "I thought I'd let you catch up with me."

The man just glowered at him. Ken pointed out that at strategic areas around the pad and trailer, he had raked out twenty-foot areas that he checked at least daily for footprints. Ken then took off again at a trot. He soon gave a hand signal to stop and take cover as he dropped to one knee. The man came up beside Ken, and Ken told him to pull the binoculars out of his pack. Ken slowly crawled to the side of a small hill. He smelled the smoke as they were coming up to the waterhole, and he didn't want to barge into something he wasn't ready for. They were about one hundred yards away from the waterhole that he had made.

Ken looked through the binoculars. It looked like they were cooking something, but what got his attention was that he recognized one of the people by the fire. He had seen him twice before and assumed he was a guide for illegals coming into the United States, but this time, as with one other time, the people he was leading didn't look like they were Mexican. He handed the binoculars to Mr. Green, and he looked at what Ken was looking at. Ken tapped him on the leg, moved back, and asked him in a low voice what he thought of the situation.

He said, "Let's go back to the pad."

Ken took him on a circuitous route back to the pad and showed him a good spot for a helicopter to land if they ever needed support and a small hill that he used to recon the pad before he would walk up to it.

Mr. Grey was there with a quizzical look on his face when Mr. Green said, "Boss, this guy has his act together. We went to a waterhole about two klicks from here and observed some activity there, and then he showed me a possible LZ if we ever have to come here."

Mr. Grey looked at Ken and asked about the raked areas around the pad and trailer. Ken told him that he would check them daily for footprints, and so far, there were none of the two-legged kind.

"Do you know how to use that thing around your neck?" he asked as he pointed to Ken's AR rifle.

"Yes," Ken replied. "Its zero is a hundred yards, and I am accurate up to three hundred yards with it." He knew this was about the maximum effective range for this rifle.

"What is your background?" Mr. Grey asked.

"Well," Ken replied, "Eighty-Second Airborne, both stateside and Vietnam, plus special forces, both Vietnam and stateside, plus ranger school."

He looked at Ken, stuck his hand out, and shook his hand. "Welcome home, brother. I'm Capt. James Bartholomew, Seventy-Fifth Rangers, and this is our squad. I have some gifts for you. We wanted to size you up, and from what I have observed and heard, I feel you know how to handle what I'm about to give you. Sergeant Michaels!" he called out.

Ken could see this startled the other members of the reactionary force. It was an unwritten rule not to use real names in the field. This made Ken stand a little taller. He felt that as old as he was, he was still one of them.

The person Ken knew as Mr. Green came over and shook his hand. "Welcome aboard," he said.

"Sergeant, give this man package group A and B," Captain Bartholomew said.

Sergeant Michaels went to the van that they had come in with, started it, and backed it closer to the trailer. "Ken, I suggest that you don't keep this in your trailer, but it must be kept in a secured area, so I guess you will have to keep this in your trailer."

There was a wooden box marked "Grenade, Fragmentation." Two wooden boxes were marked "Grenade, Smoke." When he gave these to Ken, he said there was a mix of colors in there.

"Red means a hot LZ. Yellow, you are expecting an attack. Here are three boxes of hand aerial flares, one box has parachute illumination, the other two a mix of five-star ball flares. What kinds of firearms do you have?" Sergeant Michaels asked.

"I have this AR in .223 or 5.56 and another for Betty, my wife, two 9 mm Beretta 92FSs, a Springfield M1A1 Scout in .308 or 7.62×51, a couple of 10/22 rifles, and two Mossberg 500s in twelve gauge," Ken replied.

"How are you fixed for ammo for your weapons?"

"I have some, but you can never have too much ammo," Ken replied.

Sergeant Michaels chuckled. "How true," he said. "Your AR rifles—are they civilian models?"

"Yes," Ken replied.

"Well, here are two ARs of the type we use. As you see, the selector switch is a little different from what you had in the seventies. Get them cleaned up, and we will be back in a day or two to take you and your wife to a range to zero them. We don't want you to be firing them around here. No sense in advertising to anyone that you are here. Right now, stealth is the best defense you have. We'll give you two cases of 5.56, a case of five hundred rounds of 7.62×51, five hundred rounds of 9 mm, two hundred rounds of .00 buck, and one hundred rounds of slugs for your twelve-gauges. When we leave, I want you to walk five hundred meters down the road to make sure we got off. Okay?"

Ken looked at him, and he just winked. They unloaded the gifts, Captain Bartholomew shook Ken's hand, and they left, following Jerry in his van. Ken thought, *Leave it to Jerry not to be eating dust.*

Ken told Betty that he must go down the road a bit, jumped into their pickup truck, and went after them. He saw three boxes in the middle of the road and approached them cautiously. After he was sure everything was okay, he quickly loaded them into the back of his pickup and headed back to the trailer with a big smile on his face, thinking, *Santa came early this year.* He pulled up to the trailer, and Betty came out with a worried look on her face.

"Are we doing the right thing in staying here?" she asked.

Ken could see she was troubled. "Yeah, babe. We will be all right. They will be back in a few days, and they will watch the place while a couple of them will take us to a range to try out our new firearms. I think we should take the Mossberg,s with us also so you can get some practice in with them," he said.

He went inside the trailer and got an old blanket and some towels that were cut up for cleaning rags. He stored the cases of ammo in the back area of the trailer, got his gun-cleaning gear, and went outside. He put the blanket onto the picnic table and looked at Betty.

"Do you need me to help with supper?" Ken asked.

"No." She sighed with resignation in her voice. "Go clean your new toys, and I'll call you when it's ready."

Ken had both the M4s broken down and cleaned, and to make sure they were really clean, he did them twice. He was halfway through the present on the road when Betty came out with a plate of celery with peanut butter on them for him to snack on while supper was cooking.

"What's that?" she asked, pointing to what was on the table.

"That, my dear wife, is an M60 machine gun," he said. "This will fire between five hundred to six hundred rounds a minute, but when you fire it, you do so in short three-to-five-second bursts. That way, you don't overheat the barrel. We have two spare barrels and an asbestos glove to change out a hot barrel."

Betty looked at him. "Are things that bad that we need this? I'm worried about what may happen," she said.

"Well, honey, we just continue as we have been, but we must now be more vigilant to what we see and hear," he replied. "Hey, this could all be an overreaction by the company." But secretly, Ken didn't believe it. He was thinking, *There will be many sleepless nights for a while.* He picked up a piece of celery and started chewing on it. "This is good, honey. Thanks." He thought this would get her mind off the subject at hand.

Ken went back to cleaning the M60 as Betty went into the trailer. He reassembled the M60, attached a hundred-round ammo pack to it, took it and the other firearms into the trailer, and secured them in an accessible area in the back of the trailer. He went back to the front and sat down at the dining table as Betty brought a salad to the table to start supper. During supper, they listened to a commercial radio station. It was on the AM band and was one of those news talk shows. Several callers talked about all the illegals crossing the border down South and all the crime it was causing. Then the news came on, and there was mention of rioting in some of the cities in the Midwest.

After a while, they got tired of listening to this, and Ken turned on their ham receiver and scanned a few channels. He picked up on where a guy near the border was claiming that crime was getting so bad that he and his wife were selling their ranch and were moving North, maybe as far as Alaska, just to get away from the situation down by the Southern border. Then an operator chimed in, saying he lived in Anchorage, Alaska, and that crime was the worst he had seen in ten years. He said something about the SB 91 crime bill being a joke and that criminals had a revolving door to get out of jail before the police had their arrest paperwork finished.

Ken turned the radio off, turned the CD player on, and put a disk in. The last thing he wanted was to get Betty more upset than she was. He got up and started to wash the dishes with Betty. She turned to Ken, and he grabbed her and started dancing with her to the music from the CD.

She looked at him and said, "It's bad, isn't it?"

"Yeah," he said. "The president and Congress aren't doing anything, and it seems the president is encouraging this. It's like he is setting up a situation to bring UN troops onto American soil. Something is going to happen, maybe a war with the different races or with Mexico, or maybe the economy will crash, but something is going to happen. When and where, I don't know, but this country is headed for something. What, I don't know, but we have no control of the country's situation, only ours. We must be vigilant and be prepared for what could happen to us. Rest assured, we are now very prepared."

They went to bed, with Ken knowing that he would be soon awake. The nights of full sleep for now were gone.

Two days later, around 9:00 a.m., two company vans came up the road. Captain Bartholomew got out of the passenger seat of one of the vans, came toward Ken, and shook his hand.

"Did you find anything interesting?" he asked.

"Yes, sir," Ken said everything is cleaned and ready.

"Good. Get your wife, Betty, and your new items. Sergeant Michaels and two other men will take you two to a range for target practice. The rest of us will stay here for security while you are gone."

Ken went inside the trailer and grabbed the two new ARs and the M60, while Betty grabbed a jug of iced tea and a sack of sandwiches she was making. They drove for about fifteen miles, cut off on a dirt track, and drove for about two more miles. Sergeant Michaels stopped, and Ken saw a rudimentary rifle/distance range. There were two firing pits about twenty feet apart and a bunch of silhouette targets at different distances from the pits. Sergeant Michaels got out and motioned for them to do the same.

"We are about ten miles from any building, so we can make all the noise we want to," he said.

The other two, Ken saw quickly set up a tarp on poles with a bench and table under it. Sergeant Michaels took the new AR rifles that Ken had and quickly stripped them down.

"Not bad," he murmured.

He then proceeded to lecture them for the next hour on the operation and various functions of the weapons. They had a quick break. Then they went to the firing positions. Ken watched as one of the sergeants explained to Betty what she should do, and he saw them put on hearing protection. The other one was acting as a security guard, not watching them but the country side. They put on their hearing protection that they had provided and climbed into the pit.

"I take it you know how these things work, so we will just fire for zero," Sergeant Michaels said to Ken.

Ken heard firing coming from Betty's pit, so he took up his weapon and fired three timed rounds and then fired three more. They looked over and saw that Betty was finished and had her rifle secured, so they all climbed out of their pits and went to see where they hit the target. Ken was pleased to see that he had a good tight shot group that could be covered with a half dollar, but it was high and to the left. They marked Ken's first shot round and went back to the pits to adjust his sights. He saw that Betty had to adjust her sights also. They fired another round, and Ken's zero was right on, while they had to adjust Betty's one more time. They then fired at various distances, checking shot placement after each magazine that they fired. Ken heard a full auto burst from Betty and looked over at a big grin on her face.

They climbed out, and Sergeant Michaels said, "I had you do one mag on full auto, but in a firefight, you don't want to use full auto unless you absolutely have to. It will draw attention to you, and everyone will then target you. But if things get hairy, don't be afraid to use it." He then opened the back of the van. "I brought a few other items for familiarization. Ken, I'm sure you recognize these. They are smoke grenades. The thing with these is they produce a lot of smoke and burn really hot, so once you throw one, don't pick it up until it cools off."

They then had Betty throw a few. This was so she would get comfortable for what was coming next. Sergeant Michaels opened another case and removed the taped cardboard tube that was in there.

"Betty, this is a fragmentation hand grenade," he said.

Betty backed up a bit.

"Don't be afraid of them. They are almost like the smoke grenades that we just finished throwing. We'll take a few to the firing pit and let you throw a few to see how good your arm is."

Ken went behind the van and watched as Betty threw her first live hand grenade. After the third one, she was getting more comfortable with them, and she threw two more and then came back to the van. They took a break for a late lunch, and then they showed Betty how to use the hand flares. The look on Betty's face when she fired the first one was priceless. She went running to a privacy tarp set up for her, and Sergeant Michaels looked at Ken with a questioning look, like *What did we do?*

Betty came back with a sheepish look on her face. "Mike, you should have warned me. I almost peed my pants on that one."

Betty then fired off a few more of them. Ken fired the M60 to get the feel of it once again, and they let Betty fire it for familiarization also. They then cleaned all their weapons and policed up the spent brass on the ground.

It was around five thirty when they got back to the camp trailer. Captain Bartholomew asked how they did, and Sergeant Michaels replied that Betty was a natural with a firearm and was also good with the other things. Betty's face got red, and Captain Bartholomew saw this and looked at Sergeant Michaels.

"The hand flare," Sergeant Michaels said. "You didn't warn her, did you?"

Sergeant Mike looked down and stirred the ground with the toe of his boot. "No, boss. She was doing so good, I forgot."

Then he burst out laughing, as did the rest of them, remembering Betty's run to the latrine area. They said their goodbyes and climbed into their vans and left. Ken and Betty were alone once again.

***

Sam woke up to a light rain falling. *Well, no problem*, he thought. *We're almost out of stock, and I could drop the awning on the trailer and set up under it for what we have left.* As he was making breakfast, Shirley came down from the bedroom.

"You're up early," Sam said.

"Yes. I didn't sleep well. We have a decision to make, and I'm afraid it must be made quickly."

"What are you talking about?"

"Well, the way this country is going, I think now is the time for us to sell all our properties while the market is still strong. We both listen to the radio and read the papers, and it looks like things are getting out of hand. What I feel I should do," Shirley said, "is fly to Seattle and have my old real-estate company sell our properties and use that money to build and stock our new place."

"Yes, and we could let it out that you are going to Seattle to get a bank loan for the property and to build a house. That will answer any questions the people here will have about you being gone and the money. When do you want to leave?"

"Let's open a bank account here, and that way, I can do a wire transfer of the money to this account."

"Good idea, but depending on how much you get for your properties, maybe you should buy some small gold coins so we don't have too much money in the bank in case the economy crashes or anyone wonders where all the money came from. It's Friday. Why don't you get on your computer and see if there are any flights from the nearest airport around here to Seattle?"

"If I can leave Sunday and spend a week or two in Seattle, I think I can get everything done that I have to."

Sam heard a vehicle drive up and thought, *It's early for customers* when there was a knock on the trailer's door. Shirley and Sam looked at each other. He just shrugged and went to open it. Sam saw Sally standing there.

"Come in," Sam said. "Do you want some coffee?"

"Yes, please," Sally said.

After some pleasantries, Sam looked at Sally. "You look nervous and didn't come here to chitchat. What's on your mind?"

"Well, I'm mostly by myself with my small child. The only family I have left is my brother, Deputy Barns. I was wondering if I could rent my uncle's cabin to live in from you people."

***

Betty hit the large red panic button by the trailer's door, sending a signal to the company's reaction guard force. She then grabbed the portable boat air horn located on a small shelf next to the panic button and let loose with a loud long blast.

"That isn't going to help you!" the Mexican shouted to Betty.

"No, but maybe this will."

She pulled a Mossberg 500 pump shotgun and fired off a round. Hector Mendoza dove for cover when he saw the shotgun as the rest of his gang of six laughed at him.

"What's the matter? You afraid of just one *chiquita*?" they taunted.

Ken was watching three pronghorn antelope in his scope, trying to lay out a route to sneak closer for an easier shot. *Fresh meat would be nice for a change*, he was thinking when the air horn broke the silence. Ken wasted no time. He got up from where he was at and started at a slow lope back to the trailer, where his wife, Betty, was when he heard the gunshot. He immediately dropped his small pack and started to run to the trailer. There was trouble, and Betty wouldn't shoot unless she was in danger. He came to a small hill a hundred yards from the trailer, and he got down on all fours and then crawled to a vantage point where he could see the trailer.

What he saw made his blood boil, and his instincts took over. As he eased his rifle up, he did a quick scan and saw two beat-up pickup trucks. Seven Mexicans had the trailer under surveillance and calling to Betty to put down the gun and that they would show her a good time. Ken lined the crosshairs of his scoped rifle on the head of the one doing all the talking and waited to get his heart rate down a little more from the run here. *Crack*, and the Mexican's head exploded. *Crack, crack*—two rounds center mass of the farthest Mexican. The others turned their backs to him, looking for the shooter. They still didn't know there he was. *Boom, boom, boom.* Betty was unloading her shotgun at them now, causing even more confusion. *Blam, blam.* Ken now was systematically targeting the Mexicans with center mass shots. He had his M1A1 Scout and was using soft-point hunting rounds and not steel-jacked rounds, and the damage they did was psychologically devastating on the remaining bandits. They finally got over the shock and surprise and made a run for their trucks when Betty hit one low in the leg and he fell down. Ken reloaded a fresh magazine and fired several more times, and then it was over.

He yelled down to Betty to have her give the signal if she was hurt or all right and was relieved when the okay sign was given. Ken waited a few minutes to make sure there would be no surprises when he went down there, not knowing that Betty had only wounded one. Ken backed down from the crest of the slight hill and walked wide around the ambush site so he could get a different view of the area. He stopped and got out his binoculars and looked the site over. That was when he saw the wounded bandit trying to crawl to a truck. He checked the other bandits slowly with his binoculars and verified with the wounds they had and blood in the dirt that all but one of the bandits were dead. Ken slowly got up and circled around him, knowing a wounded animal was far more dangerous. He called out to his wife in the trailer to see if she was okay. Betty replied in a very shaky voice that she was unhurt, just scared.

"Well, you should be," Ken replied, "but it's almost over."

"What?" she asked.

Ken let her know that all but one of the attackers were dead and that he was going to try to interrogate him. As Ken walked up to the attacker, he saw that the attacker was heavily tattooed, both on his arms and body but his face also and the surviving attacker was hit hard, with his legs shredded from two buckshot blasts. Ken knew he wouldn't last long.

"What were you trying to do by attacking us?" Ken asked, and when he got no reply, he switched to his limited Spanish.

The attacker spit at Ken, saying he was a dead man and his friends would rape his wife, take knives, and cut parts off her while he watched and then kill both of them.

Ken laughed at him and said, "How will this happen when all your friends are dead and you, my friend, are soon on the trip to hell?"

The Mexican then replied with pride that there were hundreds of them coming across the border and that soon, they would take back that which was stolen from them by their corrupt government. As Betty came warily walking up, Ken leveled his rifle and sent the attacker to his maker to atone for his sins. He gave Betty a long hug and felt her body shaking with sobs from the incident.

After consoling her and getting her to stop shaking, he heard the dull beating of helicopter blades. Ken took the Mossberg from his wife's hands and checked to make sure it was loaded and on safety. Then putting his arm around her shoulder, he led her back to the camper. *It sounds like the cavalry is coming this time. Better late than never.* Ken got a green smoke grenade and tossed it out and was in the trailer, holding Betty as she was shaking and crying. He watched out a window as the reaction force cautiously approached the trailer. He let go of Betty, went to the door, and watched as the force went to the ground.

"Hey, it's me!" Ken called out. "And it's all clear! the area is green!"

As the reaction force warily got to their feet, Ken only recognized two of them—Captain Bartholomew and Sergeant Michaels. The rest were strangers. Captain Bartholomew came toward the trailer as the rest of the squad checked the area and the bodies for any intel they might have.

"Looks like you had visitors. Is everyone all right?" Captain Bartholomew asked as he looked at Betty.

"Just a little scared," Betty said with a quivering voice. "What will happen now?"

"Well, several things. We will clean up this mess and load the bodies into their pickup trucks. Then we will drive them way out into the desert and dispose of them. Don't worry about the authorities. Since you all are unhurt, there are no reports to fill out."

Ken looked at him. "It's getting that bad?" he asked.

"Not yet," Captain Bartholomew replied, "but things are getting really squirrelly at the border with Mexico."

"Then what I've been hearing on the ham radios is true."

"Well, I don't know what you are hearing, but by the best estimates, several hundred—maybe as many as a thousand—Muslims have crossed into the United States and have fanned out all over the country, more than the FBI and DHS can watch. Couple these with the ones that grew up here and moved here over the years. It's estimated that there are between three and four thousand Jihadist Muslims in the United States. Some are suicide bombers, but most of them are tasked to destroy the infrastructure and cause mayhem throughout the United States. The intelligence analysts feel that there is about six months, maybe as long as a year, before things go south."

"What direction will they take? What will be their targets?" Ken asked.

"Well," Captain Bartholomew said, "the best the analysts can guess is the Muslims know that they cannot do a direct attack and take over the country, so they must do other things. Our road and rail systems are wide open. Drop a few traffic or railroad bridges across big rivers like the Mississippi, Missouri, Snake, Columbia, and others with barge and ship traffic—that would cripple the economy by stopping the shipping of grain and other products by both road, rail, and water. Most people in the big cities don't have more than a few days' worth of groceries in their home or apartments. So in about a week, most of them will have run out of food or will be dangerously low on food, and by then, it will be too late to buy any food, even if you could find some. Food riots will start then, and if they turn off the electricity—there are three power grids in the continental United States, and these are basically unprotected, either by sabotage or computer—this would shut down a lot of services. Many medicines need refrigeration, like insulin. Add to that kidney dialysis, people on life support in the hospitals, and nursing care facilities, not to mention, in the summer, the air conditioners and lights in the big cities. It's been estimated that a coordinated attack at the right time could, over a period of weeks or months, kill one quarter to one half of the population of the United States, and if it lasts longer, even more people will die—and that's without firing a shot. The people themselves will do the job for them. Gangs will, at first, fight one another for territory control, and then they will band together, forming large armies to take what they want or need to survive.

"What does this have to do with Betty and me?" Ken asked.

"Well, the powers that be know about your waterhole. They have all the waterholes around the desert mapped. They want us to set up an observation-listening post and see who uses it. They feel that your waterhole may be one of several in a trail system into the United States, so after we clean up your mess here, I'll leave a three-man team to monitor the waterhole. They will be resupplied by you from supplies we leave behind or bring to you. We want a low-key dark ops, so we felt that since you know the area and the drill, to have you do the resupply, and if needed, you will be the reactionary force until we can make it there. Before you answer, talk it over with your wife because she will be part of the operation also."

"Talk what over?" Betty asked as she walked up.

Ken was briefing Betty when Captain Bartholomew took over. "How are you feeling?" he asked Betty.

She looked at him. "I have had a better day. What will become of us?"

"What do you mean?"

"Well, there are a bunch of dead people around here. How do we explain it to the police?"

"What bodies?" the captain asked.

You could see Betty was still shaken by what had happened, but if she was worried more about the authorities than what had happened here, this was good.

Captain Bartholomew knew she would come on board with the operation. "Betty, you and Ken did really good here. Are you hurt in any way?"

"No," Betty answered. "Just worried about what we will tell the police."

"Well, Betty, don't worry about the police. They have bigger issues to worry about than a few illegal Mexicans. Did I say illegal? I meant to say undocumented Mexican drug runners. After all, in these times, we must be politically correct, mustn't we? What will happen is we will clean up the mess you and Ken made. We'll take the bodies and trucks out into the desert, and they will just disappear. But, Betty, I must know—how do you feel mentally and emotionally? What we are about to undertake doesn't have a lot of risk, but there is some risk involved. I must know. Can we rely on you to hold up to the situation?"

"Tell me," Betty said. "What just happened? Was this a random act, or were we intentionally targeted?"

"Well, this is what we want to find out and the reason for the surveillance post we want to establish. Three of my guys' will spend some time out in the sand, watching the waterhole to see just what is happening there. We want to see what traffic there is and if it is being used as a drop site or meeting site. Besides an observation post, it will also be a listening post. We have some interesting hardware with us, so we can listen on what, if anything, is being said at the waterhole, and we have some cameras and other things. We want Ken to do the resupplies of my men and, if necessary, to act as a reaction force until we can get here. Your job in this operation is to stay here and be the guard force here. There may be a scenario where we will be busy at the waterhole and you will be alone here, but if that happens, we will already be enroute here and will be only minutes away."

"I would feel better if there was another person here. I don't think I could defend this place by myself. It's one thing for you guys to be Rambos, but I don't have the training or skills you people have."

"That's a good point," Captain Bartholomew said. "I think one person here and three at the waterhole should suffice. Ken, I still want you to be part of a relief force if you feel up to it."

"Yeah, but I would feel better if I had some more equipment like a vest, MOLLE gear, and some other toys you guys have."

"No problem. I can get you and Betty geared up, and I guess some spares wouldn't hurt. What we are going to do now is to clean up your mess, and we will be back."

***

It was a busy Friday. Sam and Shirley went to the U.S. Bank branch in Potlatch and set up a checking account and a savings account. Sam was driving up U.S. 95, heading back to their trailer after seeing Shirley off at the Pullman-Moscow Airport. He was deep in thought, mentally checking off all that had to be done in a very short time, when he was startled to see a small heard of elk in the road. He managed to swerve and stop in time, avoiding hitting one and doing damage to the pickup truck. Sam managed to get back to the trailer before nightfall and was settling in for the night.

In the morning, Sam was going to move the trailer to the property and start overseeing the construction of their new home. He and Shirley decided to go with insulated poured-concrete walls for the shell and a metal roof. When questioned about the construction, Sam replied that the house would be almost fireproof if a forest fire came this way. That satisfied the contractor, and after all, it was his money. The footprint of the basement was twice the size of the house plans. The extra area was to be used as a root cellar or other storage. The roof extended about eight feet past the walls of the house on each side to make a roofed porch area that had a river rock wall thirty-eight inches high down both sides of the house. The floor was poured concrete, and underneath was a storage area on each side of the house. In winter, the porch could be enclosed with glass or plastic Visqueen to make a greenhouse to be able to grow vegetables in the winter and supplement the heat source for the house. For decoration, there would be a river rock facade at key points around the house, like under the windows, to add extra ballistic security to anyone firing from the window to the outside, and with the exception of the furnishings like rugs and furniture, the house was virtually fireproof and bulletproof. Construction seemed to go slowly at first, but Sam knew once the foundation was poured, the forms could then be set in place, and then the rest of the construction would go quite rapidly. During this period, Sam had three wells drilled around the property: one for the house, one for a garden area, and one for a barn for livestock and a work shed. A septic system was installed, twice the size normally needed. Sam explained this as a fear of a septic problem. The contractors humored him. After all, it was his money.

He stayed in the trailer since they were letting Sally and her child live in the cabin rent free. The only thing that was constant was his calls to Shirley every evening. During their conversations, he discovered that their decision to liquidate all their real-estate holdings was a correct one. During one phone conversation, Shirley said that she could see the beginning of control by liberals and special interests. She told Sam of new firearm regulations being implemented and of the minimum wage increases around Sea–Tac Airport. During Shirley's time as a real-estate broker, she always had a buyer or two willing to buy houses, duplexes, or fourplexes if the prices were reasonable. When she got to Seattle, she quietly contacted these buyers and offered them all of their holdings not at fire sale prices but at a price they would be willingly to buy for. She had movers pack a few cherished items of furniture and all of Sam's tools and had them shipped to their new home in Idaho. Every day, while Shirley was in Seattle, she would go to the Ivar's stand at Lake Union for a bowl of their clam chowder. She thought that there was no telling when she would get a chance to get some of their clam chowder again, so why not eat it while she could? Her contacts came through for her, and what they couldn't buy, they passed on to other buyers whom they knew. In two weeks, she had all 12 of her rental units sold as well as their house.

***

Ken was sitting on a folding canvas camp chair with Sergeant "Willie" Williams. They were drinking sweet mint iced tea after eating a dinner of antelope steak. The radio that one of them always carried was next to them, and their conversation stopped. There were three squelch breaks, which Sergeant Willie replied with two breaks. Then they herd four squelch breaks, and they grabbed their gear beside them and took off. All this happened before Betty knew what was happening.

As Ken and Willie trotted off, Betty went into the trailer and performed her security jobs. She turned off all the lights, filled several buckets and pots with water, and put one pot on the stove to start boiling to sterilize anything that would need sterilization or to throw into the face of anyone who got into the trailer. She then went and retrieved her Mossberg 500 shotgun, loaded it with .00 buckshot, and placed bowls of shells around the house. She then went and got her AR rifle and a satchel of magazines for it. Then she opened the trailer door and waited.

It wasn't long before she heard the crump of hand grenades and the rapid fire of an M60 machine gun and the automatic fire of AR rifles. She couldn't tell how the battle was going, but all of a sudden, everything went quiet. It was nerve-racking not knowing what happened and who was hurt.

Betty jumped when the radio in the trailer crackled with the words "Green, Green. Amber." Betty looked at the sheet of codes on the wall next to the radio and was both relieved and frightened. "Green, Green" meant there were no injuries to the men, but "Amber" meant one got away. Ken and Willie had dug a firing pit at the back corner of the trailer overlooking approach points from the watering hole and the road. Betty got her weapons and hurried there, closing the trailer door behind her, but before she left, she keyed the mic to the radio and said, "Brown, Brown," letting them know she was going to the firing pit. When Betty got into the pit, she pulled the camouflage netting over the pit and opened the ammo box in there. There was a claymore clicker in it, along with a diagram of where the claymore mines were. There was also a range card to various landmarks around the trailer and a military-style flashlight with a red lens. Betty settled in and waited. She didn't make any fast movements as she scanned and listened for movements.

Her eyes and head were hurting from her scanning the area when she thought she saw something from the corner of her eye. She slowly turned her head and scanned the area when she saw movement. It looked like someone was trying to sneak up to the trailer. Once Betty identified the threat, she slowly and cautiously raised her firearm and trained it on the figure crawling toward the trailer when a thought came over her. What if this was a diversion for others to get close to the trailer? She then continued to scan the area while keeping special attention on the stranger. Betty knew the trailer was his intended destination. He didn't waver or change his course. Betty saw that he was about a hundred feet from the trailer and that he didn't see her position. It looked to Betty like the approaching threat was slowly getting onto his feet and getting ready to rush into the trailer. Betty eased her rifle up, got a good sight, and pulled the trigger—nothing. Then she remembered the safety. She thumbed it off and pulled the trigger again. The rifle bucked, and the person started to thrash around and then lay still.

Betty stayed in the firing pit and then saw another figure coming. As she was moving to take this one under fire, she saw a red light start flashing the friendly signal. It took a moment for her brain to register this, and then relief flooded over her. It was Sergeant Willie from the listening post by the waterhole. He raised his rifle over his head and cautiously walked toward the person whom Betty had just shot. He quickly brought the rifle to his shoulder. This got Betty's attention, and she quickly brought her rifle to bear on the prone figure. Then she saw another figure coming up on Sergeant Willie, and she shifted to cover him when he turned and waved at the figure. It was then that she recognized Ken, her husband, and she was both relieved and furious that she had almost shot him. Betty climbed out of the pit and started toward Sergeant Willie and Ken, berating Ken for rushing up like that.

"I could have killed you!" she screamed. "Don't you know the procedure for approaching here?"

Ken was puffing, out of breath, and Sergeant Willie was laughing.

"Betty, you would make a great drill instructor," Sergeant Willie said. "The old man isn't in as good of a shape as he thinks he is. Let's see what you bagged."

The figure lay still, but they all could see he was playing possum. He wasn't wounded very seriously. They cautiously approached from three different directions with their rifles at the ready. The man was dark-skinned but not a Mexican. Sergeant Willie slung his rifle and pulled and cocked his pistol as he cautiously approached. He circled around to the man's head and placed the muzzle of his pistol against it.

"If you move, I can send you to hell because there will be no virgins for you," Sergeant Willie said.

He then quickly grabbed the man's arms, and producing a zip tie, he secured the man's hands behind him. Sergeant Willie then cautiously checked for a hidden booby trap or grenade before rolling him over. While his wound was serious, it wasn't life-threatening at this point if proper first aid was administered. Sergeant Willie asked him in English where he was from and received nothing in reply.

They heard someone shout, "Friendly coming in!" and then one of the men from the listening post showed up.

"Oh, good," Sergeant Willie said. "It's Sergeant Fish, our language expert. Can you talk to this person?"

Sergeant Fish walked over, first spoke Spanish and then Farsi, and finally in English said, "Enough of this charade. I'm tired and hungry, so be a nice person and answer our questions, or you will suffer the consequences. We can treat you as a combatant and treat your wound or a foreign invader, the choice is yours." He then turned to Sergeant Willie. "Ask him your first question."

"Where are you from?" Willie asked.

The person just looked at Willie with a sullen look. The gunshot startled everyone but Sergeant Fish, and they hit the dirt. Sergeant Fish stood there with a pistol in his hand, and the person on the ground howled in pain.

When the howling stopped, Sergeant Fish said, "You have another foot, two hands, knees, elbows. This can be very painful or not. It's up to you. Now what is your name?"

The man replied.

"Good," Sergeant Fish replied. "And now where are you from?"

Sergeant Fish made a motion like he was cocking his pistol and was aiming it at the other foot when the man said he was from Iraq.

"Why are you in the United States?" Sergeant Fish asked. The man said nothing, and Sergeant Fish calmly walked around to the man's foot and said, "I won't ask again. Why are you in the United States?"

He kicked him in the foot that had been shot. The man howled in pain, and Sergeant Fish kicked him again in the foot. It took several more kicks, but the story finally came out. He said he was part of a large group of people from Iraq, Iran, Afghanistan, Syria, Libya, and a bunch of other Muslim countries from the Sand Box, who were infiltrating the United States, and their job was to scout out locations where explosives could be placed to disrupt commerce in the United States—power lines, large electrical transformers, highway and rail bridges, and communication systems. Sergeant Fish asked him how many were in his group, and at first, they thought all this was just wishful thinking for a few foreign terrorists until the man bragged that his group was just one of over one hundred groups of twenty men and that some women were trained and were in the United States already.

Sergeant Fish turned and walked away. "There are over two thousand operatives here in the States, and these are just the ones this guy knows about. Sir."

Ken turned and saw Captain Bartholomew. *When did he get here?* Ken thought. *I never heard him come.*

"That's just his group of cells. I wonder how many different groups are here already," Captain Bartholomew said.

Sergeant Fish asked him, "How many groups are in here?"

The man gave no reply.

"No can do, boss. He is finding out how many virgins are waiting for him."

"I have to get this to higher-ups ASAP, and I should do it in person. Sergeant Michaels, take over. Clean up this mess and the one at the waterhole and then stand by here." Then Captain Bartholomew got into a van and took off.

Ken helped where he could in cleaning up after the fight, and during this, he saw that Betty seemed relatively calm for what had happened. The special ops guys took the bodies out into the desert, let the scavengers do their job, then they came to the trailer, and took up positions around the trailer a couple of hundred feet away. As night came, Betty started shaking, and Ken knew what was coming.

He went to her and held her close and said, "Everything is all right, the guys will pull security, and we can get some sleep. In the morning, we will have to decide what we want to do."

Then there was a light knock on the trailer door, and Ken thought Betty would jump out of her skin. He looked out and saw two of the special Ops men, so he opened the door.

One came up. "I'm Mitch, but they call me Doc. Is Betty okay?" he asked.

"Yes, just a little jumpy," Ken replied.

"Well, she should be. She isn't trained for this, You and us, we have been there, but she hasn't. May I see her?"

"Yes, come in."

He went to Betty. "Betty," he said, "I'm Mitch, the squad's medic. I would like to check your blood pressure and ask you a few questions Will you be okay with this?"

Betty agreed, and when Mitch was finished, he made sure Betty took a pill he had given her, saying it would help her to sleep.

Ken asked, "What about me?"

Mitch looked at him and said, "Take two aspirins and call me in the morning." Then he left.

The headache came, just as Ken had remembered it, and he took the aspirins. He saw Betty was getting sleepy, so he told her to go to bed and that he would clean up the trailer.

Ken awoke with a start, grabbing for his rifle. Then he remembered where he was and what had happened. He looked at the clock—4:30 a.m. *Crap. Too early to get up but too late to go back to sleep.* So he quietly got out of bed and looked at Betty. She was still out, so he went to the kitchen and quietly made a pot of coffee. He filled a thermos and grabbed some cups and then quietly went outside. Ken heard a low whistle to his left and went there first. It was an operator he didn't know, but he was appreciative of the coffee, and they sat there in the dark, sipping coffee, just looking out across the landscape. It was strange how some people could just sit and not say anything but say everything. Ken heard two more low whistles and went and gave them cups of coffee also. The sun was coming up, so Ken went inside the trailer, made another pot of coffee, and started making a big breakfast of French toast, bacon, and scrambled eggs. He knew the guys would be hungry. Betty came down from the bedroom. He looked at her and immediately knew.

"We have to talk," Ken said, "but first, here is coffee and breakfast. Eat. It will be good for you."

***

Captain Bartholomew drove very fast, breaking all speed limits, and arrived at the team's base of operations. There was a helicopter waiting for him. He quickly secured his gear, taking only his sidearm and a clean change of uniforms with him. He was airborne within an hour, headed for Fort Hood. They landed at the Killeen–Fort Hood Regional Airport, and there was an air force Learjet waiting for him. Its engines were started as he walked across the ramp to it. His bag was stowed, and as he took his seat, the airplane started moving. Captain

Bartholomew fell asleep almost immediately. He often said the fastest way to get somewhere when flying was to go to sleep.

He woke when the engines were throttled back for landing. He surmised it would be Dulles Airport, and when the jet landed, he knew he was wrong. It was Pope Air Force Base. As the aircraft's engines were shutting down, the aircraft passenger door opened, and he saw Air Force One sitting on the tarmac. General Bixby, the army chief of staff, came walking toward him. Captain Bartholomew saluted the general and was relieved of his bag by the generals and a major.

"I must apologize for my appearance," Captain Bartholomew said.

"Don't worry about it. Most of us were captains once."

He followed the general and was led to Air Force One. There was a truck with stairs against the side of it and two men at the bottom. He could see bulges under their jackets. *This will be interesting*, he thought since he was still carrying his sidearm.

As they approached, one of them stepped forward and said, "Captain Bartholomew, we will hold that for safekeeping, and we will return it to you when you leave."

Captain Bartholomew looked at the general, and he gave a slight nod. He handed over his service pistol to one of the secret service agents and followed the general up the stairs. He stepped inside the door and turned right, and Captain Bartholomew followed him to a large conference room. The president was at the head of the table, as well as all the joint chiefs of the different military branches and the secretaries of defense and state. The president looked up and motioned Captain Bartholomew to sit, which he did so rather stiffly.

"When was the last time you had a meal?" the president asked.

Captain Bartholomew looked at his watch and then up. "It's been a little over thirty-six hours ago, sir," he replied.

The president looked at the secretary of state and said, "Go find my chef, Ham, eggs—how would you like them, Captain?"

"Scrambled would be fine, sir."

"Eggs scrambled, home fries, and have him bring in a large pot of coffee and then make more. Then you come back here."

The secretary of state left and almost immediately returned.

"Captain, if you would please fill us in from the beginning," the president asked.

"We met the Bachman's soon after their first contact, which they handled nicely. Ken Bachman was a ranger in Vietnam, so that helped us tremendously."

Captain Bartholomew was almost through the debriefing when there was a soft knock at the door, and when it opened, there was a steward with a cart holding another pot of coffee. After it was delivered and cups refilled, the president asked how he had known of how many immigrants came into the country and what their plans were. Captain Bartholomew saw the faces of the chiefs of staff go rigid, concerned as to what he would say.

"Sir," Captain Bartholomew said, "the immigrants I'm referring to are foreign insurgents intent on bringing the United States to its knees by strategic sabotage."

"How do you know this?" the president coldly asked.

"Well, sir, we were able to interrogate one of them, who, as luck would have it, was a leader of a cell."

"Is this person available for our intelligence people to question?"

"No, sir. He died of injuries suffered when he tried to attack the trailer where Betty Bachman was."

"Who inflicted these injuries, Captain?"

"Mrs. Bachman did when she defended herself after he had fired at her." Captain Bartholomew saw his last statement hadn't pleased the president.

"Captain," the president said, "it seems your breakfast is ready, so why don't you go eat? And if we need you, we will call for you."

Captain Bartholomew got up, saluted, and saw a door open, so he headed for it.

***

Sam came walking toward the strange pickup truck and trailer that had pulled into the area where their house was being built.

"My, you have been busy," Shirley said as she got out of the truck.

This surprised Sam. He hadn't expected Shirley to drive here. It must have taken her two or three days driving to get here. "I didn't expect you to drive here, and what's with the truck and trailer?" Sam asked. "And what is all that in the back?"

"Well, if you have been listening to the news, it looks like things will soon come to a head, probably within six months. Is there someplace we can talk without being overheard?" Shirley asked.

"Yeah, let's go into the camper," Sam said, "and then I'll show you how the house is progressing."

"Not yet. We must talk."

Shirley headed for the trailer. Sam closed the door and grabbed a cup of coffee, looking at Shirley, who shook her head.

"No, I'm coffee-d out."

"So what's so important?" Sam asked.

"It looks like things are going to get really bad and soon, and if we are going to go to the campground and get what we left there, we should leave real soon."

"Well," Sam said, "I'm really not needed here. I had a farmer plow up an area for a garden and asked the people who live here what grows good here besides weeds, and I have planted a lot of things, including about two acres of sweet corn. We will have to eventually fence that in so the deer and elk don't eat all the corn. All that needs doing is weeding and watering, but that could wait for two weeks. When do you want to leave?"

"Can we do it the day after tomorrow?" Shirley asked.

"Yes," Sam said, stroking his chin. "I'll talk to Sally to take care of the rabbits and chickens and some other people today and ask them to watch after the place while we are gone and then hook up the trailer. By the way, what is that in the back of your truck and trailer?"

"Oh, just some solar panels, batteries, an inverter, and stuff that I thought might come in handy around here."

A big smile spread over Sam's face. "Good idea," he said.

***

Captain Bartholomew steeped through the door, and a steward was there, who motioned him to a chair by a table with a plate that had a domed lid over it. The steward removed the lid, revealing a massive breakfast. He then pushed a button by a speaker on the table and was surprised to hear the conversation in the conference room he had just left. The steward just winked and left.

The president was saying, "I want you to take turns and explain what is happening and what your branch can do to solve the problem we have. Let's start with the navy. Admiral, what does the navy have to offer?"

"Mr. President, we have our conventional forces. Our ships could patrol both the Gulf of Mexico and the Mexican coast off the Pacific, preventing arms from coming in."

The president nodded.

"But our biggest problem is these are unconventional fighters, Mr. President. If they sink a few freighters in the Panama Canal in both the east and west lanes or blow up a freighter in one of the locks, then trade with the whole world will be jammed up. Shipping will have to go around the horn of South America, increasing the cost of shipping in both money and time."

The president's head was down. He then looked up. "And, General, what does the air force have to offer?"

"Well, sir, we can provide electronic surveillance for radio traffic and personnel in the desert and, if needed, drones for surgical strikes anywhere in the world."

The president just nodded and looked at the army chief of staff. "And, General, what can the army provide?"

"Mr. President, through SOCOM, we can provide training to local groups and utilize them to protect key bridges and other infrastructure, but we won't be able to protect all of them. You will have to determine which routes need to be kept open and concentrate on those. Also, there is the electrical and communications infrastructure that needs protection."

"So, General, your solution is to train and arm the general population—Billy, Bubba, and a bunch of beer-drinking self-proclaimed militias. This sounds like a recipe for disaster, a bunch of untrained civilians given guns and backed by the power of the U.S. Government running around my country."

This last statement hadn't gone unnoticed by the generals sitting at the table. The president of the United States did not realize the assets at hand were former special ops personnel from Delta, army special forces, navy SEALs, and air force special ops.

"Mr. Secretary," the president called, "do we know who the heads of these groups are?"

"Yes, sir, We have contacts and thorough intermediaries."

"Is it possible to negotiate with these people?" the president asked.

"I don't know, sir. I could send some feelers out and see what happens."

"Okay, then this is what we will do," the president said. "Mr. Secretary, you send out your feelers and see if we can negotiate peacefully with them, and in the meantime, you generals come up with an OP plan for what you and your forces can do. Do it through SOCOM and make it so we are not violating the Posse Comitatus Act. Gentlemen, if our captain has had his breakfast, then this meeting is over. I have to continue on to Brussels, and you all have some work to do."

***

Captain Bartholomew was driving to the Bachman's trailer when several bullets riddled the vehicle he was driving. He pushed his foot down on the gas pedal and swerved to his left to the centerline of the asphalt road he was on. The maneuver saved his life as an IED blew up alongside of the road but slightly behind him. Captain Bartholomew guessed that they had expected him to stop, and he would have been directly in the kill zone.

Captain Bartholomew exceeded the speed limit going to the Bachman's trailer. There was steam coming from under the hood. At first, he had guessed that a bullet hit the radiator and prayed the engine held together to get him to the trailer. Then two miles from the trailer, the steam stopped, and the engine started knocking, and as he was pulling into the trailer area, the engine seized from lack of coolant. Hearing the racket of the engine seizing, Betty and Ken came out of the trailer with weapons, and Sergeant Michaels came from the OP by the trailer, carrying his weapon.

"Holy shit," Sergeant Michaels said as he saw the condition of the vehicle Captain Bartholomew was driving. "What happened, boss? It looks like you had some trouble getting here."

"Call the men together," Captain Bartholomew said, "right now, even the ones out at the desert OP. Tell them to pull all the gear that's out there. I don't think we have much time."

The men from the OP in the desert came trotting in with all the gear, which really—for the amount of time they had the desert OP in operation—wasn't very much in extra since each man, when he went out there, had taken his gear with him and brought it back when he returned.

"Gentlemen," Captain Bartholomew said, "when I got back to our staging area, there was a helicopter waiting for me, and I was flown to Fort Hood, where a Learjet was waiting. I was then flown to Pope Air Force Base, where Air Force One was sitting on the ramp. I was taken into it, and the president and all the joint chiefs of staff were there. I was asked to give a briefing of our action here and the intel we had received. I could tell the president wasn't happy that we didn't have coffee and donuts for the downtrodden immigrants crossing our border illegally."

There were some chuckles from the group when he had said this.

"After my briefing, there was a breakfast for me, and while I was eating, I was able to overhear the discussion about our action and what I suppose the president plans to do."

"What's that, boss?" one of the men called out.

"Well, after he questioned the chiefs of each branch of the military, he asked the secretary of state if he had any contacts for negotiation with the insurgents. It seems the president doesn't want to acknowledge that there is a serious problem with our Southern border. So with that said, on my way back to Fort Hood, General Collins flew with me. He briefed me on what he feels will happen, and it isn't good. We are to be reassigned to a new operation, and that means that, Ken and Betty, you guys won't have any backup if anything happens here. Tomorrow a representative from the company you are working for will come to

brief you on your options, and in the meantime, we will be here for
three more days, and then we must leave. Ken, do you and Betty want
to stay here with your butts hanging out?" Without waiting for an
answer, Captain Bartholomew went on. "We will help you guys pack
everything you want to take with you, and I would suggest that, after
your meeting tomorrow, you leave here as soon as you can. I would
suggest that you head west and eventually North to the Palouse area
of Montana, Wyoming, Idaho, and Eastern Washington. With your
skills, you should be able to find a position in security. The rest of us
will square away our gear, and then we will help you pack up."

Ken woke up with a start, the alarm clock showed 4:00 a.m. He was
having flashbacks of his service when he was in Vietnam more regularly
now. He quietly got out of bed, started coffee, and, when finished,
poured it into a thermos and went outside. There was a security guard
posted at the firing pit dug by the trailer, and he got his gear and went
there with the coffee. The sentry on duty was glad for the coffee and to
have someone to talk to.

"What do you think?" Ken asked.

"Well, if it were me and my wife, I would haul ass as soon as I
could. I would head west to Phoenix and then to Las Vegas, maybe
spend a few days there—I know there is a great RV park next to Sam's
Town on the Boulder Highway—and then go North up to Salt Lake
and then Idaho."

"That would be quite a trip," Ken replied.

"Yes, but up in the North, there won't be too many of these Muslims
up there, not yet anyway. Stay away from California, Western Oregon,
and Western Washington."

They talked a little more and watched as the sky began to lighten
with the sun coming up. Ken got out of the pit and went to the trailer,
quietly opening the door. He started frying bacon and scrambling fresh
eggs from their chickens. When he had had enough, he started making
breakfast burritos for the guys.

He had a large stack on a plate when he heard a vehicle approach.
Quickly grabbing his firearm and gear, Ken quickly went to the firing
pit. The vehicle stopped just outside the trailer's compound, and he

heard the satellite phone bell on the outside of the trailer start to ring. Betty soon opened the trailer door and called out that it was a company man coming to talk to them. Ken climbed out of the firing pit and told the ranger in it that there was a plate of breakfast burritos in the trailer and to come and get them and pass them out to the rest of the guys whom he saw were emerging from their firing areas. As Ken walked to the trailer, the company vehicle came forward, turned around, and stopped, pointing back the way it came. The company man got out of the SUV-style vehicle. Ken noted that this was someone he had never seen before. He came walking over to Ken, holding his hand out to shake Ken's.

"You must be Ken Bachman," the man said, shaking Ken's hand.

Ken noted that he had a firm grip and that his hand was calloused, like a working man's hand. "Yes," Ken said, "and that's my wife, Betty, standing in the door. And who might you be?"

"I'm Jerome Walker. I'm the vice president of operations for the company. Is there someplace we can talk?" he asked.

"Yes, we can sit at the picnic table there. Anything you have to say can be said in front of our new friends," Ken replied. "Betty! There is a big plate of breakfast burritos on the counter. Would you hand them to me and then come out to hear what Mr. Walker has to say to us?" Looking over his shoulder, Ken called out, "Chow time, guys! It isn't much but beats cold MREs. You can sit at the table if you want."

Only Captain Bartholomew took Ken up on the offer to sit at the picnic table, the rest of the rangers grabbed two burritos each and went to their firing pits, providing cover for the meeting. Mr. Walker looked at the dwindling pile of burritos, and Ken saw this.

"Help yourself, Mr. Walker. We can make more."

"From what we hear and what I see, you guys had some trouble here. We can reasonably expect a little problem with theft, but what happened here is more than we expected or what your contract covers. So what the board has decided is to close this well for now and remove all the equipment that we can. We have a larger security force coming along with heavy equipment to load what we are taking. Now that brings us to you and your wife. We are willing to buy you out of what's remaining of your contract along with a bonus for the trouble you had, and if you can stay two more days, there will be another bonus for that."

"How much are we talking about?" Ken asked.

"It will be around $20,000," Mr. Walker replied.

Ken saw Captain Bartholomew was trying to get his attention. He looked at him and asked, "Do you have anything to say, Captain?"

"Yes. First, I feel $20,000 may be a bit low, but if Mr. and Mrs. Bachman were paid an additional $10,000 in cash if they stay the extra two days, I think it would be fair for them."

Ken looked at Mr. Walker and saw that he was deep in thought.

"After all," Captain Bartholomew went on, "they put their lives on the line for this company twice."

Mr. Walker looked up. "Twice? I know of just one, the one we had here a few days ago."

"Yes," Captain Bartholomew said. "About two months ago, there was an incident here, and Ken and Betty handled it by themselves very professionally."

"Yes. Now I remember an incident paper came across my desk, but I didn't realize how serious it was," Mr. Walker replied.

"Ken is a former army ranger who served in Vietnam. He has been around death and firefights before, but for Betty, that was her first firefight, and it was very traumatic for her."

Mr. Walker was looking down, deep in thought. He looked up. "Okay," he said. "You spend two more days here, and we will add ten thousand to your twenty thousand." Then looking at Captain Bartholomew, he said, "When you get out of the army, look me up. We might have a job as a negotiator for you." Getting up, he said, "I'll be back in two days with the work crew, and I'll have your money then."

"Mr. Walker," Ken said, "ask Hulio, one of your maintenance men, to come out here and pick up our chickens."

***

Sam and Shirley were driving down Interstate 17 as they passed by the town of Black Canyon.

Sam turned to Shirley and said, "You know, if we don't stop for a long lunch and push a little, we could be at the campground over in Globe before dark."

"That sounds good. I'm getting a little road sore from the trip down."

"Yeah, me too, but we have to do it if we want to get back before July. Have you taken notice? Since we have been on I-17, there have been a steady stream of campers, U-Haul trucks, and cars pulling big U-Haul trailers heading the other way."

"No, I hadn't really noticed."

"Watch," Sam said. "See? Here comes another string of vehicles. Trucks pulling cars on trailers or trailers with a car following, pulling a trailer, and look at the motor homes and fifth-wheels. It almost looks like an exodus. I wonder what's up."

For the rest of the trip to Phoenix, there was a steady stream of traffic going the other way, with little going to Phoenix. They made really good time getting to the campground just outside of Globe, Arizona. Sam pulled up to the camper staging area and went into the office.

"Well, look what the coyote dug up," Peter White said. "Hi, Sam. You guys are back early, I wasn't expecting you for another five months if at all."

"What do you mean, 'if at all'? What's up?" Sam asked.

"Well, I'll come by later and fill you in, and I have someone I want you to meet. You can go to your regular spot, and we can fill out the paperwork later. Do you have a CB radio in your camper?"

"Yes. Why?"

"Well, most of us are monitoring CB channel 2."

It was just getting dark. Sam and Shirley had a specific spot they wanted the wheels of their fifth-wheel trailer to be on, and it took a little maneuvering to accomplish this, but they finally had their camper where they wanted it. Shirley was getting a quick dinner going, and Sam was moving a picnic table to their area when Peter came up in a golf cart with another man in the right seat.

Peter got out and walked toward Sam when Sam said, "You must be doing better to afford a golf cart for you to run around in, and what's with the armament?"

"Well," Peter said, "there is more to it than just transportation."

Then the CB radio in the golf cart started. "Net Alert. Net Alert. Strangers at the chicken coop."

"Sam, if you have a shotgun, get it. There are *no* other ATVs or vehicles like this. If any come by, shoot them."

Peter then turned, and Sam saw that the person in the golf cart had slid over into the driver's seat and turned it around. Peter jumped on the back where the golf bags would go and pulled an AR-style rifle out of the front of the cart.

"Who were you talking to?" Shirley asked as Sam hurriedly went into the trailer.

"Peter, and I guess things are a little hairy around here." He grabbed a Mossberg 500 with an elastic stock clip that held five extra shells and headed for the door.

"What's going on?" Shirley asked with concern in her voice.

"Turn off all the lights and stay in here," Sam said as he went outside. He took a position between the trailer and his pickup truck and hunkered down, watching the road by his trailer.

Then there were several shots from the area of where the camp recreation pavilion was, a cement-block structure with clothes washing and drying machines, a pool table, a soda machine, a ping-pong table, and His and Hers restrooms and showers. Sam looked in that direction when he heard a high-pitched engine head his way. It came into sight and was a John Deere Gator six-wheel ATV. Sam lifted the shotgun up, remembering what Peter had told him, and squeezed the trigger. He wasn't sure if he hit anything, but the blast and fire coming from the barrel lit the area briefly, and the ATV swerved into a concrete parking stop that was placed on the edge of the gravel road in the park. It caused the driver to be catapulted out, and he skid to a stop halfway into the road.

Sam ran over, and as the person was getting up, he gave him a butt strike across the back of his head, knocking him out. Sam then went and found the key to the Gator, turning it off, and pocketed the key. He knelt down beside it and waited. There was an occasional shot from the recreational pavilion, and soon, everything was quiet. Sam looked at the still form in the middle of the camp road and determined he must have hit him hard since he wasn't moving yet. Sam stayed low and scooted over to the prone body, and just as he got there, it moved. Sam hit him again behind the head with the butt of the shotgun, went back to the ATV, and knelt down again.

Peter and his passenger rounded the corner of the road from the recreation pavilion and headed to Sam and Shirley's trailer. About a hundred feet from it, they stopped and called out for Sam. Sam had seen them coming and repositioned himself and was just a few feet from them when he answered their call. The passenger fell out of the golf cart, bringing his rifle up to the ready, when Sam yelled, "Friendly!" The rifle came down but not by much as Sam stood up with his shotgun over his head. Only then did the passenger lower his weapon. They went up the road and found what Sam had done and were happy at what they saw. They quickly secured him with zip ties and duct tape. Peter went over to the Gator, looked it over, and then asked Sam if he knew where the key was for the Gator.

Sam said, "Here in my pocket where it will stay."

"Good. Let's load this shit into the back of the Gator and run over to the pavilion. You know your way around here," Peter said to Sam. "Don't use any lights. We will be right behind you." Peter then got on the CB radio in the golf cart and said, "Net Call, Net Call. Situation green. Go amber."

Sam could hear several doors open and close, but no lights were visible, which was strange since people in the campground always had the light by their camper door on at night. As Sam pulled up to the cement-block pavilion, he saw several pock-marks on the wall. Peter jumped out, opened a double door to the pavilion, motioned Sam inside with the Gator, closed the door, and secured it.

"Sam," Peter said, "go tell Shirley you are all right and then come back here. Tell her there is a poker game or something but come back here as soon as you can."

As Sam left, he had a chance to size up Peter's passenger, the person Peter had wanted him to meet. Sam trotted to his trailer and stood to the side as he knocked on the door.

"Shirley, it's me, Sam. Turn off any light and let me in."

"How many lumps of sugar do you like in your coffee?" came the challenge.

"None. I like it hot, like you," he replied.

"Open the door," Shirley replied, and he stood there in the doorway. "Are you okay?" Shirley asked with a slight quiver in her voice.

"Yes, but I need some aspirin. I have a headache. Don't turn on any lights until we black out the windows."

"What happened?" Shirley asked.

"I don't know, but I must go to the recreation pavilion right away, and I think I'll find out then what's going on around here."

"What should I do for supper?"

"Somehow, right now, I'm not too hungry, but I will be later. Make two of your great hoagies for me. I got to go. I'll fill you in when I get back, and make sure all the windows are covered with two layers of blankets or dark towels."

After Sam picked up a five-round box of .00 buckshot and another one of slugs, he left and trotted at port arms back to the recreational pavilion. He beat on the door and identified himself, and the door was opened by the stranger. The door was closed and locked, and a weak light came on. Sam saw that his prisoner was hanging by his bonds around his wrists from a roof rafter in the pavilion. His head was down, but he was breathing.

"Sam," Peter said, "this is Ken. He and his wife, Betty, came in here about a month ago. I was hoping you would get here a little early, but this is earlier than I had hoped for."

"What's up, Peter? It feels like I walked into a war here."

"Well, Sam, in a way, you have. With the borders being open and all the illegal people crossing, many of them were getting welfare and supplemental aid. Well, the government cut many of those programs and money, and that didn't make people happy, so they started to riot.?"

"You mean the Mexicans rioted?" Sam asked.

"No, it was the others who thought the 'gubment' owed them a living. With the Mexicans, it's the younger kids, the teenagers, and the twenty-year-old's. They are the angry ones. They don't have the patience to work their way up the work ladder. They want it all right now. Then the gangs came across the border and set up shop. They started running marijuana into the states that legalized the recreational use of it. The states taxed it so much that an underground market developed, and they pressured the head shops to sell their product, and if they went to the police or refused, nasty things happened to them. Then the Muslims came in. Al-Qaeda and others came across the border, and then there was sabotage to water and electrical systems. Down closer to the border, things are really bad. It's really like a war zone, with gangs controlling different parts of counties." Yes, counties. They graduated from towns and small cities to whole counties. If you don't have the right sticker or window hanger in your car, you risk being shot at. Ken here was down in Texas, guarding an oil well pad. I'll let him tell you his story."

"What do you want?" Ken said. "The CliffsNotes or the full Monty?"

Sam said, "the situation being what it is, I'll take the CliffsNotes, and later, you can fill me in."

After ten minutes, Sam said, "That's quite an experience you and your wife had. The way you handled yourself, it looks like you have had some military training."

"Yes," Ken said. "I was in Vietnam for a while."

"Me too," Sam said. "Welcome home."

They shook hands.

"Well, now that old homecoming is over, look who's awake. Sam, you must have really clocked him for him to be out this long."

"Pete, he wasn't out. He was listening to Ken here and getting intel on us."

"That makes a problem for us. Come outside for a minute so we can talk without ears around."

"What are we going to do with him? We cannot feed him, and we cannot let him go to report back to his buddies what we have here."

"Well, Sam," Pete said, "I have a Case tractor with a bucket on the front and a backhoe on the rear. I can, in a very short time, dig a twelve-foot-deep hole. I'll make it big enough for four bodies."

"Good," said Sam. "I'll question this guy while you are gone. Oh, by the way, is this the first time this has happened?"

"No," Pete said. "Soon after Ken showed up, the raids started. It was a few chickens at first. We thought it was hungry locals. Then I received a visit from four Mexicans and someone who I think was a Muslim. I listened to them and then ran them off. That night, a trailer burned, with two very nice people losing their lives. Ruth and Jacob Petrovich. They were from Pittsburg, Pennsylvania. He worked most of his life in the steel mills and foundries, and she kept a large garden. They were the ones who took care of your weed patch while you were gone, and they did a good job of it. We ate plenty of fresh veggies from it all summer. What's left of their trailer is still here. After that, we set up a radio net with CB radios. If you have a sideband radio, that would be great. Then we made sure everyone blacked out their windows on their campers. All but two complied with this request. Jacob had us get chickens. He said he liked fresh eggs, and the manure was good for the garden. He built a good pen for them and got thirty straight-run peeps. I asked him if that wasn't too many chickens, and he said with luck, there would be a fifty-fifty mix of roosters to hens. It turned out he was close. We got nineteen hens and eleven roosters, so when the time came, we had a chicken barbecue with ten of the roosters. We had plenty of eggs for a while. Then more and more people came in—refugees, you might say—from close to the border. When the fire happened, many of them left the next day. We have nine camper couples and four children between two of the couples left here."

"Tell me about the two who won't black out their windows," Sam asked.

"Well, I don't want to prejudice you. I think we should have a camp-wide meeting at noon tomorrow here."

"That doesn't give me much time to question our guest."

"Well, we caught one of these once before we did everything we could to make him talk, but he said nothing."

"What did you do with him?" Sam asked.

"We shot him and then buried him."

"Was he Muslim or Mexican?"

"Well, we think he was a Mexican. This one is Muslim. They have different fears of death."

"Are there any farms around here with pigs?"

"Why, yes. About a mile from here, there is a farmer with about a dozen pigs."

"Do you know him? I mean really know him?"

"Not really. I have his phone number. What do you have in mind?"

"You don't want to know. Can I get there with this thing?" Sam pointed to the Gator.

"Yes. Like I said, it's only about a mile down the road on the left. Give him a call and let him know I'm coming, and let's load this dirt bag in the back."

By now, the guy Sam had captured was fully conscious. He asked him a few softball questions, and he was quiet and surly. Sam pulled into the lane at the farm and talked to the farmer. When he heard what was going on at the camp, he was more than willing to help. Abdul's— or whatever his name was—eyes got wide when he saw the pig pen. Sam asked Ben, the farmer, if he had a tractor with a boom or bucket on it.

"As a matter of fact, I do have a bucket on one of my tractors. I use it to clean out my pens."

They tied Abdul to the bucket and raised the bucket over the outside part of pig pen. He swung there like a side of beef. The pigs came out of the barn, curious as to what was happening. He was high enough that they couldn't get to him. Sam told him if he answered his questions, he would kill him quickly and give him a decent burial, but if he lied to him or refused to answer his questions, he would slowly feed him to the pigs.

Sam asked a softball question, like where he was from, and he replied with an epitaph, so Sam had the farmer drop him a little lower to the pigs. They were really milling around now, and some were standing with their forefeet on the backs of others to try to get to Abdul. One of the pigs got lucky and got a toe. The scream, Sam couldn't tell if it had come from Abdul or the pig, but he started to talk. Sam got all he wanted from him, only having to lower him one more time. He had the farmer tip the bucket, dropping him into the pig manure with the pigs. It was over in a few minutes. Sam found out from the farmer that it was just him and his wife. They never could have children. He thanked him for his service and went back to the campground, his trailer, and Shirley. She was pissed after making the sandwiches that Sam wouldn't eat one, but for some reason, Sam wasn't hungry. He went to bed, telling her everything was all right and that he was tired.

Early in the morning, Sam went to the campground office, surprised to find it open. He looked for Peter and found him in his office, studying a road map of Arizona and a Rand McNally book on his desk.

"What's up?" Sam asked. "You planning on taking a trip?"

"I'm looking at what's going on in states around us," Peter said as he put the map down. "What did you find out from our friend last night?"

"Well, after a little persuasion, he was quite vocal. It is amazing, what is being planned and how it's being done and who is behind it."

"Now you have my attention. Fill me in."

"Well, for beginners, he wasn't no run-of-the-mill Muslim. He was the regional administrator or mullah. His job was to secure this county and another county by controlling the small towns and remote properties. This will cause the bigger towns—and eventually the cities— to fall in line either by conquest or fear or people moving somewhere else to escape the violence. Like I guess you are planning."

Peter sheepishly looked up. "Yes. We cannot fight them all."

"You're right. This is what we have to do."

For the next hour, Sam laid out his plans to Peter.

"It sounds like it would work, we are having a camp meeting at noon in the pavilion. I'll make another net call and remind everyone."

"Where is Ken's trailer?" Sam asked.

"Down the road you are on," Pete replied.

"Thanks."

As Sam left, he heard Pete make another net call reminding everyone of the meeting and to pass the word to others. He walked to his trailer and saw that the curtains on the windows were open, so he knew Shirley was up. He stopped at his trailer to talk to Shirley.

As he walked in, Shirley looked at him and said, "You're up early. What's up?"

"I went to the office and talked to Peter. There is a meeting at noon at the pavilion, and it might get interesting. I'm going down to Ken and Betty's trailer. Do you want to come with me and meet them before the meeting at noon?"

"Sure," Shirley said.

They walked down the road.

"Wow! What happened to their trailer?" Shirley asked.

"They had some problems and I guess barely got out from where they were with their life."

"What were they doing?"

"They were guarding a remote oil well site in Texas and were raided by a Mexican gang. Ken gave me a brief rundown last night. Hello!" Sam called out.

The trailer door was opened by Ken. Sam could tell he had a firearm nearby. He came out, and Sam introduced Shirley to him. Ken called Betty to come out and meet their new neighbors. Betty and Shirley hit it off right away and went off by themselves. Sam turned to Ken and filled him in on what was going on here.

"Well, after the fire, we decided to set up a camp watch and use CB channel 2 for general communications, with seven up on the sideband for any critical communication. All but two couples went with the program, and they are a bunch of batty liberals who think the president is the messiah whose word is golden and anyone who wants to close the Southern border is oppressing our brown neighbors. They stay to themselves and won't do anything to help defend the campground."

"How are the rest of the people here?" Sam asked.

"Well," Ken said, "for the most part, they are okay. Only one other guy has had any military time, and that was in the guard, but his unit went to Iraq, so he has a little combat experience. The rest, while well meaning, are mostly followers."

"You know there is a camp meeting at noon at the pavilion, don't you?"

"Yes."

"Well, I'm going to fill you in on a little of what will be said so you will be of support if you desire."

As Sam was finishing talking to Ken, he saw Shirley and Betty coming toward them, talking like they were lifelong friends. He didn't know how she did it—maybe a sixth sense—but Shirley always seemed to know when Sam finished talking to someone and then to appear.

"I'll see you guys at noon then."

They shook hands all around. On the way back to the trailer, Sam looked at his watch. "Wow! It's only 9:00 a.m. Let's go look at the garden and see how it made it through the summer."

As they got there, Sam could smell the tomato plants before he saw them, and they were huge, with many red ripe ones and dozens of green ones. There were string beans, radishes, carrots, and other items that had been planted while they were gone. Sam stood up from pulling a weed and saw a motor home pulling a horse trailer and a pickup truck pulling a stock trailer come up the road. He gave a low whistle to get Shirley's attention, and they both kind of stared. It was an older class C Winnebago with one of the side windows missing and bullet holes along the back of the horse trailer. As they were backing the horse trailer into a vacant spot, Shirley and Sam walked over to introduce ourselves. The pickup with the stock trailer stayed on the road, which was no problem since there wasn't but one person at the end of the road. A slim young man in his late twenties got out of the Winnebago, and a young woman somewhere in her mid-twenties got out of the pickup.

"Hello. I'm Sam," Sam said, holding his hand out, shaking his—it was a nice firm grip of a working man. "And this is Shirley, my wife."

"I'm Joseph and this is Rebecca, my wife. Can you give us a hand?"

"Sure. What do you need?" Sam replied, thinking he needed help to connect his utilities and sewer hose.

"Here. Grab a panel."

Sam noticed three metal pipe-like panels on each side of the trailer. They were chained to the sides, and each leg stuck in a pocket to hold them. They got all six panels unchained and set them up, two on each side of the trailer, extending back from the gate, and one across the back, making a long chute. The sixth panel was kept on the trailer. Joseph then opened the rear door to the trailer, and two cows with calves and four steers came tentatively out of the trailer, along with three goats. The two calves and goats romped around as the two cows and steers looked for some grass to graze on. Joseph went to the back of the pickup truck, got a bale of broom hay, cut it open, and tossed it over the fence. He then got a rubber tub and placed it inside of the corral, and then he got a hose, hooked it up to the camp's water system, and filled the tub with water.

"There," he said. "That will hold them for a while."

"Joseph, this is quite a setup you have here."

"Call me Joe."

"Well, Joe, this is quite a setup you have here."

"Yes. My grandfather provided calves for rodeo roping, and he built this trailer to haul calves around the circuit. Three nights ago, we were glad to have it."

"How's that?" Sam asked.

"Well, we had some visitors to our small ranch five days ago. They wanted us to give them half of our cattle for protection. I told them to come back later with a truck, saddled one of our horses, rounded up what few cattle I had, drove them into our barn, and closed the door. I then hooked our cattle trailer to the pickup and backed up to the cattle chute behind the barn. I then got our camper out of the shed, and Becky and I started loading it with food, clothing, kitchen equipment, my guns, and all my ammo, which isn't much. Well, the next day, they came back with a truck for half of my cattle. I told them I changed my mind and to get off my property. One of them pulled a rifle out of the car that accompanied the truck. That's when I reached inside of the door of my house and grabbed my Marlin .30-30 rifle and the shooting started. I shot two of them. One was the guy with the gun. The rest took off, we finished loading everything we could think we needed into the motor home, and loaded as much feed and hay into the back of the truck, the front of the cattle trailer, and the horse trailer that we could and hooked it up to the camper."

"Then three nights ago, we heard some shooting at our neighbor's house about a mile away. At night, sound travels far on the prairie. Then we saw their house and barn on fire. That's when we started loading our cattle and Becky's three milk goats. We had more to load, but they came in fast. The chickens and rabbits were left behind, we opened their cage doors before we left. There were three pickup trucks and a cattle truck. I know some Spanish to get by with some of the local Mexicans, but two were shouting in a language I had never heard. There were some Mexicans. They were driving the cattle truck and knew what they were doing. The others started shooting up the house, and they set fire to it. I shot one of the Mexicans and closed the back door on the cattle trailer. It was already hooked to our pickup, and I told Becky to take the shortcut to the Interstate. I went back into the barn to get our two horses when they set fire to the barn. I got the horses into the horse trailer and took off with the Winnebago, pulling the trailer. I followed Becky, and I guess they saw me leave and started firing their guns at me. Some were full auto."

"I followed after Becky and met her at an overpass that was built over the Interstate so ranchers could get to their land on the other side of the Interstate. Becky's great-grandfather helped build that stretch of the Interstate and erect the fence in that area. He and the other workers that lived in the area built a hidden gate in the fence, saving the local people there a ten-mile trip to get onto the Interstate. We went through the fence and closed it back up. If you don't know about it, you wouldn't know it's there, and with it being dark and us driving without lights, they wouldn't find it until late morning. That's if they bothered to chase us at all."

"We drove all night, and as the sun was coming up, we stopped at a wooded area, and we got out and checked on everything. That's when I found the bullet holes in the back of the horse trailer. My heart sank at the sight. I opened the door, and the horses were shot up pretty badly but amazingly still alive but barely. I couldn't get them to come out of the trailer, so I got my pistol and put them out of their misery. This really upset Becky since she really those horses. I tied a rope to their hind legs and to a tree and drove forward. I closed the rear of the horse trailer and checked on Becky and the cattle. Since she had left first, everything was okay with them. We took off again and drove until we couldn't stay awake any longer, and besides, we had to milk the goats. And here we are."

"Well," Sam said, "that's quite an experience, but I'm afraid you went from the frying pan and wound up in the fire."

"What do you mean?" Joe asked.

"Come to the meeting at noon in the camp pavilion and be armed with at least a pistol, both of you."

The whole time Joe was telling Sam their story, Becky was holding onto Joe's arm. Shirley went to Becky and hugged her and told her things would be better. Sam shook Joe's hand and left with Shirley, and they went to their camper. Once they got into their trailer, Shirley said they had had quite a scare and an experience.

"How bad is it for us here at the campground?"

"Not quite as bad as they had, but it will get bad. Start picking and canning all the vegetables you can from the garden and don't unpack."

After a light lunch of a salad and sliced tomatoes and onions with vinegar and parsley from the garden, Sam and Shirley walked to the camp pavilion. Once there, they saw most of the people from the campground were there, and was surprised that the farmer and his wife were also in attendance. Sam saw that there seemed to be a distinct line drawn, and there were two very distinct groups, although one was a bit smaller. Peter White, the owner of the campground, got up and called everybody to order. There were folding chairs for them to sit on, and up front, there was a table and a small podium, and in the background behind the table were an American flag and the flag of the State of Arizona. Peter had them stand and led them in the Pledge of Allegiance. Then he bowed his head, and they recited the Lord's Prayer. Sam took notice that there were a few people who, while able to, didn't stand or participate in this little ceremony.

"I called this camp meeting to stop any rumors and to bring everyone up to date on what has happened. Last night, we were attacked at the chicken coop by some illegals, and there was some loss of life."

One of the women from the small group stood up and said, "Don't you mean you murdered them? If you would do what our group here suggested, they would still be alive, and we wouldn't be having this meeting."

Pete looked at her with a disgusted expression and said, "Why don't you explain what you dictated to me for everyone to know your group's position?"

A man stood up. Sam guessed he was her husband. "We talked with you that these people crossing the border aren't illegals but refugees from their country looking for a better life. If we set up a food and watering point for them, then they will leave us alone and move on, and there won't be any bloodshed."

Sam saw several heads shaking and only one pair of heads nodding. It looked like Joe was about to jump up, so Sam quickly got up and started to walk up to the podium.

"I think you might have some good points there. We just got in from a long road trip and haven't had a chance to stock up on food, and Joe and his wife just got here also, and they are low on food, so how much extra food do you guys have?" Sam said, looking at their little group.

"Well, we don't have enough to feed a large group of people," he said.

"I see," Sam said as he scratched the right side of his nose with his right index finger.

He saw Shirley do the same. It was a hidden signal they had for the other to follow the lead of the other person.

"I tell you what I will do," he said. "I'll kick in $100."

"Shirley jumped up and said, "I'll give another hundred."

Sam turned to Pete and said, "I'm sure, Pete, the camp can spare a hundred for this good cause."

Pete just stared at him.

"That will be $300. Do you guys think you can go into Phoenix to a Sam's Club and buy some rice, beans, and other staples? And you will have to go to a Walmart and pick up a turkey fryer to cook all this and some bottles full of propane. Do you guys think you can do this important step while we prepare an area for these refugees to rest and eat overnight?"

Their faces broke into broad smiles, and it looked like they were beaming.

"Take your time," Sam said, "and if you go over the budget, I'll kick in some more money when you get back. Take your time and don't skimp or forget anything. Take off while there is time, and we will organize things here, and why don't you spend the night in Phoenix so you don't have to rush and forget anything?"

They excitedly jumped up, and you could hear them chattering like a bunch of monkeys making a list of items they were going to buy as they left. Shirley escorted them to the door and made sure they were gone and then closed it. Pandemonium broke out.

"What the hell did you just get us into?" several shouted.

Sam put his hands up and said, "Quiet. What I'd just done was to get the idiots out of here. Now we adults can get to the real plans. My best estimate is that we have six or seven hours at best, so there cannot be much if any discussion on what I am about to propose. As I see it, we have three choices. Those of you who have family close by, you can try to go to them, but I would strongly recommend not going South or west, only North or east. I feel we are at a demarcation line, and it is slowly moving North. The other choice is to stay here and die or watch your wives and daughters get raped and then be killed, or you can throw in with Shirley and me. While we were gone, we were in Eastern Washington, Idaho, and Western Montana. We found a nice piece of property in Idaho. It's sixty acres with a cleared area for crops and a garden and woodland for firewood for heating and cooking. Before we left, I designed a house to be built. It's a ranch-style house with a basement, four bedrooms, two and a half-bathrooms, two septic systems, three wells, a solar system, and other goodies. Those of you who want to you are welcome, but all I ask is those of you who want to go to your family, help those of us who are going to try to make it to Idaho to get packed and loaded. Are you with me?"

A teenager stood up. "Are we going to give a name to our group?"

Sam looked at him, perplexed at first. Then it made sense. They would need a call sign on the highway, so he asked, "Any ideas."

A woman in her late twenties stood up. "Do you know what a group of baboons is called?"

Someone yelled out, "A congress!"

"Now do you know what a group of scorpions is called? A tornado. That is what anyone will get if they mess with us."

"All right," Sam said. "When we travel and from now on, we will use the call sign Scorpion. We have a lot of work ahead of us. Shirley, my wife, could use one of the children to help her harvest all the vegetables in the garden to be canned later." He looked at the farmer. "James—is that right?"

"Yes," he said. "James Monroe and my wife, Ruth."

"Okay. Are you with us, or do you have other plans?"

"We have no family close by. Both our parents have crossed over, and any other relatives are back east, and we're not too close with any of them, so we are with you."

"Okay. What help do you need, and what assets do you have or need?"

"Well, I have a flatbed truck with sides, a pickup truck, a stock trailer, and a flatbed trailer. If I bring all my animals, I could use another stock trailer. I have a milk cow with a calf, two heifers, a dozen well-fed pigs . . ."

Sam was taking a sip of coffee when he had said that and almost choked on his coffee.

James looked at Sam and smiled and went on. "Some goats and chickens."

"Joe has an empty horse trailer. Would that be of help?" Sam asked.

"Yes, we can put the pigs in it, the goats and cows into my trailer, and the chickens into a cage for a day or two."

Sam turned to Peter, the campground owner, and asked, "Peter, that Case tractor you have—what else do you have?"

"Well," he said, "I bought it at an auction with a tilt bed equipment trailer and a Ford 7000 five-yard dump truck to pull it. I also have the camp garbage dump trailer and a small flatbed trailer I use to move tables and other items around the camp."

"You have a dump truck and trailer to haul your Case and your pickup truck to pull the flatbed but no driver for it."

That was when one of the parents of a teenage boy stood up, saying, "My son, while he only has a learner's permit, really does know how to drive. He could fill in for a driver."

"That's good," Sam said, "but we still have a trailer that needs a tow vehicle."

Peter spoke up. "The Petrovichs came in here with a long trailer pulled by a Ford F250 pickup, and it's a four-wheel drive with a warn winch on the front."

"Well, that settles the truck and trailer, but who will drive it?"

Shirley spoke up. "I can do it."

"Good," Sam said. "Any other trailers or vehicles without drivers? What we will take will be necessary items—first fuel and then food, and that also includes feed for the animals, firearms, and defense and then anything we need to use to can or preserve food, clothing, and, if we have room, anything else."

Pete spoke up, "the camp has fuel tanks both Diesel and gasoline and a propane tank."

"How full are they?" Sam asked.

"The propane is a five-hundred-gallon tank, and I just topped it off. I have a three-hundred-gallon diesel tank, half full, and a five-hundred-gallon gasoline tank, about three fourths full."

"Okay. We will take all three with us."

"But I leased the propane tank."

"Don't worry. I don't think anyone will mind in two or three more days. Joe, can you help the Monroe's load their livestock and anything they have that we can use? Ken, can you help Pete load the tanks and then secure the Case to the trailer? Is there anyone here who doesn't want to go with us?"

An elderly couple stood up.

"I'm Dale Heckman, and this is my wife, Miriam. We have our grandchildren with us, and we feel we should try to contact their parents and try to get to them."

Sam looked at the other couple, and they said, "I'm William Rodgers, and this is my wife, Mary, and our son, Aaron, and Samantha, our daughter."

They said they didn't have anywhere to go or anyone alive who they were close to and that they were just driving around, doing odd jobs that they got from Workcamper and other similar sites. They were homeschooling their children, so they figured they would tag along.

"Good," Sam said. "How about you two help the Monroe's load." He looked at Dale and Miriam, the elderly couple with the grandkids, and said, "I just ask that you help us get ready, and when we leave, you stay at the back of us so that when you must turn off, no one will follow you by mistake."

"No problem," they said.

"Good," Sam said. "This meeting took us an hour and ten minutes. We have five maybe six hours to get out of here before the liberals get back here."

Shirley and Sam rode back to their trailer in the Gator that Sam had inherited.

"This is nice, and we can really use it in Idaho. We have to figure out how to take it with us."

At the trailer, Sam asked Shirley if she would be okay by herself for a while, and she looked at him.

He said, "I want to go into town to the hardware store and see if they still have any garden seeds and anything else, we can use."

"Yes," she said. "We will need all the seeds you can get. I can make out okay. Go."

Sam turned onto Hill Street in Globe, Arizona, and looked for a parking spot near the hardware store. There was activity all over the place. Many of the stores had half-off signs in their windows or on the sidewalk, and people were going about with a purpose. He was in luck. Someone was pulling away from the front of the hardware store as he got there. Sam got a front-door parking spot. He walked in and headed to the garden department. Surprisingly, there wasn't anyone there. He found a sales clerk and asked him what was going on. He said it was the monthly farmers' market and auction. Since they were never back this early, Sam didn't know this happened.

"How is everything else?" Sam asked him, trying to find any news of the trouble that was coming this way.

"Almost everyone comes in here at one time or another, and I haven't heard of any problems in the area."

Good, Sam thought. *We still have time before the panic.* He then asked if there were any garden seeds left in the store.

"Sure," he said. "It's late in the season, and there isn't too much left, but we still have some. What do you want?"

"Well, what do you have?"

He took Sam to a back room. "This is all we have. We have, carrot, radish, lettuce, and other seeds this size in one-pound boxes for bulk sales, peas, sweet corn, beans, and larger seeds in five-pound boxes, and field corn in twenty-five-pound bags."

"How many do you have?" Sam asked.

There wasn't much left since it was at the end of the season, so Sam bought all that they had. He then looked around and saw ten rolls of barbwire and fifteen sheets of three-by-four-foot Plexiglas. He got them and five rolls of one-inch chicken wire, four by fifty feet in length. He went through the hardware store, buying things he thought they would need, from chainsaws to hammers and nails. By the time he was finished, he had quite a pile. It dawned on him that with the fifth-wheel trailer hitch bolted to the bed of his pickup, there wasn't much room for cargo, but they managed to get it all on and tarped and tied down.

When Sam got back to the campground, he saw that everyone was busy. He dropped the ramp on their trailer and packed some of the supplies that he had just bought in there. He then drove the Gator up the ramp and tied it down. He then unloaded the rest of items he had gotten from the hardware store from the pickup, storing them in the Gator and the back of the trailer. He hooked up the trailer to the pickup and disconnected the service lines and filled the fresh-water holding tank on the trailer. In the meantime, Shirley had harvested all the vegetables from the garden. She had basically just pulled the plants up, roots and all, and had them on a plastic sheet in the trailer. Sam looked at the mess.

She said, "I thought we didn't have time to be neat, and why leave this for the people coming? We can clean this later."

"I'm going to see how things are going with the rest of the camp," Sam said and took off on foot.

He found Pete and two other men behind the office. They were finishing loading the gasoline bulk tank into the camp's garbage dump trailer next to the bulk diesel tank.

Pete turned around, saying, "Sam you got here just in time. All the work is done."

"Good," Sam said. "I'll go to the farm and see how things are going. Pete, can I borrow your golf cart? I have the Gator secured in my trailer, and my truck is hooked up to my trailer."

"Yeah, go ahead and take it, but it will be a long slow trip."

"Oh, Pete, pass the word for everyone to fill their fresh-water holding tanks. We will need the water for the cattle."

Pete was right. It was a slow trip to the farm. At times, Sam thought he would have to get out and push the golf cart. When he got there, he saw James and Joe had the stock loaded and were catching chickens.

"What help do you need?" Sam asked.

"Well," James said, "I would like to take more feed, hay, and straw. Who and what is available at the campground that we can use?"

"I have an idea," Sam said. "I'll be back as soon as I can." He jumped into the golf cart.

"Bring some help when you come back."

Sam picked up the radio microphone and called the campground. Sally answered his call. He told her to get Pete on the radio and call him back. After about what seemed an hour but was only five minutes, Pete called Sam on the CB radio. He asked if the Case was on the trailer yet.

"Yes, boss," he replied

"Is it hooked up to the dump truck yet?" Sam asked.

"It soon will be. Why?"

"Come over here with the dump truck and trailer and some manpower."

Within fifteen minutes, Sam saw the dump truck coming up the lane to the farm. The Case tractor with the bucket on the front and backhoe on the rear was chained to the trailer, and it looked like everyone from the campground was with them.

"Okay, what's up?" Pete asked.

Joe spoke up. "We want to take as much feed, hay, and straw as we can. Pull up to the barn, and we will load as much of the bagged feed as we can. Then I'll toss down hay bales. You guys stack them in the truck, and we will put a layer of straw bales on top. They are lighter, and if they get rained on, it won't hurt them. We can also put hay and straw on the trailer. Let's get going."

Sam pulled Pete to the side. "Why is everyone here?"

He looked at Sam and said, "We have everything ready to go there. This is the last job to do."

"Good," Sam said. "Let's go help."

They finished at the barn. The truck and trailer couldn't hold any more, so they went and helped James and his wife, Ruth, pack their house. When they finished, they had an hour to spare.

Sam said, "Let's all go to the campground for one quick meeting."

He looked, and the golf cart was chained to the trailer, so he rode the running board of the dump truck to the campground. When they got there, they had one last meeting.

Sam said, "We will all stay together. Keep about thirty feet clearance from the vehicle in front of you. If anyone stops, we all stop. When this happens, those of us who have firearms will form a perimeter. No one can get within ten feet of our vehicles. We will stop at a gas station as we go through town. I want everyone to fill your tanks, and we will try to put as much as we can into the camp's gasoline and diesel tanks. Does everyone have credit cards for fuel? We will take as much fuel as we can because there is no telling about the availability of fuel once we reach the Interstate. When we came in two days ago, there was a steady stream of vehicles heading north on Interstate 17, so I'm afraid we might see gas stations without fuel. Also, there are bound to be vehicles either broken down or with flat tires, out of gas, or with busted axles from carrying too much weight. As hard as it sounds, we cannot stop to help anyone, or we will be stranded ourselves. How many of you have CB radios in your tow vehicles or motor homes?"

A few hands went up.

"Okay. I want you two to be the last two vehicles. Then I want the farm vehicles with Pete and the dump truck in front of them. I will take the lead, and I want a radio halfway between me and Pete. We will use channel 7 as our travel channel. I don't want any unnecessary talk. Security and silence will be our edge. We have about four or five hard days of driving to get to where we are going, but believe me, it will be worth it when we get there. Remember, if anyone gets tired, don't be a hero. Call, and we will take a break for a while. It's not worth having an accident because someone fell asleep while driving. When we do stop, we must put out security front, back, and on each side. Let's gather around and ask the Lord to watch over us on our journey."

They had a brief prayer and then took off to their vehicles. Sam pulled into the gas station in town, topped off both his diesel tanks, and then moved out of the way. He noticed that James and Ruth Monroe were missing. This upset him since they needed to stay together for group safety. Sam went to the rear guard and asked what had happened. He was told they had said that they had something to do at the farm and would catch up. Sam then saw them pulling in and was headed over to admonish them for not staying with them when the town's volunteer fire department siren went off. He looked at Ruth and saw that her shoulders were heaving, and she was crying and holding onto James. Sam saw James's eyes were red, and tears were rolling down his cheeks. He went over to them and hugged both of them. He asked if they were all right with fuel and was assured that they were. James said that he and Ruth had talked it over, and they didn't want to leave anything behind.

With the excitement of the firetrucks leaving town, they were able to fill all the vehicles and the fuel tanks that they had brought from the campground. They formed up and took off for Phoenix and Interstate 17. They made it through Phoenix, and while it wasn't as bad as Sam had feared, you could see smoke from several large fires around the city.

The riots were starting. Instead of going up Interstate 17, Sam got on the radio and informed everyone that they would take U.S. Route 60 to U.S. Route 93. This would cut a hundred or more miles from their trip. All along the way, there were signs at gas stations in the towns saying, "No Gas." On the north side of the town of Wickenburg, Sam radioed that they would start looking for a place to logger for the rest of the night. The animals needed to get out and be fed, and Sam felt everyone was tired.

It was around midnight when they pulled into an area, and Joe, James, Peter, and two other men set up the corral and helped feed and water the livestock. Sam asked Joe and James how the animals were holding up, and they agreed that they would lose some, but most of them should make the trip. Sam found Ken and asked him if he would stand guard with him. Ken agreed. Sam went and asked for volunteers for guard duty from 3:00 a.m. to 6:00 a.m. and got three to volunteer. He told them to get some sleep and that he would wake them at 3:00 a.m.

There was intermittent traffic going north on the highway all night long, but many of the vehicles weren't loaded like they were refugees. Sam woke the other guards up at 3:00 a.m. and told them, since there were three of them, for one to go to either end of their convoy and for the other to walk to one end, and when he got there, that person was to walk to the other end, and then that person was to walk back and to do this for the rest of the night. Sam felt that this way, it would keep them awake longer.

It was six fifteen when Sam heard a pounding on their trailer door. He jumped up, grabbing a shotgun, and opened the door to find Ken there, grinning.

"Wakey, wakey, boss," he said.

Sam got dressed and went out to find many of the people were just waking up. He looked at Ken.

Ken said, "I couldn't sleep, and I thought everyone else needed a few extra minutes after yesterday."

"Thanks," Sam said. "Will you be okay?"

"Yes," he said. "It happens at times for me."

Sam looked at him. "Yes, I know what you mean," he replied. "Let's eat a quick breakfast and get loaded. I would like to be on the road by 8:00 a.m. We will stop around noon to water the animals and get a quick lunch break and then get back on the road again."

James came by with a bucket of milk for anyone who wanted some. Some of the women and children were unsure, but after they tasted fresh milk compared to store-bought milk, they rapidly changed their minds. They took off a little after 8:00 a.m. after everyone had topped off their fuel tanks from the tanks in the trailer and headed for Las Vegas.

They made it to Las Vegas and resisted going into town for a little R&R and gambling. From what Sam could see, the situation in Las Vegas was almost normal. The people here still didn't know—or they didn't care—what was happening to the South of them. They stopped and topped off all their fuel tanks again at a Terrible Herbst gas station, and this drew some curious looks and stares because they had made quite a show with all their vehicles, especially the ones with bullet holes in them. There was a brief meeting to discuss if they wanted to take U.S. 93 or Interstate 15. It was decided to take I-15. They were hoping to make better time driving instead of going through a bunch of small towns and running the risk of drawing more attention to their group.

They picked up I-15 and headed for Salt Lake City. They spent the night south of Salt Lake City and left the cattle out again for the night. Traffic wasn't as bad as it had been coming out of Phoenix, but Sam set up roving guards again. This time, Ken said he would like to get some sleep, and Sam left him. James came by with more milk for anyone who wanted some. Sam felt that they were now ahead of the panic crowds and that they would make it to their homestead without any problems. They still had a long way to travel, and he hoped they could make it without losing any of the animals they had with them. He felt that they would need all that they had.

***

The president of the United States was sitting in the situation room. The chief of staff, all the different heads of the military, the secretary of state, and several other people were sitting in chairs around the table, while their aides or seconds were sitting in chairs with writing arms on them, seated behind their respective bosses, taking notes. The choices were not good, and the solutions were even worse. The country was under attack, and the president knew deep inside that he was responsible for it. He had allowed the Southern border of the United States to be left open for his party to garner the Hispanic vote, but with the Hispanics also came other people. The radical Muslims crossed the border with the help of the Mexican drug cartels, and now there were thousands of them in the United States, ready to destroy the infrastructure. If they targeted the electrical grids and if they blew up some bridges over the major rivers in the United States, things would be snarled for a long time. Now he, the president of the United States, must figure out how to defend the country and use the "Fourth Estate" to blame it all on the Republicans.

***

They were passing through North Salt Lake when Sam heard, "Scorpion Lead, Scorpion Lead, this is Stinger. Come across the CB radio."

Stinger was the last vehicle in their group or convoy, so he called back, "Scorpion Lead. What's up? Is there a problem?"

Stinger replied, "No, but I'm picking up a weak call for Scorpion on our scanner. It's on channel 7. Do you want me to answer them?"

"Who all knows our call sign—" Sam replied when someone broke in and said, "The only one not traveling with us who knows our call sign is Dale and Miriam Heckman."

"Okay," Sam replied. "Contact them and give them our position and the first rest stop we come to. We will pull in and wait for them."

They pulled over at a West Bountiful Park and waited for the people who were trying to contact them on the CB radio to catch up with them. They used the time to find a gas station and refuel their vehicles, a few at a time so they wouldn't draw too much attention to them. They also used this time to set up the corral and let the animals out for awhile. Fortunately, while some people in the area were tense and they got a lot of stares, they were able to refuel all the vehicles and even were able to get an extra hundred gallons of gasoline and diesel into their bulk tanks. While they were waiting at West Bountiful Park, Shirley asked Sam when he thought they would get to their new home. He looked at her with a questioning look, and she said that the way things were, they should try to time the delivery of their household items from their house that they had sold in Seattle that were in storage and have them delivered to their new home.

"Good idea," Sam said. "I'm hoping to get there if we don't have any problems around the end of June or July 1 or 2. Why not have them deliver our stuff on July 2?"

Shirley went and called them when the Heckman's pulled into the park. He went over to their motor home and saw what looked like bullet holes and a broken window.

"Hi, Dale. It looks like you had some problems. We would like to talk, but we must get moving. The livestock was reloaded into the trailers . We can talk tonight, and you can tell all of us your story and what it was like. If you have any problems, we are on CB channel 7. We also use it to inform everyone if there are road hazards. How are you fixed for fuel?"

Dale said he had half of a tank.

"Well," Sam replied, "we will be heading north on Interstate 15. We will hold our speed to fifty so you can refuel and catch up with us. Let me know when you catch up, and I will start looking for a place to lay over for the night. I'm sure everyone would like to hear your story, and you can tell everyone at once about your trip then."

Sam shook his hand and gave the start-up signal to everyone, and they got back on the road.

They were slightly north of Plymouth, Utah, when they had finally found a deserted place large enough to hold their group. They circled their campers and trailers, reminding Sam of how the settlers had done in in the 1800s as they crossed the country in wagon trains. They got the cattle unloaded, fed, and watered for the night. After doing it for several times, they now knew who did what and had the corrals up in record time. They also were good at reloading the animals and securing the corrals for the move out. It now became a challenge to see how fast they could set up and then reload and tear down. Because of the dry area they were in, they didn't have a campfire but a large charcoal grill.

People were sitting around and talking when Sam got up and said, "As we all know, we picked up another member of our merry caravan— Dale and Miriam Heckman and their grandchildren. I know many of you want to know their story, so I will turn it over to Dale."

Dale got up and cleared his throat. "When you guys left, we left soon afterward. We had to dodge a few firetrucks but instead of heading north, we went west on Interstate 10 to Los Angeles. As we traveled on the Interstate, we saw isolated fires and smoke from fires in the countryside all along the way. We didn't like the thought of what was happening, and we pressed on, only stopping for fuel and to change drivers. As we passed through Indigo, California, there were many fires and people in vehicles getting onto the Interstate. Many were headed to Los Angeles, but some headed back the way we came. Traffic on the Interstate started to slow with all the people on it.

"We pulled off for fuel and found out that there was rationing going on at the gas station. Too many of the people were filling their vehicles, and the fuel at the station we were at was running low. I asked the attendant if there was a Walmart or hardware store nearby, and with luck, there were both. We went into the Walmart, and people were stocking up on food, and almost all the guns were gone, as was most of the ammunition. I was able to get three five-gallon fuel cans and a trailer hitch rack to be put on the back of the motor home to hold the gas cans. We then went to the grocery section and saw most of the canned goods were gone, but we did manage to get several cans of Augason Farms food and several packages of spaghetti and jars of spaghetti sauce. We also got all the Spam that was left on their shelves and several cans of tuna along with anything else we thought we could use. We were able to fill two shopping carts. Then we paid for it with a credit card, thinking they won't be good for too much longer.

"We stopped at another gas station and were able to top off the motor home with fuel and fill the three gas cans. As we were headed back to the Interstate, we heard on the CB radio that there were problems on the Interstate. Vehicles were running out of fuel and were starting to block the lanes because they didn't pull to the side of the road and this was causing several accidents. We didn't get on the Interstate but stopped at a small convenience store and bought several maps of the area and surrounding states. We continued to our son's home on secondary roads, but as we got closer to his place on the outskirts of Los Angeles, we started to see homes that were burned, and then we saw a firetruck that was burned and looked like it had been shot up. Because of all the stupid gun laws in different states, all we had was a Mossberg 500 shotgun for defense. I pulled into a parking lot of a church that was still standing and had Miriam, my wife, keep a lookout while I got the gun from where I had kept it hidden and several boxes of .00 buckshot and slugs and loaded the shotgun. I put it on the floor between us and had Miriam roll down her window. I was thinking if anyone shot at us, I didn't want glass flying around.

"The closer we got to my son's home, the worse it looked. There were shells of burned-out homes, and then we started to see bodies in yards. I had Miriam close the curtains on the motor home so our grandchildren wouldn't see more of the carnage than they had to. We noticed that there were houses that seemed to be untouched but had some sort of graffiti painted on the side. We pulled onto the street where our son and his wife lived, and my heart beat a little faster. We saw that their house was burned. I stopped in front of what was left of their house, dreading the worst. I got out of the motor home, looking around, when a neighbor whose house that was still standing that was next to theirs came to me. I asked what had happened, and he said that the gangs had carved up the city into territories.

"'They came by demanding food and any firearms that we had. I showed them our pantry, and they took almost all our food. Then they painted their gang sign on my house. They said that they were in charge of the area. We were spared because we were Hispanic. Only Hispanic homes were spared. All the others were looted and anyone there that didn't go along was killed and their homes were burned. Your son and daughter-in-law were not home at the time, so they broke into their home and took all that they could carry. When your son and his wife came home, I told him what had happened. Sampson asked me to keep an eye on the place and that they would soon be back.

"'In about an hour, Sampson returned, towing a fourteen-foot enclosed cargo trailer with a Ford F250 four-wheel drive pickup truck that had a shell over the bed of the truck. I had never seen the truck or trailer before. His wife, Megan, also pulled in with their Ford Bronco, and it was pulling an eight-foot enclosed cargo trailer. Sampson backed his trailer up to the garage door, and with several tries, Megan was able to back her trailer beside Sampson's trailer. Sampson went into the open garage door, and the garage was a mess. I borrowed tools from him on occasion, and I knew he kept his tools and garage in order. Everything had a place. The floor was strewn with tools and hardware from the organizers he had stacked on the shelves. If anyone in the neighborhood needed a nut or bolt, they didn't have to run to Lowe's or Home Depot. They could come here, and chances were that Sam had it, and he would never accept any payment for whatever you needed, if it was a nut or bolt or a wax ring for your toilet. He got two five-gallon buckets, a broom, and a dust pan and swept up all the hardware and hand tools, putting them in the buckets. He said this stuff will come in handy soon. He loaded the empty organizers.

"'Then he looked at me and said, "Jack, you cannot ever mention what you are about to see. Watch this."

"'He pulled on his workbench, and it and the pegboard connected to it came away from the wall. He had a false wall, and behind it, he and Megan started pulling boxes out and, using a hand truck, started loading the two trailers. I gave him a hand, and there were boxes and eighteen-gallon Rubbermaid totes. Some were really heavy, and some weren't quite so heavy.

"'He then looked at me and said, "Jack, you can never mention what I am about to load next."

"'He then started stacking ammo boxes marked with the different calibers, and I could tell by the sound they made that they were full.

These went into the back of his pickup, and some went into the Bronco. Then he started pulling plastic gun cases out. These also went into the pickup and Bronco, with more going into the pickup.

"'We took a short break, and I looked at him and asked, "Did all this come from between the wall?"'

"'He looked at me and smiled and said there was a small stairway in there that went down into a walled area in the crawl space and that there was a dug-out area behind the house where he always kept a small stack of two-by-fours and other wood to keep people off the top of the area he had dug out. This was where he had his secret stash in case anyone from the government came snooping around, and since this was California, not many people would understand all the guns, ammo, and food. Sampson then asked me how I was fixed for food, and I told him that the gangs had taken most of my food. He frowned at this and asked me why I was staying, and I told him that the wife had diabetes and that we needed to stay close to where she got her medicine.

"'Sampson looked at me then and said, "You know there will come a day when insulin won't be available."'

"'He looked at me, and I said, "I know, and we will cross that bridge when we get there."'

"'Your son then gave me two boxes marked, "One-month food supplies" and a tote with pinto beans and one with rice in it. He said, "If you are careful, this will last you and your wife three months. Go to Walmart and get a propane camp stove and all the propane you can buy. Put it on your credit card because soon, they won't be any good. Do you have a firearm?"'

"'I told him no, so he gave me an SKS rifle and five hundred rounds of ammo for it and showed me how to use it. He said that I should talk to the neighbors and see if they were willing to set up a neighborhood defense force for when the gangs came back again and to strip the guns and ammo from the gang members that we killed. He shook my hand and wished me and my wife luck and said that with any luck, the hiding place will survive, and I looked at him. He said that if we decided to leave, they were going to the Palouse area of Idaho, that they had a cabin there, that he would constantly monitor CB channel 12, and that his call sign would be "Jawbone."

"'I gave your son a quizzical look, and he said, "Sampson killed ten thousand Philistines with a jawbone of a mule." It may come to that. We both chuckled about that.

"'As we walked out of the garage, Sampson then said that I should get my garden hose out. I looked at him, and he said that he was going to burn what was left of the house. I asked him if I could go through his house first.

"'He looked at me and said, "Only if you promise to burn it before the gangs come back."

"'I told him I would. Then he then opened an ammo box and gave me a roll of silver quarters. He said that they would be the currency of the future.

"'He then said, "If my parents come by with our children, tell them where we went and to call for me on CB channel 12. I hope they have enough sense to go to our cabin instead of here."

"'We shook hands, and they drove off. For two days, I went through Sam's house, looking for anything I could use or trade, when I heard that the gangs were making patrols. I got out my garden hose and set fire to Sam's house, just as he had asked me to. The smoke quickly brought a gang patrol, and I was there, hosing down the side of my home, when two heavily armed gang members came to me. They looked angry and asked what had happened, and I said another gang had come by just a few minutes ago, telling me that they were in charge of this area and that when they had found this house empty, they set it on fire to show us who was in charge.

"'I looked at them and said, "Just who is going to be our protectors?" This really got them angry, and they asked me how many of them were there, and I said, "Only ten, but we have no guns or any way to protect ourselves, so we are at the mercy of you people, but we need to know who we are to support with the food from our gardens." They asked me which way they went, and I pointed down the street. They then took off, trying to catch a ghost.'

"I asked him how his wife was with her diabetes, and he said that they couldn't get any more insulin and that she had passed away a day ago. I asked him if he wanted to come with us, and he said no, that his wife was buried behind their house, and that there was another grave dug in the back.

"He looked at me and said, 'Do you know who the most dangerous person is? A person who has nothing to lose or live for. I have some surprises for those gang bastards when they come back. I will take out as many as I can before they kill me.'

"I looked at him and saw a broken man, and I knew he meant what he had said. I shook his hand and wished him luck, and we had a short prayer, and we left. On our way here, we ran into a little trouble. When we were getting fuel, some people tried to attack the gas station, but they had some guards stationed around it, and the guards took care of the problem. That's where the bullet holes in the motor home came from. The farther away we got from Los Angeles and California, the better things got. We remembered that you said you had a place in Idaho, so we looked at a map and saw that this was the most logical way for you to get there. We were hoping that we could join up with you and your group, at least until we find our son and daughter-in-law."

Dale sat down, and Sam stood up. "Wow, that was quite a story. You know that we are headed to some property we recently bought, but the living quarters won't accommodate everyone, but those who want to stay would have to live in their campers probably throughout the coming winter. You will also have to work to help support the group, and if you don't know how to use firearms, you and your wife will also be required to learn how to use firearms and be willing to defend what we have, and that might mean taking another life. Do you think you can do this?" Sam asked. "If you feel you cannot do this, you can tag along until we get close to our farm, and then you will be on your own to try to find your son and daughter-in-law, but be advised that the Palouse area stretches from Eastern Washington State to Western Montana and from the Canadian border to parts of Wyoming. It's a large and, in some places, remote and rugged area. Your chances of finding them will be difficult at best. If anyone has any questions for

Dale and his wife, now is the time to speak up, and I do mean *any* questions, no matter how insensitive they may be."

Bill Rodgers stood up. "I don't know about how the rest of you feel, but Dale and his wife helped us to get loaded and ready to bug out at the campground. I feel that they have a place in our group, providing they are willing to work and defend it." He then sat down, and there were murmurs among the group and nodding.

Sam stood up and said, "The offer still stands, you have tonight to discuss it with your wife, and let us know in the morning how you stand. Be careful if you leave your camper during the night because we have guards posted to protect the cattle and sound a warning if it looks like anyone is trying to steal from us."

Miriam then stood up and said, "I was raised in a Christian home, and the Ten Commandments say 'Thou shalt not kill.' How does this and the Bible stand with us possibly having to kill someone?"

Everyone was quiet, and there it was, the one thing that was on many people's minds, now out in the open.

Ken Bachman stood up. "This is the same question I had when I got to Vietnam. I asked the chaplain assigned to our unit the same question. He sat down with me and showed me several passages in the Bible where murder is sinful but where to kill someone who is trying to kill you isn't murder. In Luke 22:36, Jesus says, 'The one with a purse should take it and likewise a bag, and the one without a sword should sell his cloak and buy one.' We should not take joy in taking another life but in defense of your life or, in today's world, your food and supplies since without them, you will die. Killing someone will not be sinful."

Sam agreed that before they would leave in the morning and after they had the cattle loaded, they should have another quick meeting on this subject. Ken sat down, and Sam looked around, and Rebecca Wolfman stood up.

"I grew up handling guns, so I have no problem with them, but some people might be uncomfortable with or around them. Now is the time to come to grips with our situation. You can liken what is happening now to the 1800s, the women had to stand up and help defend the homestead while their husbands were either on a cattle drive or working on the range or in the field. We will need people who not only cook, garden, and can what we grow but also will be able to defend the farm while the men are gone doing whatever they have to do. I think we need a few more discussions before we get to Sam and Shirley's place so everyone knows what will be expected of them. Tomorrow, when we have our morning meeting, we can start the process, and then we can discuss it among ourselves while we are driving, and tomorrow night, we can have another campfire meeting."

Rebecca sat down, and Sam looked around.

"Anyone else?" he asked. "If not, check who is on guard duty and what times."

Everyone got up and joined hands and had a group prayer before going to their campers for the night. As everyone went to their camper, Sam was happy to see that some people had stopped and talked to the Heckman's.

Sam's alarm clock went off at 3:30 a.m. because his guard shift was to start at 4:00 a.m. and run to 6:00 a.m. He went outside with a cup of coffee, an AR rifle with a duplexed thirty-round magazine, and a pistol belt with two ammo pouches with two thirty-round magazines in each pouch. He liked this shift since he was an early riser anyway. There was a unique quietness to this time of the morning, a stillness and, at times, a unique smell for the upcoming day. Sam was paired with Ken Bachman. Ken knew that Sam was a steady, reliable man. They had a brief discussion and decided to make irregular patrols around the campsite, Ken going clockwise and Sam counterclockwise. Ken's starting point would be the corrals and Sam's opposite from the corrals. Ken would be on the outside, and Sam would be on the inside of the perimeter that the campers had made. Close to 6:00 a.m., Sam noted that there was activity in most of the campers as he did his patrol. He rapped on the campers with no sign of activity, waking them up to a new day. By seven thirty in the morning, most of the group were outside, having eaten their breakfast, with coffee cups in their hands. Some started to the corrals, and Sam stopped them.

"Let the animals enjoy a few more minutes of freedom before we load them and pass the word to everyone that we will have a quick meeting." Once everyone was gathered, Sam asked, "Well, did you discuss what we talked about last night?"

There were nods.

"We are about two days from our place, so you will have to decide if you want to stay with us and work as a small community for mutual support because from what we have heard from the Heckman's and what little we can get on the radio, it looks like things may go downhill in the country real soon. There is no telling what these invaders will do, and there really is no telling what, if anything, our government will do. So far, our president is sitting on his hands. It's almost as if secretly, he is hoping for something to happen by the American people so he can declare martial law and become a dictator. Last night, we discussed what roles the women could play with our group. It's almost necessary that everyone become familiar with the handling and operation of firearms. The men, besides field work, will need to have scouting patrols and a reactionary force in case the gangs or insurgents come our way. Like I said, we have about two more days, maybe less, so today think about what your role will be if you decide to stay with us. That's it for now, so let's get the animals loaded, and let's get going."

It took a little longer than usual to load the animals. They knew what was ahead of them—more hours in a cramped trailer—and some of them needed more persuasion than normal to go into the trailer. They stopped twice for fuel during the day, and every time they stopped, they drew a lot of stares and attention. Sam tried to use truck stops or gas stations along the Interstate for this, but at times, there weren't any available, so on those occasions, they had to go into a town. They were asked questions about what they were doing, and Sam had warned all the people to not say anything about where they were going or why but to say that they all happened to be going the same way, so they decided to go as a group in case of an emergency with one of the vehicles. They had another meeting that night, and the discussions were about what awaited them when they got to Sam and Shirley's place. Sam said that they should make it by the end of the next day, and then they could see what was waiting for them, and then they could make a decision if they wanted to stay with them or try to make it to a family member's place or go it alone.

It was a long hard day of driving, and as they went up U.S. 95, they caused many a head to turn, especially when they went through the smaller towns. Sam wanted to get to their place as soon as they could because they had lost two pigs and a heifer calf, and he didn't want to lose any more. It was getting increasingly difficult to get the livestock into the trailers in the morning. It was around eight thirty in the evening when they hit Potlatch and turned off 95 to Onaway. Sam wanted to go through these towns at night when there weren't too many people out on the streets because they made quite a parade of vehicles. The people in the area didn't have much to talk about, and Sam didn't want them to be the talk of the town gossips.

As they pulled into their home site, Sam was relieved that the house, barn, and workshop at least had roofs on them. He got on the CB radio and told the drivers with animals to go to the barn area and the rest to find a level spot to park for the night. He then went to the barn to see what they had available for the animals and was pleased to see a mixture of pens and stalls as he had laid them out. They backed the trailers with the animals up and unloaded the cattle into two of the pens and the pigs into another pen. They put two tubs into the pen with the cattle for water and put a bale of hay into the two mows at either end of the pen for them to eat. It seemed that the animals knew their journey was over as a few bucked and pranced. In the pig's pen, they put some troughs for water and one for feed. They too sensed the trip was over and were exploring their new home.

After they had this finished, Sam called everyone together and said, "Well, we made it. Let's say a prayer of thanks for our safe arrival."

They all bowed their heads as Sam gave thanks for their safe trip and asked for a blessing on their new undertaking. He then said tonight they wouldn't need any security guards and to have a good night's sleep because in the morning, they had a lot of work to do. His goal was to get there by July 4, and today was July 1. It was a minor miracle, with the distance they had covered, that they didn't have any serious problems.

They said their thanks and good nights as everyone headed to their camper. Everyone was bone tired.

Sam awoke to fresh coffee and bacon frying, He looked at the alarm clock, and it was 7:00 a.m. He got dressed and went to the kitchen area, where Shirley was finishing making breakfast.

"Morning, sleepyhead," she said.

"Morning," he replied as he kissed her and sat at the table.

Bacon, eggs over easy, toast, and coffee—this was usually his standard breakfast for as long as he could remember. He finished his second cup of coffee and got up.

"What are you going to do?" Shirley asked.

"Well, let's see who else is up, check on the animals, see what we have in the barn and shed. We have to unload the trucks and trailers of hay, straw, and feed and then check out our new house," Sam replied. "What's on your agenda?"

"Well, I want to see our new house and then check out what, if anything, is left of the garden we planted before we left."

As Sam left the trailer, he looked at his rifle and pistol hanging by the door. *Strange*, he thought. *I don't think I will be needing these for a while.* He walked out into the sunshine. As he started to walk to the barn he saw Sally's car and wondered how she and her little daughter would fit into their group. Sam continued to the barn. When he walked into the barn, he saw Ken, Joseph, and James looking around the bottom of the barn.

"Well, guys, does it meet your approval?" Sam asked.

"Well, boss," Joe said, "it will do."

"It's well built," James said.

"And laid out nicely," replied Joseph.

"How are the animals doing?" Sam asked.

"They all seem to be looking okay. In a day or two, they will be at home here."

"Good," Sam replied. "What I need from you two is a list of supplies for the animals, feed, medicine, whatever you can think of. Enough supplies for a year. Ken, I have a GPS. What I want you to do is grab Peter and Bill Rodgers and do a surveillance patrol about a half-mile radius around the building area. I'll help you get the Gator out of the back of my trailer and use that. Look for tire tracks, trails, logging roads, footprints, and anything that doesn't look right. Go armed, and until we can dig out the radios, you won't have any comm, so be careful. We will do a wider check later, but for now, we need to know if anyone is watching us. I'm going to check the maintenance shed and see how that turned out. Then I'll be in the house, setting things up. Try to be back before 3:00 p.m. if you can."

As they took off, Sam went to the shed. It had a hard-packed dirt floor except where the office area was. That had a finished concrete floor with a full bathroom, hot water, and heat and was large enough for two people to bunk in it if it was necessary. As Sam was looking around, he heard a vehicle come in the driveway. Instinctively, he reached for his pistol and remembered it was in the trailer. He walked out and saw it was Deputy Barns. Sam walked over to him with a smile on his face and shook his hand. Sally came out of her cabin and came over to them.

"How are things around here?" Sam asked.

"You guys created quite a stir last night," he said. "You all are the talk of the town." "Yes", Sally said "I thought there was a parade coming in here." Sam looked at Sally, "Sally I plan on having a group meeting at 5 PM in the Maintenance building, can you and your daughter be there?" "I'll try to make it", Sally said then gave Jessy a hug and left.

A frown came to Sam's face. "I tried to come in late so no one would see us."

"Well, you were seen," Jesse said.

"Oh, well," Sam said. "We couldn't hide here forever. How are things here?"

"Not good, the sheriff thinks there will be trouble and wants me to take stock of what resources I have in this area and how many men I could rely on to defend this area."

"What information is the sheriff basing this on? A hunch? Or does he have hard evidence?"

"After you guys left, the sheriff attended a meeting of all the county sheriffs down in Boise. When he came back, he briefed all of us deputics on what was covered. It seems our government has been resettling what they call refugees in various states, and Idaho is one of these states. The problem is that they are Muslims. They tend to stay together and do not want to assimilate into the towns they are sent to. One of the sheriffs said they have a large group in his county, and he and his deputies, along with some trusted civilians, are closely monitoring them. This sheriff said they have what looks like a military training camp on three hundred acres with about a hundred people now in training, but they don't know how many have been trained there already. Once these people get trained, they leave, and another group shows up. Sometimes there are as few as thirty, and sometimes they have as many as a hundred and not only men but also women and children as young as about ten years old attending this camp. Officially, it's listed as a religious retreat summer camp, and outwardly, it looks like a Boy Scout camp, but there are areas hidden from the main area where explosions and gunfire were heard, and they have a military-style obstacle course. He said it has all the earmarks of a terrorist training camp, and it's here in Idaho. He went on to say that they have two three-man teams monitoring the place 24-7. They have followed the people when they left the camp. Some went South to Utah. Others went to Seattle, but many went east to Iowa, Illinois, and other states. But the scary thing is we have a terrorist training camp here in Idaho."

"So what is the sheriff going to do about it?"

"Nothing he can do for now, they aren't harming anyone or breaking any laws. but if anything happens, it will be the first place that will be closed, and from the way it was said, it will be closed without warning."

"Well, right now, I have three of our group doing a half-mile perimeter patrol around our place to see what is out there. Actually, I hope they only find animal tracks. It's too early for us to set up a security guard, although if we had to, we could because we had to have a security guard at night on our way up here."

"Tell me about your trip from when you left here until you came back. What did you see and hear?"

"Let's get some coffee and find a place to sit. This could take a few minutes."

So over several cups of coffee, Sam told him about the traffic that was heading North while they were going South and how it reminded him of refugees leaving an impending war zone. Sam then told him of the trouble at the campground and of the attacks there, of the problems some of their group had before they met up, and of the fires in Phoenix and how they had circled the campers and posted guards at night. Sam also told Deputy Barns that he felt that there was going to be some sort of trouble soon. He said he didn't have any hard evidence, but things they had seen and heard were stacking up.

"You know," Sam said, "when a large airplane crashes, it usually isn't just one item that brings it down but a series of little incidents that mount up to finally create an unsurmountable incident, and this is how I feel now. I cannot put my finger in any one item but a national debt closely approaching $25 trillion. One-third of the people who can work are supporting the other two-thirds who can work but choose to not work and suck off the government teat with food stamps, welfare, rent subsidies, and other free giveaways that others are paying for. Then there is the fluid Southern border with not only Mexicans but many other nationalities crossing with impunity, and instead of integrating in the American culture, they are staying in their own groups, and now you are telling me that there is a Muslim ISIS training camp in Idaho and in other American states. Then the stock market is overblown, and many banks are overleveraged. If there was a financial crisis, our stock market and banking system would collapse like a deck of cards. You also have the news media fanning the flames of discontent with their one-sided news coverage. Then there is the just-in-time delivery of our groceries to the supermarkets. Many people don't have three days' food in their house, let alone three weeks. If the food trucks stopped running in a week to the big cities, there will be food riots."

"Stop," Deputy Barns said. "You more than made your point."

Shirley came out, waving a cell phone. "The moving company is on the phone. They need directions here."

"Ask them where they are," Sam said.

"They are in town and need directions," she said.

"Well, I'm going to town," Deputy Barns said. "I'll find them and lead them here."

Sam looked at Shirley. "Well, you have your work cut out for you."

"What do you mean me?" she asked.

"I have tons of work out here. The first is spotting our trailer and then unhooking our truck, getting everyone else's RV spotted out of the way, getting them busy unloading all the equipment we have, and other chores. I feel we are running out of time."

Sam looked at his watch. *Wow—only 9:00 a.m. and so much to do.* He went to all the campers and told them that he would like a meeting in the equipment shed at nine thirty. When the people came in and saw no seats to sit on, they went to their campers and brought camp chairs into the shed to sit on.

Sam looked around and said, "We have a lot of decisions to make, and we must make them now. I will give people a chance to talk as long as they don't monopolize the time because right now, time is important, and we do not have much of it. First, you will notice there are three members missing. I have them doing a scouting and security patrol in a half-mile radius around our place here. I want to know who or what is close to us. Next, the Heckman's—are you going on to your son's place, or are you going to stay with us? You don't have to answer that now but later today. For the people who are staying, I would like you to bring your RVs through the shed, one at a time, unload any supplies you are willing to donate to the good of the group, and repack your RV with supplies like pots, pans, bedding, and so on for a quick departure if we need to leave. Food will be combined, and if we ever have to bug out with our vehicles, we will draw from our group's stockpile. We will first organize each RV and inventory what is in them. Then we will park them in the woods behind the buildings. We must unload what supplies we have for our livestock into the barn, and I have asked James and Joseph to provide me a list of supplies they need for the cattle and chickens. We planted a garden before we left, and we will need some people to weed it and see what is left after the deer and elk have had free range in it for the past two weeks. The garden will have to be weeded, and any food that is ripe will have to be harvested and canned or preserved in some way for winter.

"Sleeping arrangements—without the Heckman's, there are thirteen of us. I have said the Heckman's have until the end of the day to decide if they want to leave. That goes for anyone else, but for sleeping arrangements, we have the RVs, but come winter, they will get really cold. The shed here has room for two people and is heated, and the barn could house some people during the summer and the main house. Once it is organized, we can put everyone into it. It will be tight, but it can be done. The last thing I have for now is security. We will still have to be security conscious. We will stand out in the small community. We are already the talk of the town gossips, so we must be careful for now who we talk to and what we say. In a few days, I feel we will need a security or observation post in case of trouble, and we must decide where it will be and then build it. Are there any questions?"

Mary Rodgers stood up. "If we decide to leave, what do we leave with?"

Sam stood up and said, "You will leave with what you now have. Right now we don't have any extra supplies to give out at this time."

Dale Heckman stood up. "What if we leave and cannot find our son and his wife? Could we come back?"

Sam said, "Yes, the group that came here will always be welcomed as long as they agree to our standards. Anyone else will be put to a group vote."

Mary Rodgers stood up again. "Sam, no offence, but the way you talk, you will be a dictator here. Is this how this place will be run?"

"I'm sorry if I come across like that, but we have things to do, and someone must keep track of what must be done. I have asked for input from James and Joseph as to what they need for the animals, and for now, it would be natural for them to take care of the livestock until others can be trained. I will always be open to ideas and suggestions, but we must remember this will not be a democracy. There is a storm brewing, not a rainstorm but something much worse, and we are way behind the power curve in being trained and prepared. There is a lot that must be learned, and I will have the people who know what they are doing do the instructions. Once we get trained and things settle down, there will always be room for discussion. This is not a TV reality show. This is real life, and what we do will affect everyone in one way or another. Everyone here, in one way or another, will rely on what another person does, whether it's taking care of the animals, working the fields or garden, preserving or harvesting what we grow, or defending the operation. We also will have to do an inventory of all the firearms and ammunition that we have, and I will have the people with a military background set up a target range and get everyone checked out in the weapons of their choice. We were lucky getting here, but as the Heckman's said, things are a bit rough in some places, and it could get rough here, so for now, until we can get people trained in different functions, it might seem like I'm a dictator. I would rather you all felt I was the commanding officer and various people are lieutenants and sergeants. I feel responsible for all of you who stay, but everyone must realize you must pull your own weight here to the best of your ability for us to survive."

There was a brief siren wail from outside.

"It looks like our meeting is over for now, but Mary, James, and Joseph are with the animals. How about you oversee running the RVs through the shed and get them organized? Get someone to help you to do this. Remember, you will have to live in them for a few more days until we can get the house organized. Then we can see what sleeping arrangements we have. Our supplies from our home in Seattle are here, so Shirley and I will be busy for a while, and from now on, everyone must have at least a sidearm and two magazines of ammunition for it on them at all times. Let's have another meeting later, let's say around 5:00 p.m."

Sam quickly went outside before any more questions could be asked and saw Deputy Barns and a tractor-trailer truck and a large van in their courtyard. He went to their trailer and strapped on his Beretta 92FS and went to the house.

Shirley looked at Sam. "Why the sidearm?" she asked.

"Well, I think things are going to get squirrelly soon, and I want people to get accustomed to carrying at least a sidearm. The trucks are here from Seattle with our household goods, so I guess I know what we will be doing today."

Sam left their trailer and walked over to Deputy Barns. "How are things in this area of the county?" he asked him as he walked up to him.

"Well, now everything is quite—almost too quiet. You know, like the calm before the storm. Are you guys coming to the town's Fourth of July party? It would be a good way for everyone to get to know one another. It's a potluck. Names ending with A to G, bring a vegetable dish, H to P, bring a salad, and Q to Z, bring a dessert."

"That's a good idea. Where and what time?"

"The town park, and everyone starts showing up around one. There will be a band and games for adults and kids, and there will be a side of beef and a pig being barbecued."

"That sounds good. Most of us will be there, but now we have to supervise the unloading of the trucks."

Shirley was like a drill sergeant, telling the movers where to put the boxes and furniture. The trucks were emptied quickly, and the movers started to unpack the boxes when Shirley stopped them. She told them that she wanted to unpack the boxes at her leisure and that they were free to leave. Sam looked at her, and after the workmen left, she said she didn't want them to see what was packed in some of the boxes, especially the ones that he had packed.

"We will be having a group meeting at 5:00 p.m. When you come, be sure you also have a weapon with you," Sam said as he headed for the door.

"Where are you going?" Shirley asked.

"I'm going to help unload the trucks that have hay, straw, and feed for the animals into the top of the barn and then unload some of the fencing supplies from our trailer so we can get a pasture set up for our cattle. We also have to set up the solar system you bought and a dozen other things."

At 5:00 p.m., the people started to come to the equipment shed and found seats wherever they could. Sam stood up and looked around. The age group ran a diverse range, from ten-year-old children to sixty-five-year-old men and women.

"Folks," Sam started, "The first thing I want to do is introduce all of you to Sally Barns Gilmore and her daughter Kathy. This property used to belong to her uncle who passed away last month. She is a substitute school teacher and she agrees, she will be part of our group. She is living in what was her Uncles cabin." "Now we have a lot of work ahead of us to get ready for winter. We all know what is happening to the South of us, and right now, food and supplies are still available, but we must get this place ready and organized. This means we must be as self-sufficient as we can be, and we must start training in defense of this place. But now I need a report on how things are going. First, James and Joe, how are the animals?"

Both James and Joe stood up, and James replied, "The animals are settled in, and we both feel we won't lose any more from the trip, but we need T posts for the barbed wire you have to finish the pasture areas."

"Good," Sam replied and wrote that on a tablet he had. "And, Mary, how did the RV organization go?"

Mary stood up and replied, "We stripped the RVs of all the usable gear and then reloaded them with the basic equipment to keep them operational if we need to leave in a hurry. Plus, there is enough nonperishable food in each unit for the owners to last thirty days. We have an inventory of firearms and ammo and who owns them, not including what you have. It's here on a spreadsheet." Mary gave the list to Sam and sat down.

"Ken, what did your trip around the property reveal?"

"We used the Gator, and that made it easier, so we did a sweep around the immediate area and then tried to follow the property lines. It was pretty much guesswork on that. We didn't see any evidence of people trespassing, but we did see game trails. It looks like elk and deer hunting should be good here for a long time. We did see a neighbor in his field cutting hay and our fields need to be cut and bailed very soon"

"Good job guys, today I was informed by Deputy Barns, the local sheriff's deputy here, that there will be a Fourth of July party in town, but we cannot let this place be unguarded. From now on, we must be vigilant here. We will find a location for an observation post and staff it 24-7. I will rely on some of you younger former military men to scout this out, but for now, we will leave two people behind tomorrow for the security of what we have here."

There were moans from the group.

"What I have in mind is if there are volunteers to stay back, it would make things easier, but if not, the adults will draw straws, and the short straws stay. I have some portable radios so they can keep in touch with each other, and we have CB radios and cell phones to contact one another if we are needed back here. Are there any volunteers?"

A few people looked around.

Then Ken stood up. "I would like to attend the picnic, but I'm sure there will be fireworks, and I wouldn't like to be around them, so I'll volunteer to stay behind."

Peter White stood up. "I don't have any family, so I'll also stay and let the people with children go to the picnic."

"Okay," Sam said. "I think with these two people behind, everyone else can go to the picnic."

There were cheers from the rest.

"We have a lot of work to do before we go. It's a potluck picnic, so we must bring some food with us, and the two staying behind, we have to find observation and firing positions for you."

Joseph stood up. "I would like to stay also to take care of the livestock and help with security if needed. I'll stay near the barn and shed."

"Good idea," Sam said. "Anyone else? If not, we have our work cut out for us."

Peter stood up. "We can use the backhoe part of the tractor to dig some firing pits, and then we can cover them with logs and brush. We can make them more functional later."

"Okay, you people with military background, go look for two locations for firing pits to cover the farm buildings and house. The women will be making something for us to take to the picnic."

After the meeting was over, Ken came up to Sam. "Sam, when we were guarding the oil well pad, we ran into some trouble and met some people from the Seventy-Fifth Rangers. They gave me some items that

I kept out of the inventory. I didn't know how some of the people we have here would react to what they are."

This had Sam curious. "You were in the military," Sam said.

"Yes," Ken replied. "I was in Vietnam. Then I went into special forces, and I completed the ranger program."

Sam looked at Ken and replied, "De oppresso liber."

This startled Ken. He snapped his head around and looked at Sam with a quizzical look.

Sam replied, "So was I."

"Who else has military experience?" Ken asked.

"Well, I haven't talked much about this with the others, and maybe I should, but I think Joe and James might have military experience. Ken, what is it that you have that's not on the inventory?" Sam asked.

"Well, I have an M60 with two spare barrels and about two thousand rounds for it, a case of frags, a case of mixed smoke, and some aerial hand flares."

Sam looked at him for a minute and then said, "I have enough rifles and pistols to outfit all the adults with a rifle and pistol, and if we can sort out which of the children we can train and trust, I have a firearm for them also. This doesn't include what weapons were brought with the rest of the campers. For now, we keep this information to ourselves until after the picnic. You and I know what's coming, and I think the others do also but aren't ready to admit it, but for now, let's get ready for the picnic."

For the rest of the evening, there was a lot of activity. Peter got his tractor running and dug two hasty firing pits that overlooked the compound, and the women started baking and cooking for the picnic.

The sun came up around six o'clock, and everyone helped with either the barn chores or finishing the firing pits. Around 11:00 a.m., they assembled, and Sam told the adults going to town to make sure they had either a rifle or pistol, but, preferably both, with them. They loaded their goodies for the picnic and climbed into pickup trucks, the children sat in the beds of the trucks with one adult, and the rest of the adults crammed into the cabs of the trucks. Sam made sure they had radio communication between the vehicles and the guard force as they headed out.

They went to the town of Onaway and found out that the town of Potlatch was having the parade, and that was where the picnic was being held. As they got closer to Potlatch, they started to see more traffic, and then there was someone in an orange vest directing traffic to a side street. They easily found the picnic grounds and went to the parade route to watch the parade. They all stayed together, and this caused a few people to stare or comment among themselves. For a small town, the parade was a big item. There were firetrucks from different volunteer fire departments from the outlying smaller communities, the mayor in a convertible provided by the local car dealer, floats for 4-H and FFA being pulled by tractors, children riding bikes with bunting woven in the spokes, veteran groups with older war veterans riding on floats pulled by farm tractors or flat-bed trailer trucks, and marching bands from schools and one drum-and-bugle corps. Any person could tell by the show of groups that the area took the Fourth of July and their patriotism seriously.

As they were walking back to the picnic area, they were still in a group since they didn't know too many of the locals here in Potlatch. Deputy Barns saw Sam and came over to him. Sam introduced him to the group, and after pleasantries, Deputy Barns pulled him to the side.

"Sam, I don't want to have this get out to too many people. I know what you guys went through down South, so I'll fill you in on what's happening here and elsewhere."

Sam looked at him. "Here and elsewhere?" he asked.

"Yes. Let's go over there and talk. Tell your group you'll catch up with them."

Deputy Barns led Sam toward an area with a bunch of military tents and antennas set up and a sign saying it was an ARRL field meet. There were several generators running at a distance, with wires running in different directions and into the tents. Deputy Barns told Sam that these guys set up at all outdoor functions and used these events to talk to people all over the world. They also, used these events to try to recruit people into ham radio and use it for training. As they walked up, a young man was at a table with what looked like a logbook and fliers to hand out to people who might be interested in ham radios. Jesse walked up and told the young man to go get Ben and then led Sam off to an area away from the noise of the generators. An older gentleman came walking toward them.

"Good afternoon, Jesse!" he called out. "Is this the guy?"

"Yes. Sam, meet Benjamin Owens. He is the driving force with ARRL in this area. Ben, fill Sam in on what you heard this morning."

"This morning, around six o'clock, I went into the radio room at my home and tuned up my radios. I picked up a signal from a ham in Anchorage, Alaska. It sounded like there was a battle going on there between troops from Russia and the local civilian militia and military. I did manage to contact him briefly, but it looks like they were using the holiday to cover their attack, thinking many of the military and civilians there would be away from town or the military bases, fishing and camping. We have been trying to raise anyone from Alaska, but it seems everyone went dark for now."

Sam looked at Deputy Barns. "This is serious. What are we going to do here?"

"Well," Deputy Barns said, "This isn't on any of the national TV news channels yet, and I feel we should quietly get ready for trouble here."

"What do you mean?"

"Well, our great liberal governor has told the president that Idaho would we willing to accept five thousand Muslim refugees."

Sam looked at Jesse and said, "Oh crap!"

"Yeah," Jesse replied. "Things could get a little hairy here."

Sam then told him of the trouble Ken and Betty had and the trouble they had at the campground and that there were Muslims involved in both incidents. "With the Russians in Alaska and the Muslims in the South, we might need to form a militia here in case anything happens."

Deputy Barns looked at Sam. "Yeah," he said. "Let me talk to the sheriff and see what he makes of this. In the meantime, keep quiet about this. We don't need a public panic on our hands."

They walked over to the picnic area, where Sam saw that their group had commandeered two picnic tables for them to use and put them close together. There were games and face painting for the kids, and a band was setting up on a wooden bandstand. They delivered their food to the people setting up the food area. Sam saw Sally Gilmore there, said hi to her, and introduced some of the people in their group to her. Two of the women in their group volunteered to help with the food, and their offer was readily accepted. Sam felt that this was a good way for them to break the ice and be accepted into the community.

Later in the afternoon, Geraldine Atkins, the real-estate agent and auctioneer, stopped by their tables to say hi. Sam introduced her to the people in their group who were there. He was sitting in a camp chair they had brought with them, listening to the music, which was mostly patriotic in nature, and just dozing off and on when he felt a kick on the leg of the chair. He opened his eyes, and his wife, Shirley, was standing there, and she just nodded to the side. He looked past her, and the hairs on the back of his neck stood up. This would happen to him in Vietnam just before they would walk into an ambush. The band was still playing, and the people were having a good time. Some of the young and older couples were dancing to the band's music. Sam got up and walked toward James Monroe and caught his eye. James got up and followed Sam to their vehicles. Sam opened the door to their pickup, pulled out his Beretta 92FS 9 mm pistol and its holster, tucked it in the belt behind his back, put a three-magazine ammo carrier on his belt, and then pulled his shirt out to cover it.

James looked at Sam and asked, "What's up?"

Sam told him he had a bad feeling and to quietly tell the others to come here, one at a time, to get armed and that he would wait for them. Sam then checked his AR rifle and made sure that it had a thirty-round duplexed magazine in it. He did this by taping two magazines together. One by one, the others came by, and Sam told them to quietly get armed but not to show that they were armed and that they would need one person to stay with their vehicles. As Sam slowly made his way back to their area, he saw Deputy Barns slowly making his way to him. He was shaking hands and briefly chatting with people, but Sam saw he wanted to talk to him, so Sam slowed down even more. Deputy Barns finally got to him, shook his hand, and quietly asked if he was armed.

Sam looked at him and said, "Yes, and so will be all my people."

"Good," he said. "We will need two people at the ARRL tents"

"Okay. Just let me talk to Shirley, my wife."

When Sam found her, he filled her in on what he thought was going to happen and told her to make sure the women had the children into their area and to be ready to get to their vehicles if something happened. She told him she was going to get her large diaper bag and then pass the word. Sam knew she always kept a pistol in that bag along with other items. He walked over to the ARRL tents and asked the young man at the information table if he could get Benjamin and that he would stay at the table. Benjamin came out of the tent followed by the young man, and he pulled Sam off to the side and told him that they heard from some Hams in Anchorage, Alaska that things were bad in Alaska. Sam looked at him and asked what kind of security he had there at the site. He replied that they usually didn't have any problems, so they didn't have any security. Sam told him that Deputy Barns wanted him and another man here and, if any of his people had any firearms in their vehicles, to quietly go get them. Sam relieved the young man at the information table and answered a few questions and handed out a few fliers.

It was 8:00 p.m. and just starting to get dark. The town's fireworks show was about to begin when Sam saw a bearded young man with a white hat walking toward him. It looked innocent enough, but he could see he was looking around and back and forth. Sam stood up, and just then, the first firework went up, and the man pulled out a pistol, but Sam was ready and faster and shot him. Then all hell broke loose. There were several explosions and gunfire in the picnic area, which ended quickly. People were screaming, and Sam heard gunfire by the generators. He made sure the man he had shot was dead, took his firearm, turned the table over, and was kneeling behind it when Benjamin came up to him.

"We shot one trying to sabotage the generators," he said, "and it looks like you got one also."

"Yes, I think his mission was to shoot the people in the tents and destroy the equipment. Do you guys have this area secure?" Sam asked him. "I want to try to find my wife and see what damage was done."

"Go," he said. "We have this area secure."

Sam hurried to the picnic area to the tables where they were. He was surprised that it still had strings of lights lighting the area and didn't see any of their people there, but there were two women wearing Muslim-style head scarves who were very dead. He wondered, *If the men get seventy-two virgins, what do the women get?* He then went to their vehicles and saw most of their people there, with Shirley and Ruth Monroe watching over the children. They were both armed, and Shirley had Sam's AR rifle, while Ruth had a lever-action .30-30 Winchester. Sam asked Shirley where the rest were, and she said that when the shooting had started, everyone came here, but now they were in the picnic area, helping the wounded as best as they could. He told both Shirley and Ruth to stay here and to not let anyone who was not with their group near the vehicles.

Sam left and went to the picnic area, coming across two partially dismembered bodies. He could see there was nothing he could do for them. It reminded him of a mortar attack when he was in Vietnam. Sam soon saw more people. They were in a large tent with lights that was set up as a beer garden, and that was where they were taking the wounded. He spotted Deputy Barns. His clothing was bloody, and Sam could tell he was shaken but not hurt. He was directing people, telling them what to do. Sam came to him and asked if he was injured. He replied no.

Sam asked him what he wanted him to do when a shot rang out, and Deputy Barns fell to the ground. Sam immediately fell down and crawled to Deputy Barns. He saw he was breathing. As he looked at Sam, he said that was the second time his vest had saved him, and another shot rang out, followed by a scream. He told Sam to see if he could find the sniper. Sam got up and ran to a trash can. Just as another shot rang out, he fell to the ground, looking around and judging from the shots that there were only two areas where the sniper could be. He got up and sprinted to the vehicle area, which was out of what he thought was the sniper's vision.

Shirley came to Sam, crying. "I thought you were dead out there."

"No," he replied. "Deputy Barns was hit, but he had his vest on. He said it was the second time today his vest had saved him, but he will be sore for a few days. I need the rifle."

She looked at him. "Be careful out there."

Sam kissed her and was about to leave when Geraldine Atkins came up. She said she had a hunting rifle in her car. He told her to get it and to come back here. Just as she returned, there was another shot. Sam looked at her and asked if she was ready to go hunting, and she surprised him by saying she not only was ready but also had an idea where the sniper was, and there was a house that overlooked the picnic area and from where the shots were landing. That was the only place they could be. They left, staying out of sight from where Geraldine thought the sniper was, and came up to the side of the house, where there were no windows. They were discussing what to do next when two more men with rifles showed up.

Sam said, "We could use two people to lay down suppressive fire into the windows, where the sniper could be hiding, and I would need someone to come with me as we clear the building."

One of the men said he was a former marine and had training in clearing buildings. He also had a small tactical flashlight, so Sam told him that they both would do that, and Sam told Geraldine and the other man to get in a flanking area and take random shots at the sniper. Just before they left, the marine said to call him Ed.

Sam replied, "Sam."

They found a door and checked it for booby traps, and surprise, surprise—they found one. Ed looked it over and said it was just like the ones they had used in Iraq and quickly disarmed it. They carefully cleared the downstairs area and found the owners of the house in the basement. The husband and wife, both elderly, had their hands tied behind their backs and were beheaded. Sam had seen a lot of atrocities conducted by the Viet Cong in Vietnam, but this was barbaric and pissed him off. Ed told him that it happened over in the Sand Box more than the people in the United States knew. They cautiously went back up to the first floor and looked at the stairs to the second floor. This was an older home, with the stairs going up the side of a wall, ending in a hallway at the top—a perfect killing zone for anyone who came up the stairs.

They could hear a steady shooting from outside when all of a sudden, the firing increased outside. *More people must now be firing at the sniper*, Sam thought. Just as they were ready to go up the stairs, they heard movement from upstairs, and two men came running down the stairs. Ed and Sam both fired, and they toppled the rest of the way down the stairs. Ed grabbed Sam and pulled and threw him behind a wall into the living room when an explosion occurred on the other side of the wall. One of the shooters had a body bomb on him. It was obvious now that their mission was a suicide mission, and they didn't plan on being captured. Ed got off Sam, and as he shakenly got up, Sam was about to thank Ed for saving his life when Ed said that he had seen it before in the Sand Box, where snipers were wired with body bombs to kill anyone near them if they were wounded or captured. This was new ideology for Sam from what they had in Vietnam.

Sam's ears were still ringing from the explosion when he heard Ed call out that they were okay and that they were going upstairs and to stop shooting. They cautiously went upstairs, and whenever one of the old steps creaked, Sam cringed. They quickly cleared the top floor. Ed called out that the house was secure and that they were coming out. Deputy Barns came cautiously through the door, looking around. Sam could see the stress on his face, his uniform bloody from the victims of the attack. Sam went to him, asking how he was holding up. He could see in his eyes that he was going into shock over what was happening. He looked at Sam, saying that he thought all the attackers were dead.

As Sam came out of the house that held the snipers, he could hear people crying and mothers and fathers calling out the names of their children. He looked around and realized how dark it had become as he headed to where their vehicles were parked. He saw Shirley coming toward him with tears in her eyes.

"I heard an explosion," she said.

He hugged her and said that he was all right and that one of the snipers had a body bomb that detonated. He asked if any of their group were hurt.

She looked up at him, saying, "Not seriously."

It was because of his observation and warning to gather all the children at the vehicles, who we were spared any serious injuries. Sam gave her a quizzical look.

She said, "Only scrapes and bruises as the children were thrown under the trucks by their parents."

"Let's get everyone together for a head count and situation report. Then we will go help the rest of the townsfolk."

The younger children stayed at the vehicles, but the older teenagers, Sam felt, could be of use as runners and exposure to what they were now facing would be a good learning experience. They now had to grow up quickly.

They headed to the tent where the beer garden was set up, and Dr. Jethro Smith, the county coroner, was busy since he was the only doctor available. There were people all over. There was an area with young children. Some were crying. Several women were there trying to console them, and two were sitting there, just staring off into space. There was a row of blanket-covered bodies. Sam counted fifteen, and two of them looked like children. There were several women working as nurses, but Doc Smith was working alone. Ed, the guy who had helped Sam clear out the snipers, came up.

"Doc, I had some combat medical training. Can I be of some help?" he asked.

"Yes. We need blood. We will have to do person-to-person blood donation. Find volunteers and use a marker to write their blood type on their foreheads."

Ed took off, and it didn't take long for him to have a line of men and women willing to give blood. Deputy Barns came up, and he looked like crap. Sam could tell he was under a lot of stress, and he wasn't walking too well. He was taking short breaths and holding his side. He gingerly sat down as Sam bent over him, helping him take off his vest and shirt. His chest and ribs were black and blue. Sam saw where three bullets had hit his vest. He went into the tent and got some ACE compression bandages and wrapped his ribs. It was all that they could do at this time. Deputy Barns looked at Sam with tears in his eyes.

Sam looked at him. "This isn't your fault, Deputy. You must put this aside and show courage for the rest of the community."

He looked at Sam and tried to take a deep breath, but the pain kept him from doing so. "How many are dead?" he asked.

"I don't know yet," Sam lied, "but it could have been worse. The ARRL radios are intact, and none of the people there were injured. I believe we took out two terrorists there and two snipers in the house. I don't know how many more were involved in the attack. Doc Smith is using the tent that was the beer garden for a hospital and operating room since it was well lit, and we have guards around it as well as people helping as they can. Have you been in contact with the sheriff yet?"

"No. There wasn't time to do so."

"Well, I'll walk you over to your car to use the radio, or maybe it'd be best to call him on a cell phone."

Deputy Barns looked up, and Sam could see he still was in shock over the attack.

"I think the phone would be best in case anyone is listening on your frequency."

"Good idea," the deputy replied.

Sam asked, "Do you have a cell phone?"

"No. Mine took a bullet and is ruined."

"Well, here is mine. Give him a call."

***

Farhad Hafeez was just inside a tree line on a slight hill overlooking the picnic area. On September 11, 2001, he was only twelve years old, living in New Jersey, when Muslim freedom fighters crashed airplanes into the World Trade Center. He felt a sense of pride. Finally, the evil Americans were getting a taste of what they were doing to his country. His parents moved from Syria four years earlier because of the war in the area where they had lived. The other boys in his class in school didn't want anything to do with him and constantly taunted him, and after September 11, 2001, the taunting got worse. He couldn't wait until he graduated so he could go back to his friends in his homeland. He got a part-time job after school at a Bodega run by Muslims who lived in the neighborhood. He gave half of what he earned to his parents and saved as much of the rest of his pay as he could. He didn't tell his parents of his activities other than he had a part-time job. He rented a mail drop at a UPS store and went to the local library, where they had free computers for the public to use. It didn't take long for him to make contact with an Al-Qaeda group. He received training through the internet on how to get false passports. When he turned eighteen, he applied for and received a U.S. passport. Soon after he graduated, he took most of his money from his bank account and purchased an airplane ticket to France. Once there, he would meet up with people sympathetic to the cause. They would then help him get to Syria. When the time came to leave, he wrote a brief note to his parents. He hoped they would understand and be proud of him, going to learn how to fight the morally corrupt Americans.

Farhad didn't know it, but at every stop in his journey, he was being evaluated. This was to find out if he was a CIA mole and to what extent his training was so they would know where to send him for their best use. He wound up at a training camp where his skills and abilities soon made him stand out with his instructors. It seemed that he had a natural knack for leadership. He received additional training on how to be a cell leader. He was supposed to leave the training camp for an assignment, but because of his skills with the American language, he was kept there for several months to help train other students in the American language and the ways of Americans. It was here that he had developed his plan to create a massive attack on the United States and bring the whole country to its knees. At the camp, he had access to computers, and he worked tirelessly on his plan. He almost became obsessed with his plan. Before he was finished, his inordinate use of the computer came to the attention of other instructors, and he was soon questioned about it. He then showed his supervisors his research and what he had accomplished so far. There were some who thought it was too large and would fail. They wanted to have small one- or two-people units who would shoot up a church or school, but there were others who could see the greatness in his still-emerging plan.

A few months after he had explained his plan to the camp leader, one of the higher-ranking Al-Qaeda leaders came to their camp and sought him out and have him explain his plan. By then, he had expanded it further and had more detail. He showed them where, at eight to ten locations, they could cripple the electrical grid for the whole country, and this would last for years in some areas. He then showed some strategic bridges that carried either vehicles or trains and that if these bridges were blown up, they would curtail the movement of food and goods to the cities. It took him most of the day to conduct his briefing because with Google Earth, he could provide pictures of many of the locations he was talking about, and when he was finished, the leaders who had come thanked him for his intelligence and asked him to continue with his plans while they discussed the merits of his plan with others. They looked at a satellite schedule for their area and saw that they were coming up on a period of an hour where there would be no satellite coverage of their area. The leaders timed their departure for this time.

Farhad continued to work on his plan, but after a month without any word from the leaders, he was wondering if he was just wasting his time. Farhad was coming out of a building. He had just taught a class on using different electronics for detonating bombs. He saw a car pull into the compound and immediately go into a roofed-over area to hide it from satellites. Four men took brooms and rakes to remove the car tracks. Then Kafeel, the leader of the camp, came out of his office and went to greet the arrivals. Farhad could see from the way Kafeel acted that the visitors were important people. He then saw Kafeel point toward him, and he became uneasy. They started walking toward him, so he walked toward them.

"Farhad!" Kafeel called out. "These are very important men within our group. They have heard about your plans and were sent here by our great leader to learn more. How soon can you get your plans and do a briefing for these people?"

"All of what I have done is on two of these thumb drives. They contain the exact same information, and all I have to do is plug them into a computer that has a projector connected to it, and I can explain everything I have planned."

"Good, good," Kafeel said. "Let us go eat lunch, and then you can explain your plan."

The call to prayer had just started when Farhad finished his briefing, and they all went to prayer. After prayer, Kafeel came to Farhad and told him the visitors would be spending the night and would want to ask him some questions in the morning. Farhad slept fitfully that night. In the morning, after his morning prayers and meal, he was sought out once again. They went to a building that wasn't being used that day and sat down.

"Farhad," Kafeel said, "the briefing you gave us yesterday was different from what we were briefed a month ago. Can you explain?"

"Yes. When I first explained my plans, I hadn't fully developed them. I have had more time to do research, and I now feel I have a plan and a diagram to bring the evil United States to its knees. My plan started small, with just fifteen or twenty small cells working independently from one another, with none of them knowing what the other cell was doing in case of a breach in security. At first, I was just planning on destroying the electrical grid, but when I researched where the main points of attack should be, I saw a pattern where, at key points, if bridges were destroyed, not only would they prevent cars, trucks, and trains from using them, but also, if they fell in bigger rivers like the Mississippi River, the Delaware, and others, we could also prevent boat and barge traffic from using them. Couple this with a coordinated attack on groups of people in different parts of the United States, and we could create chaos for years.

"I know this is an aggressive plan, and we will need many trained people to carry it off, but it will make the 9/11 attack look small. In one day We can make a massive strike. We will have to train as many as five thousand fighters. They cannot know anything except their target, where its location is, the date, and the people in their cell. To get that many people into the United States, we would have to use several routes—one through Mexico and up through the Southwest, another through Canada and down from the North. We can use the Caribbean Islands and boats into Florida and immigration measures. We would use a day where Americans do outdoor parties and picnics and do it close to the American presidential election for the most effect. My suggested date would be at July 4. It's their Independence Day. In five years, it would be a Monday. That year, many people will be away from their homes on what they call a vacation, government agencies would be closed, and many military men would be gone from their bases to be with their families. Also, since it would be a Monday, our cells would have two days to prepare their equipment without drawing attention to themselves. They just tell nosy neighbors that they are going camping in the mountains or to the beach or to visit relatives. We have five years to train and get everyone into place. Could you and Kafeel allow us some time to talk between ourselves? We will let you know what we decide before we leave."

Kafeel went to his office, while Farhad went to a class on leadership. The next day, a messenger told Farhad to go to Kafeel's office. Once he got there, he saw the two leaders there. As Farhad walked to Kafeel's office, he saw that there were two sentries posted by his door. This caused Farhad to have some concern about why he was summoned to the camp leader's office. Farhad knocked on the door of Kafeel's office and was immediately told to enter. As Farhad entered, his worries eased a little when he saw that there were no armed guards in the room. Everyone was seated at a table that was set up to the side of the office. The Al-Qaeda leader stood up and gestured to Farhad to sit at the table.

"Farhad," he started, "I have looked over your plan, and I feel, while it is a large and aggressive operation, with some more work and planning, your operation would be an excellent chance to bring the decadent American country to its knees. We will scour our organization for English-speaking people whom we can use as instructors, and we will turn this camp into an English speaking only camp. We will start training as many people as we can here, and at other camps, we will also train people. I feel that depending on their size, each cell will have one or more people as fluent in the American language as we can get them. Some of them will get jobs with people sympathetic to our cause, and being able to speak the American language, they will blend in with the people in their neighborhoods. We have some cells already in the United States waiting for an assignment, so we will have to train less people than you envisioned."

Farhad was watching his cell attack the infidels. He hadn't expected such a quick response to his planned attack. His leaders wouldn't be happy that he had lost all his people, but they were with Allah in paradise now. They had fought well and killed many, but he hoped that more of his group would have survived. It was up to him now to complete their mission for this area.

It was still nighttime, and under the cover of darkness, he went to their van, parked on a side street away from the target area. His first target was a cell phone tower there in the town. It was easy to cut the chain-link fence surrounding it. He placed his explosives around the base of the tower and set a timer for sixty minutes and went to his next target. Farhad didn't like being around high-voltage electricity, but he knew if he carried this out and the other cells were able to do the same, they would cripple the whole United States. He kept low and only walked on the gravel walkways. There were four huge electrical transformers. He and his cell had scouted this location months earlier. He wished he had another person to help him. It took him two trips to the van to carry the explosives into the area. He looked at his watch. He was behind the schedule set for the cells, but he knew he would be successful with his attack. Checking his watch again, he set the timers to go off when the cell tower explosives would go off. He left and closed the fence as he did at the cell tower with some wire. It wasn't perfect, but a casual glance would not show any problems.

He then went to his last target. It was an older nondescript brick building. Many years ago, it had housed a large bank of switchboards and had many telephone operators working there. They would have connected people, trying to make phone calls to businesses, families, and friends. Now the building was a large junction box. This was where all the fiber optic cables for communication for this part of the state came together. There were no more operators who, when things were slow, would eavesdrop on people's conversations. It was unmanned, and just a padlock secured the building. If he could destroy this building and the cables, it would be weeks—maybe months—before any computer or telephone service could be restored. He set the timer on the explosives and cans of gasoline to detonate ten minutes after he left. He knew it would not give him much time to get as far away as he wanted, but it was a risk he had to take.

The sky was already getting gray. The morning sun would be coming up in less than thirty minutes. Farhad turned onto U.S. Route 95 and headed north to Coeur d'Alene and the safe houses around the lake nearby. As he passed the road to the training camp, he was tempted to turn on it and go to the camp, but that wasn't part of the plan, and he was going to stick to the plan. After all, it was mostly his plan.

***

"I need to make an accurate situation report," Deputy Barns said. "Sam, will you come with me to my patrol car so I can get a tablet? Then we will go talk to Doc Jones and get the results of the attack."

As the deputy and Sam walked toward his car, Ed came up and asked what he could do.

Sam said, "Go around and find out how many people attacked us and if they are still living or dead. Get someone to help you to gather their weapons, whether they are in operating condition or not, and any ammunition that may be left. Deputy, I think we should go by the ARRL tents first and find out what they know or have heard. Then we will go to Doc Smith."

They walked to the ARRL tents, and the place was bustling. You could hear many voices. There were two guards stationed outside of a ring of concertina wire that now surrounded the tents, and the area was lit by several portable flood lamps like you would see at construction sites. Sam wondered, *Where did they get the wire and lights, and how did they set them up so quickly?* A guard moved to bar their entrance to the tent, but a good stare-down by Sam and Deputy Barns made him change his mind. They got the attention of Ben, and he came toward them, motioning them to go outside.

"What can I do for you?" he asked.

"We're here to find out what you know or have heard on the radios."

He said, "I thought that was why you were here. I have the traffic log with me, and things are not good. There have been attacks up and down this part of the country. It seems that not counting Alaska, the West Coast has had many attacks, and they all seemed to be coordinated to happen within an hour of one another. These attacks range from as far South as Arizona to us here in Idaho, Washington, Oregon, Utah, and other states to the east. This is a widespread attack on not only areas of the western United States but all of the United States."

They thanked him and then went to see Doc Smith. There were several generators running at the beer garden tent. They were supplementing the lights from the few outlets that were available at the picnic area. It looked as if things were starting to settle down, and there wasn't as much frantic activity as there had been an hour ago. They found Doc Smith in what looked like a recovery area talking to a woman whom Sam thought was a nurse, or she was acting as one. He looked up and came toward them.

"Let's go outside. I need a break," Doc Smith said. "It's been a rough night."

"I don't want to sound flippant," Deputy Barns said, "but what's the statistics? I am about to call the sheriff and make a report."

"Well, there are now eighteen adults who are dead and three children. There are twelve people with various injuries, two with catastrophic arm or leg amputations, one other whose arm I had to amputate. The rest of the injured are various bullet or shrapnel injuries. I am reasonably confident that if we can get some of these medevacked to either Coeur or Boise, they will fully recover. We just don't have the antibiotics needed, and we have basically run out of all our medical supplies. We raided the First Care Trauma Center in town for all their medical bandages and supplies. If nothing else happens, with the exception of two or three cases, we should be okay. I would like to be able to send five cases out, and if we can, like I said, get more antibiotics, then we won't lose any more."

They thanked Doc Smith and headed to a quiet area. They found a picnic table and sat down. Ed came by with three other people—two men and a woman. They were all carrying firearms.

"Deputy, from what we discovered, there were seven attackers, and they are all dead. Five were men, and two were women. Two were the snipers in the house, two tried to attack the ARRL site, and two—a man and two women—were at a picnic table in the middle of the crowd. They had rifles, pipe bombs, and explosive vests that they detonated, we think, when we started shooting at them. Things could have been much worse if they could have detonated the pipe bombs. We found them in a picnic basket. Here are their weapons, the pipe bombs, and what ammunition we could find."

Deputy Barns and Sam thanked them, and the deputy told them to help where they could. Sam gave Deputy Barns his cell phone, and as he called the sheriff, Deputy Barns hit the speaker button on the cell phone, so Sam could listen to what the sheriff had to say.

"Sheriff Emmerson," the voice on the phone said.

"Sheriff, Deputy Barns here at Potlatch."

"Deputy, how are things there?" the sheriff asked.

"Well, we had some trouble here, and now that things are secure, I'm checking in with a situation report. We had an attack just as our fireworks started by whom we believe were some Muslim terrorists."

"You are the third town to report in with a report like this. What is the casualty report?"

Deputy Barns read off the list and asked for medevac help for their most injured.

"Deputy, I saw on the caller ID that you are not using your official cell phone. Is there a reason for this?"

"Yes," Deputy Barns replied. "My cell phone was in the vest pocket of my protective vest and took a round. In fact, my vest saved me from three rounds. I'm sore but not seriously injured."

There was a pause, and then Sheriff Emmerson said, "Deputy, enact Plan T for TANGO. I repeat—"

There was an explosion, and the cell phone went dead. Then there was another larger explosion, and some of the lights at the picnic area flickered and went out, as did all the streetlights and lights in all the houses nearby. Then there was a third muffled explosion, and they saw a fireball and smoke coming from town.

Deputy Barns looked at Sam. "Oh no, now what is happening?"

"What did the Sheriff mean by 'Enact Plan T'?" Sam asked.

Deputy Barns said he now had the authority to ask for volunteers to form a civilian security force for this area. "They would have semi-legal authority and report to the sheriff through me. We must notify Ben over at the ARRL tent that his group is now activated and that they are now under our control. Then we must go see what the other explosions were all about."

Sam looked at him with a quizzical look.

"Yes, you and your group kept more of the townspeople from being killed during this attack and the people won't forget the service your group provided. The town and this area will need people like you and your group."

They walked over to the ARRL site, and the security team out front recognized Deputy Barns and Sam and left them into their area. Ben came out of the tent, looking at the deputy.

He said, "I guess we're activated?"

Jesse looked at him. "How did you guess?"

"Well, all the cell phones are dead, as are the landlines, and the power for the area is down. From what we are monitoring on the net, this is not an isolated event by a bunch of local radicals but a full-blown attack on the United States."

"How is that?" Deputy Barns asked.

"Well, we have been monitoring events across the country, and there have been attacks in other parts of the country. The electrical grid across the country has been attacked and, in many places, destroyed. It will take six months to a year to repair, but in some places, it is still working, as well as the phone service. It's being reported that many but not all cell phone towers have been blown up. Microwave, fiber optic, and other means of communication have been damaged in many areas.

Some bridges have been destroyed or damaged in an effort to block river traffic on the Mississippi and Missouri Rivers. Train tracks and train bridges have been damaged, but only two have been destroyed, and many bridges and roads on the Interstate highway system have been severely damaged. In short, someone has tried to knocked us back fifty to a hundred years, but they failed in many places."

The brochure table that was knocked down during the attack had been righted, and the chairs were set up by it.

Deputy Barns sat down. "This is a serious situation," Jesse said. "How many people know about this?"

"Well," Ben started, "there are riots in the major cities—Chicago, Detroit, Milwaukee, Saint Louis, New York, New Orleans, Tampa, Miami, San Diego, Los Angeles. In all the major cities, when the power and phones went out, there was looting, burning, and gunfire. In short, it's a mess."

Deputy Barns put his elbows on the table and lowered his head into his hands, rubbing his eyes. He looked up. His voice had resolve in it when he said, "Ben, we are activating one of our emergency plans. You are now in charge of the local communication. Sam and I are going to see what the other explosions were about, but we will be back. Keep as much of this as you can under your hat for now until we know more of what is happening."

Jesse and Sam went to the deputy's patrol car. Leaving the area, they headed downtown. As they passed the town's volunteer fire station, they saw men pulling chains at the doors, trying to open them. There was no electricity, so the only way to open the doors to the fire stations now was to use the manual backup system. They continued on to where the fire was.

Jesse looked at Sam and said, "This isn't good."

"Why is that?" Sam asked.

"Because this is the telephone-switching building for this area of the state. All the landlines and fiber optic cables go through this building. In essence, all communications for this area are now destroyed, and it will take six months or maybe longer to replace and repair the damage."

A small breeze started, and a building next to the phone building started to burn, and sparks started to fly through the air. The firetrucks started to arrive. There were two pumper trucks, a water tanker truck, and a smaller brush firetruck. As Jesse walked over to a man with a white helmet, Sam followed close behind.

"Chief," Jesse said, "the wind is starting to pick up. I think we should have the brush truck do a patrol in case any of these sparks start a brush or forest fire."

The chief looked at Jesse. "Deputy, I already thought of that and have some men and women patrolling with their cars with radios to call here in case there are any other fires."

Sam could sense that there was something between Deputy Barns and the fire chief.

"Well, Chief, if you need anything, if I can help, let me know," Jesse said and then turned and, with Sam following, went to his car.

"What was that all about?" Sam asked when they got into the car.

"Oh, that was Chris Manley. He thinks that because he is the local fire chief, he is exempt from speeding laws. I give him a speeding ticket about once a month, and he is angry about that."

Instead of heading back to the picnic grounds, they continued to an electrical transformer yard. This was a large one, almost an acre in size. It was a mess. Several of the large transformers were damaged, with large gaping holes in them where an explosive was placed. Others had shrapnel holes in them, leaking cooling oil, and there were several wires lying on the ground. They didn't get out of the car but surveyed the destruction at a distance while safely in the car.

"In the briefing the sheriff gave us," Deputy Barns said while turning the car around, "he said that with these types of transformers, they were going to be a prime target of terrorists because it will take over a year to make one. They are custom-made, and each one can cost a million or more dollars to make. It looks like we will be in the dark for a year or more. I know Bert at the Conoco station has a generator. He can pump gas from his underground tanks, so anyone with a generator will have electricity until the gasoline runs out. We will have to figure out a rationing system for the gas, and I will have to tell Chief Manley that he should put an armed guard on the fire companies' bulk fuel tanks."

"I gather he will love that suggestion," Sam said.

"Yeah, I'll have to be very tactful when I tell him," Jesse replied. "Let's head back to the park and see how things are."

As they pulled into the park, Sam saw the sky starting to get light as the sun was coming up. Things were not quite as hectic as they had been when they left, and Shirley and Doc Smith were sitting at a picnic bench. In the twilight before dawn, Sam could see the strain in both their faces. Deputy Barns and Sam walked over to them, and Sam was surprised to see they both had cups of coffee.

"I sure could use a cup of joe," Sam said. "Where did you find it?"

"The ARRL tent has a pot going," Doc Smith replied.

As Sam was about to get up, he felt a hand on his shoulder.

"You stay here with your wife. I'll get us both a cup of coffee or maybe something a little stronger if I can find anything," Deputy Barns said.

Sam looked at Shirley. "How are you holding up?" he asked.

"It was rough at first, not knowing if anyone from our group was injured, but no one was. Your observation and getting everyone to the vehicles paid off."

"Where are they now?"

"Ken and one of the people from town are in a house overlooking the park for security. The rest of the group, I told to go back to the farm and fill in the people whom we left behind on what happened here, set up a protective perimeter around the place, and get some sleep."

"Good," Sam said. "I don't know how much longer I will be needed here."

"Not much longer," Deputy Barns said as he came back to the table with a thermos of coffee and two cups. "I haven't heard anything official, but I'm guessing the governor will be declaring a statewide emergency or possibly martial law. If that happens, I'll have to see what will be covered."

The coffee tasted good and was strong, Sam guessed he had gotten it from the ARRL site. They sat drinking in silence for a few minutes, each of them in their own thoughts. Sam looked up and stiffened a little. Deputy Barns saw this and turned around to see Fire Chief Manley walking toward them.

"Great," Deputy Barns muttered. "Now what does he want? How's the fire?"

He came toward them. "It's mostly out, but we have a few hot spots to take care of. But you know, the destruction of the old phone company building destroyed all the communication we have in this area of the county."

"Yes," Deputy Barns replied, "but that's not all. The electrical transformers have been destroyed, and unless people have generators or other power, there is no electricity for this area."

Chief Manley looked at Deputy Barns, and his shoulders sagged a little. "What does that mean?"

"Well," Deputy Barns said, "I don't want to tell you what to do, but those five-hundred-gallon tanks of diesel and gasoline you have behind the fire house will be prime targets for theft. You might want to post an armed guard on those tanks."

"Well, for once, I agree with you, Deputy, but my guys are all volunteers with family here. They would be reluctant to prevent a family member from taking a few gallons of gas."

"So, Chris, what are your suggestions?"

"Well," Chris said, turning his head to look at Shirley and Sam, "if we had a guard force that had no personal ties to the community, newcomers whom we could trust to guard the fuel stores . . ."

Sam didn't like the way this was going. "Listen," he said, "yes, we are newcomers, but in light of what just happened, we have lots of work to get settled in. We have to plant gardens and cut fields of forage for our animals. Plus, we will have to guard what we have from scavengers."

Deputy Barns looked at Chief Manley for a reaction as he said, "What if a few people from the community helped you with your planting and other chores that need immediate attention?"

Chief Manley's head snapped to his right, and he stared at Deputy Barns.

Sam lowered his head, took a long sip of coffee, and replied, "Deputy, I and, I'm sure, all the folks with me appreciate your offer, but this is our elk to skin. However, we will discuss this with the folks back at the farm and see what we can do for the community." Sam finished his coffee and looked at Deputy Barns. "If you have no need for Shirley and me, we will be heading home."

"No, go," Deputy Barns replied. "We have some cleaning up to do around here. I'll come by your place later, maybe tomorrow."

"One of our men, Ken, is helping with security. Can you send someone to replace him so we can take him with us?"

"I'll see what I can do," Deputy Barns said and left.

A short time later, Ken came walking toward them, carrying his weapon at a low ready position.

"Come on, Ken," Sam said. "Let's get in the truck and head to the ranch."

On the drive back, Shirley looked at Sam and asked, "If we are going to provide guards for the fuel supply, why didn't you accept their help on the farm?"

Sam thought for a second, but Ken answered, "OPSEC."

"What?" Shirley asked.

"Operational security," Sam replied. "Enough of the town knows what we have. I don't want more people to know everything that we have."

"Oh," Shirley said. "Loose lips sink ships."

"Yeah," Sam said. "From now on, we must be careful of what we say to other people. Even the ones we think we can trust may say something to someone else, and they say something, and before long everyone, knows what we have."

Sam turned off the state road onto a dirt road that led to their driveway. When he turned onto their driveway, he was met with a barricade made from six-inch-diameter trees lashed onto X's with barbed wire curled around them, blocking half of the driveway, and about thirty feet in was another barricade like the first one, blocking the other half of the driveway, making him slow down to negotiate the two barricades and making an S turn to get in. He didn't see any guards but sensed eyes on him. Sam looked to his left and saw a hand come out of what looked like a bush. He wondered, *How the heck did they get a ghillie suit so fast?* He pulled into the farmyard—he thought, *Maybe we should start calling it the compound*—and stopped the pickup truck. Peter came up to the truck. Sam saw he had a pistol on his hip and one of the AR-style rifles slung on his shoulder.

"Peter!" Sam called out. "In thirty minutes have everyone meet in the equipment shed, including Rambo, out by the gate."

They had everyone but the Heckman's in the equipment shed. They had left the day before to look for their son and daughter-in-law to try to get their grandchildren to their parents. Sam stood up and looked around.

"Folks, last night and early this morning, a broad area of the continental United States was attacked by who are believed to be Muslim terrorists, and in Alaska, they are fighting an attack by Russian troops. Here in the States, the electrical grid has been damaged in several areas to an extent that it could take a year or more to get electricity in some areas. There have been several bridges destroyed and many damaged over some major rivers, causing barge traffic to come to a standstill in areas and disrupting truck traffic. Cell phone towers have been destroyed in many areas, making cell phone use spotty across the country, and fiber optic cables have been destroyed, seriously impacting internet, computer use, and communication. In our area, the electrical transformers for this area have been destroyed, and it is estimated to be a year or more to replace them. The fiber optic switching building has been destroyed, and so were several cell phone towers. We have been asked by the sheriff's deputy here if we would consider providing security for the fuel tanks at the fire station because using a local, they might not be willing to stop their friends and relatives from taking fuel from the tanks. It's important that we and the town have reliable fire service. At first, my thoughts were to decline, but I feel we could use this to our benefit. But I want to hear from you guys. What do you think of the arrangement?"

There was silence, and Sam saw several heads looking down, like schoolchildren not wanting the teacher to call on them.

"Ken," he said, "what are your thoughts?"

Ken stood up, and Sam could see he was gathering his thoughts. "Well, this is similar to what Betty and I did in Texas. There, we protected an oil well. This would just be smaller. But there, we had electricity and other services provided, and here, we would need gasoline to power our generator. We would need water service and septic service. Then how would the townsfolk think of us? Would they turn on us or see us as protectors?"

He sat down, and Sam looked at Joseph and James. "How would this affect the care of the animals?"

Joe stood up. "Well, James and I can take care of them easy enough, but we must think of bringing in fodder from the fields for the animals for winter season."

"Do we have enough people for this and the gardens?"

Shirley stood up. "With the help of the children and the women, we should be okay for now, but we must realize the animals and the gardens will soon, with what is happening, have to feed us, and we will have to feed the animals."

Peter stood up. "How will the loss of two people affect our security?"

Sam then stood up. "We could use the intel we get from the citizens by way of Ken and Betty if they choose to volunteer for this post, and they could be a forward listening post. If anything came from town, they would be the first to warn us. Plus, they would have the townsfolk to back them up, and they would be able to lead a reaction force to us if we needed one, or we could be a reactionary force for the town. It could go both ways. That's if Ken and Betty agree. Think about it until tomorrow morning.

"We have several problems that must be addressed now, and both are critical. First, we don't know how far these attacks go, and second, we need a massive amount of food for all of us here. While we have the animals, I don't want to start slaughtering them yet. In fact, we should try to start breeding them as soon as we can to increase our protein larder. But I think we should send two teams to Costco to fill up with all that they can buy and haul. There are Costco's in Coeur D, and across the border, there is one in Spokane, Washington. There is also one south of us in Lewiston. We can send a team of two and a pickup truck to each location and buy as much nonperishable food as they can."

Peter stood up. "Why can't we use the dump truck for one truck? After all, it will haul a lot more than a pickup, and then we can send two pickups and three people the other direction, and the high sides on the dump truck will hide what we have."

"That's a good idea," Sam replied, "but I have a mission for the dump truck and a trailer, but I like the idea of the high sides for security. So the pickup trucks should take tarps and rope to cover their loads, but we will send four people with two pickup trucks to Coeur D and one pickup with two people to Lewiston. From now on, we must think of security. That's why I want two people to go with each pickup, and those who are going should have sidearms and a shotgun with 00 buckshot. I feel there might be some chaos at the stores. Also, we don't know if they have electricity at the stores, so take a pen, tablet, and cash in large and small bills so you can make the exact change. While our cell phones may not work, you can use the utility function on them as an adding machine in case their cash registers don't work.

"This little foray will also give us some firsthand intel on what is happening not only in our area but also outside of our immediate area. Now all we need to do is to decide who is going and what they are going to buy. Shirley, why don't you, after this meeting, get with the women and see what they need? Peter, you get with the men and see what they think they need, and I want Joe and James to get together and make a list of what you need for a year for the animals. Besides the steers and pigs, don't forget the chickens and goats, and get something for rabbits and any other small livestock that you think we should have. Then, Peter, you take either Joe or James with you and see what animal feed you can also get. This is important, we don't have much time, so let's break here. Get into your groups, and let's come up with a list of supplies we need—and not just food but clothing for winter and any other item that may come to mind."

Sam then looked for Shirley, walked to her group, and listened for a few minutes, and when there was a break in the conversation, he said that they could use decks of cards, board games, coloring books and crayons, storybooks, DVDs, music CDs, and anything to keep everyone occupied when they were not working. "And don't forget sewing supplies."

After about forty-five minutes, Sam called everyone to order. "I want the people who have the lists to get together and consolidate your lists and make two copies so both groups will be looking for the same items in case something is missing at one location or the other, and it won't hurt to have double of some items. James and Joe, figure out which one of you will stay behind because until more people are trained to care for the animals, I don't want both of you gone at once. Then get with Peter and hook up a trailer and see me before you leave." Sam looked for Shirley, and he took her off to the side. "How much cash do we have?" he asked.

This caught her off guard. "Why?" she asked.

"Well, someone has to pay for all this, and I don't think many people have much money with them."

Shirley looked up. "Maybe we should pass the hat and see what we get."

"Folks!" Sam called out. "There is one thing we haven't discussed yet, and that is how we are going to pay for all this."

Peter called out, "Since we are all going to benefit from this, maybe we should pass the hat and see what we collect!"

"Okay," Sam said. "Folks, listen, we don't have enough to last us a year, so we need supplies—all kinds of supplies—and we all will benefit from these supplies. This will be our first trip to the stores, so while we will primarily devote most of the time looking for long shelf-life foods like rice, beans, and canned foods, if the situation allows, we will have another shopping trip for clothing and other items, but first, we must make sure we can feed everyone, and that includes the animals. We will be able to harvest some items from the gardens that were planted, but that won't be for a few more months. What we planted will not feed us all, and we will be able to harvest deer or Elk as they come to the gardens, but we will need more until we can plant more next spring. If we work hard together, then Joe and James feel we will be able to feed the animals and ourselves, but we must make it to next fall. So with all this said and since all of us will benefit, Peter White will pass the hat to help offset the cost of these supplies."

After a while, Peter came to Sam and Shirley. "This is what I collected. Everyone gave something, but some didn't have much to give since their money is in banks and they relied mostly on credit cards during their travels and ATMs for cash as they needed it."

Sam, Shirley, Peter, and Betty counted the money, and it came to $2,300.

"That's not much," Betty said.

"Yes, but it's something. I think each pickup truck should have $3,000 and Peter should have $5,000 for animal feed and supplies."

Shirley looked up. "Will that be enough?" she asked. "This is our first trip out, and I think we should get as much as we can because we don't know what will be available next week."

"Okay," Sam said. "Then let's give each pickup $5,000 also." Sam stood up. "Folks, we did well. We collected enough so that each group will have up to $5,000 to spend to purchase what's on our lists. Peter, I want you and who's going with you to take the dump truck and trailer and head to Lewiston with the pickup that is going that way, and you can stay in contact with your CB radios. All of you traveling, use the same call signs that we used getting here. Who is going to Coeur D? And remember, I want either James or Joe to stay behind."

Shirley stood up and said that she wanted to take Betty with her too.

"Okay," Sam said, "but I want Ken to stay here with me."

William and Mary Rodgers asked if it would be okay if they took their children with them and went to Coeur D with Shirley and Betty so they could get more clothing for them. Sam thought for a few seconds and replied that he would like to have their son, Aaron, stay and help at the farm since there was a lot of work to do and they could use the help while they were gone. Rebecca Wolfman stood up and said that she and Ruth Monroe would like to go to Lewiston and that James Monroe would accompany Peter White to Lewiston to look for feed. She said this way, there would be three sets of eyes looking for what the farm needed.

"Okay," Sam said, "but remember, your first priority is the list you have and then anything else. Is there anything else to cover? If not, let's have a quick prayer for safe travel."

Everyone gathered in a circle and held hands as Sam led them in a quick prayer for safe travel. He told the people going to make sure they had a full tank of gas and also a spare full five-gallon can of gas and to make sure everyone had their firearms and, before they left, to see him, and he would give them the money collected. Sam and Shirley went to their house, and Sam took the extra money needed from a gun safe in the house that came from their former home in Seattle with their household items to give to the shoppers. Shirley asked for an extra two thousand, saying in case she saw something that wasn't on the list that she thought they needed. Sam and Shirley walked out of their house, and Sam gave the money to the other shoppers and wished them a safe trip, telling them to keep their eyes open and to observe what damage, if any, they saw and what was happening in the areas that they were going to. As the shoppers left, Sam walked toward the barn, looking for James, and Aaron came toward him.

"What are we going to do?" he asked.

"Well, there are a lot of things that need doing, but let's find Joseph and see what he needs done right away, and then we will see what we will do."

As they walked into the barn, Joseph was finishing feeding the pigs and climbed out of their pen.

"Joseph!" Sam called out. "What chores do you need done around the barn right now?"

"Well," Joe said, "what we need to do is to set up some sort of schedule for the barn. The cow needs to be milked twice a day, eggs gathered at least once a day but preferably twice a day, and the food and water checked for all the animals. Then we have the field work. We don't have a mower or rake for the tractor to cut grass for hay, so for now, if we had scythes, it would be time-consuming, but we could cut grass by hand for hay. Our ancestors did it, as do the Amish, so we can also. It's too late now, but next spring, we will need to plant several acres of wheat, barley, oats, and corn for animal feed, and then we will need a way to get it ground into feed for the different animals. There should be a company that comes to farms that does onsite custom grinding. We will have to find out who does this and then get that set up, but for now, I'm finished around here until around four this afternoon when the cow needs milking again. If you don't mind, I would like to take your Gator, look around at the fields, see what kind of condition they are in, and figure out a planting scheme for next year."

"Sure, no problem," Sam said, "but take a pistol and rifle with you and a radio in case of trouble."

Aaron and Sam then went looking for Ken after checking the garden area and his trailer. They went to the road block to their compound and found him there.

"Ken!" Sam called out, and a bush walked toward them.

When he got to them, Sam asked him if he would be willing to take Aaron someplace safe and teach him the basics of firearm safety and how to shoot, take one of the hand radios, and let Joseph know what they were about to do so he wouldn't worry about the shooting. Sam then headed to the checkpoint setup at the entrance to their property. He didn't think anything would happen yet, but he felt that a good example about security must be set for everyone. He was surprised that there was a rudimentary foxhole-type position there that looked like it was dug with the backhoe that was attached to the back of the tractor that they had brought from the campground. The dirt from the hole was in a pile behind the pit, and Sam thought that some logs should be cut and a roof over the pit constructed. He thought that if done right, they could have the roof elevated slightly, allowing for observation and a field of fire in all quadrants. As Sam settled in, he saw someone had brought a tall stool to sit on, and as he looked around the pit, he saw that it was really Spartan if some small logs and boards were on the floor with a scrap of rug on top. *That would be nice, and the walls, if they were reinforced with either logs or boards to keep the dirt from falling in, would also be nice.*

As the day wore on, Sam caught himself starting to doze off, so he did a slow look around, and not seeing anything, he stood up to stretch when a small fist-sized rock fell into the pit. *Grenade!* he thought and jumped out of the pit to a chuckle from behind him.

Ken was there with a shit-eating grin with Aaron beside him. "I thought I should come to relieve you."

Sam went behind a tree and relieved himself, all the while trying to regain his composure and berating Ken, telling him he could have been shot.

"No," Ken replied. "You were sound asleep. I know we have had a long day, and you didn't get any sleep last night. Joe is either in the barn or workshop. He wants to talk to you. I'll stay here with Aaron and show him the ropes of sentry duty."

"Well, since there will be two of you here, why not get the tractor and a chainsaw and make a proper bunker?" Sam then explained what he had in mind.

"Good ideas," Ken said. "Why not send Joe down with the tools after he talks to you?"

Sam slung his rifle and walked to the barn, still berating himself for falling asleep, but Ken was right. It had been a long two days, and he wasn't as young as he once was. Sam found Joe in the equipment shed, but the word *shed* was a misnomer. It was a block-and-metal building with a hard packed dirt floor. It also had an office area that had a full bath, a cement floor, and heat and could sleep two people easily.

"What's up?" Sam asked as he walked in.

"I'm looking for some chain. There are a few stumps and large rocks that need to be removed to make some of the cleared area ready for planting. If we also remove a few trees in one area, we can have another area for planting."

"Well," Sam said, "what can we plant now to be harvested this year?"

"Not much," Joe said. "It's July. If we hurry, we could get carrots, red beets, peas, beans, and a few other vegetables, and if you have any turnip seeds, the cattle will eat those, or we can. There are some fruit trees in one area that need pruning when the time comes, and if we can get a chipper, we can chip the trimmings to use to smoke meats."

"Have you had anything to eat yet today?" Sam asked Joe.

"Yes, I had some leftovers from the picnic that we were able to save and bring back with us."

"Okay then. Get the tractor a chainsaw, an ax and shovels, go to the road block, and help Ken and Aaron build a good fortification. Ken knows what is needed. I'm going to grab a bite to eat and then come down and help. I think we need to get this done now, and before the people come back from shopping, tomorrow we can start on the fields."

Sam went to his house to see what he could put together for a lunch as Joe got the tools and tractor with its bucket and backhoe and went to the end of their lane. Sam found a can of Campbell's bean-with-bacon soup and, while it was heating, found some bread and luncheon meat and made a sandwich with it. When the soup was ready, he put some saltine crackers in it and sat at the dining table to eat. It felt good to get off his feet.

After eating, Sam went to help build the bunker at the entrance to the property. When he got there, he saw that the hole was made larger. It was big enough for four or five people to be in there without bumping into one another. In fact, there was room for a cot and an area to relieve themselves when nature called. In order to get into it, you entered from the back and had to make two ninety-degree turns to get in. The pit was about five feet deep with a small log-and-board floor for when it rained and snowed. There was an eighteen-inch gap all around between the pit and roof, and the roof had a small mound to it with at least two feet of dirt on top. By cutting some pine boughs and spreading some leaves and planting tufts of grass in a few months, it would be almost impossible to see it if you didn't know it was there.

As they were finishing up, Joe looked at his watch. Wow, I must go. It's time to milk our cow."

Sam looked at Ken. "Do we need Aaron here?" he asked and gave a wink at Ken.

Ken looked at him with a puzzled look for a second. Then his face brightened with a grin. "No, I think you and I can finish up here. I think it's time Aaron found out what a cow's teat was and how to milk a cow."

Joe, Ken, and Sam enjoyed Aaron being embarrassed and sent him with Joe to milk their only dairy cow. Sam thought that they would have to find a bull at some time and get her breed. Ken and Sam finished up and headed back to the toolshed as Joe and Aaron came out of the barn with a bucket of milk.

"Well, how did he do?" Ken called out.

Aaron's face turned beet red, and Joe said, "Once he found out he wasn't hurting her, he started doing all right."

They fed the rest of the animals for the night.

"They should be good until the morning," Sam said. "I would like Aaron to pull some guard duty but right now not by himself. So if one of you want to go with him, then you can get a little sleep, but have him wake you if anything happens."

Ken said he would do it, and Sam said he would be down in about two hours to replace them.

"And, Joe, get some sleep and relieve me in about four or five hours."

Sam went into his new house and took his shoes off for the first time in over twenty-four hours. He set an alarm clock and lay down on the couch. The alarm clock was ringing. It felt as if he had just fallen asleep. He went to the bedroom for a fresh pair of socks, went into the kitchen, and poured a cup of cold coffee to drink. Shirley didn't know how he could drink cold coffee. For her, coffee had to be piping hot.

Sam would tell her, "You get used to things like cold coffee, and someday you would be glad to even have that." Sam remembered many nights of putting the cocoa pack, instant coffee, creamer pack, and sugar packet from a box of C rations into a canteen cup then some hot water to get him through a cold night.

As Sam laced his shoes, he thought, *What have we gotten into?* He grabbed his rifle and, slinging it over his shoulder, went to the checkpoint. As he got closer, he walked so that whoever was on guard would see him. He thought that maybe they should have a set of challenge words and procedure so no one got accidently shot. As he entered the bunker, he called out so they knew he was coming in. He saw that Aaron was awake but a little sleepy and that Ken was sound asleep in a corner. Sam kicked his foot, and Ken was instantly awake.

"Just like old times," Ken said.

"Yeah," Sam said, "just like old times. Anything happening?" Sam looked at Aaron.

"No, just a few local people driving down by the road, but none came this way." "I know it's boring sitting here," Sam said, "but this is good information on what traffic goes by down by the road."

Sam looked at Ken, and Ken said, "He'll do okay for now."

"Good," Sam said, "The shoppers should be getting here in a few hours, so why don't you guys get something to eat and some more sleep? I'll hang out here for a while."

Sam settled in, looking around the surrounding area for different landmarks, possible firing positions of an attacking force, and the different sounds of the forest—the bird calls and the squirrels hunting nuts or whatever squirrels hunted in the leaves. Sam saw Joe coming down the road and then heard a low whistle. Sam gave a low whistle back, and Joe came into the bunker.

"Not bad," he said.

"Yeah," Sam said. "It'll do, and a few odds and ends, and this will be really comfortable."

"How are you feeling?" Joe asked.

"I'm a little tired," Sam replied. "I'm no longer used to twenty-four-hour or forty-eight-hour days. I must be getting old."

"Go get some sleep. I'll be okay."

"Good. When they get back from the shopping trip, we can find out how things are outside of our area and then decide what level of security we will need."

Shirley quietly opened the door to her new home and saw Sam lying on the couch in their living room with a blanket over him, sound asleep. She quietly went over to him and started to tickle him under his nose. Sam made two swats at his nose before his eyes opened and sat up.

"Good, you're back. What time is it?" Sam asked.

"It's 9:00 p.m.," Shirley replied.

"Nine," Sam said. "I would have thought that the people we had sent South to Lewiston would have been here by now. This has me worried." Sam got up, gave Shirley a kiss, and then put his shoes on, putting his sidearm on his waist. "Let's go and unload your supplies."

"I'll be right out," Shirley said, as she went to the bathroom.

Sam saw the pickup trucks by the equipment shed and was pleased to see they were loaded to the cab roof with a tarp covering the loads.

Ken came from his trailer, looking around. "Where is Peter and the people who went to Lewiston?" he asked.

"I don't know, and I'm worried," Sam replied. "Let's get these trucks unloaded and gassed up. I want to go look for them. They should have been here by now."

Aaron came trotting up as the tarps were being untied.

Sam looked at him and said, "Go down to the bunker and have Joe come here, and you stay there on guard. I'll fill you in later as to what I want you to do."

As they were unloading the trucks into the tool/work shed, Joe came, and Sam told him he was concerned that the Lewiston group hadn't gotten back yet, and he wanted to take a group to go look for them.

"After the trucks are gassed," Sam said, "we should take some tools, jacks, tires, fuel in cans, oil, tow chains, tow straps, tie-down straps, and coolant."

As those items were being loaded, Sam told Shirley to organize the rest of the people and, until they got back, to set up defensive positions around the compound and have one person monitor CB channel 7. "I know the range won't be far, but when we get in range, we would be able to let you guys know what's happening so you won't be worrying any longer than you need to."

Ken came up. "Boss," he said, "we have two trucks ready. If it's okay, Betty and I will take the lead, and you and Joe can follow about two hundred yards behind."

"Okay," Sam said, "and let's be on CB channel 8, and we all have our weapons and spare magazines for them. Let's bring a lot of ammo since we don't know what we will be getting into."

Ken said, "Wait a minute," and took off at a trot with his weapon at port arms.

In a few minutes, Sam saw him coming back with a small satchel slung over his shoulder.

"Okay, boss. Let's go."

As they went past the bunker, Sam stopped and filled Aaron in on what was happening and told him not to get too trigger happy. They left and went through Onaway and Potlatch and headed south on U.S. 95. It was dark, so they weren't going really fast, and also, they didn't know what was in front of them. After about fifty miles of driving, Ken and Betty stopped, and Sam stopped also. They called on the radio that they see the dump truck pulled off the road on a wide turnout and that they would drive past it and then come up from the rear. They watched as Ken and Betty went past the dump truck and then turned around. As they approached from the rear, Sam's group approached from the front. Sam stopped about a hundred feet from the front of the truck. Ken and Betty stopped a hundred feet from the rear. Sam had Joe get out on the passenger side and to cover him as he got out of the left side. Sam was thankful that he had the presence of mind to remove the light bulb from the truck's courtesy light so it wouldn't come on when either door was opened. He quickly got out and scurried behind the pickup.

"What now?" Joe said.

Sam looked at him and then called out, "Peter, James! It's Sam and Joe! Are you around?"

***

As Farhad turned into the driveway of a nondescript house by Lake Coeur d'Alene, the house was like many others along the lake, a two-story frame house with an attached three-car garage. It had a solid six-foot-high wood fence across the front of the property and a driveway that, after turning off the street, made a slight curve so people were not able to completely see into the property. Best of all was the garage, and as he approached the attached garage of the house, the garage door opened for him. Farhad entered the three-car garage. There were two other vans already in there. He turned off the engine and slowly got out of the driver's seat of the van. He was met by several members of other cells. All of them were in good spirits as they gathered around him. One of them opened the side door of his van and, not seeing any others, turned to look at Farhad. Seeing his head bowed, he knew that for his cell, the attack didn't go well.

Farook Al-Sabib entered the garage from the house and, seeing the garage door still opened, called out to close the door so the infidels wouldn't see them. He looked at Farhad, motioned for him to enter the house, and then told the rest to give him and Farhad some time alone.

Farook put his right arm out, saying, "Come, my brother. Tell me of your adventure."

Farhad went with Farook into the kitchen.

"Please sit down. Would you like a coffee or tea?" Farook asked.

"Yes, tea please," Farhad replied as he sat at the kitchen table.

"Tell me," Farook said as he brought a cup of tea to the table, "how did your project go?"

Farhad bowed his head and clasped his hands in front of him on the table as he gathered his thoughts. Looking up, he started his narrative. "At first, everything in our plan went as we had practiced. We got into our positions and were ready to attack. But when the time came to attack, there was a small group of infidels who were alert and were armed. We did manage to cause many casualties. There were many dead and many more injured, but the Americans were able to kill all our brothers and sisters. I felt it best not to reveal myself since the Americans seemed to be organized in their defense, and I still had the rest of the plan to carry out but now I was alone. I did manage to destroy the electrical transformers for the area and their communication center for the area. But I feel I failed by not bringing any of my team back." Looking at Farook, Farhad asked, "How did the rest of the plan go?"

"Our grand plan had some great successes and failures," Farook replied. "From what I have been able to learn, many of the cells were either captured or killed or failed in one way or another to carry out their mission. Our goal of crippling the Americans did not happen as we had planned, so now we will resort to an alternate plan that was developed for this reason."

***

Peter raised his head and looked around, and then Sam saw James's head pop up.

Sam called out again, "Peter, it's Sam and Joe! Are you okay?"

Peter waved out of the truck's window.

Sam turned to Joe. "Keep an eye on the area and me. I'm going up to the truck."

As Sam was approaching the truck, the driver's door opened, and Peter came out and walked to the back of the truck. He was there only a minute or two and then came forward, zipping his pants to meet Sam.

"Is there a problem?" Sam asked.

"No, The reason I stopped is that I hadn't had much sleep, and for me to continue, I was afraid I would fall asleep and have an accident, and I didn't want to jeopardize all this stuff."

"Weren't you worried that someone would steal what you have on the truck?"

"No. Why should they? Even though there is some damage, it's business as normal in Lewiston. Many places are running off generators, and some people were injured, but their casualties were not as bad as we had suffered."

As they were talking, Sam saw Ken and Betty. He waved them up front and explained to them that they had stopped because they were too tired to continue driving safely.

"Peter, where are Rebecca and Ruth?"

"They also pulled over a few miles back for some sleep."

"Well, how are you feeling now?" Sam asked.

"I'm good. I feel I can make it to the farm."

"Good. We will go and try to find Rebecca and Ruth, and then we will be back to the farm. When you get there, let everyone know that there isn't a problem and that we will be in soon." Sam looked at Joe, Ken, and Betty. "Let's go find the other sleeping beauties and get everyone back to the farm."

Sam and Joe headed to their vehicle as Ken and Betty headed to theirs. When Ken and Betty got into their vehicle, Sam called them on the CB radio, telling them they would continue south in tactical mode and do the same procedure when they came across Rebecca and Ruth.

After about eight miles, the CB radio came to life. "Scorpion 6, Lead, we have them in sight. Passing them now. We will turn around and cover from the rear."

"Roger," Sam replied, and Joe slowed down.

As Sam and Joe approached the front of the pickup truck Rebecca and Ruth were in, they put their headlights on high beam and tooted their horn. Rebecca and Ruth both popped up and put their hands over their faces and let out a scream. It was then that they realized that they were parked, and so was the vehicle in front of them, and no one was going to be killed in a head-on collision. Not knowing what was happening, Rebecca and Ruth pulled out pistols and got out of the truck, hiding behind their doors with their pistols, pointing toward the bright lights. It was then that they heard Sam calling their names. Ruth was still angry at what they had done, making them think that they were going to have an accident, that she fired off a round from her pistol just to scare them and make them duck their heads. The lights went out on Sam's truck.

He called out, "Don't shoot! It's Sam and Joe! Don't shoot!"

Rebecca heard someone from behind say, "It serves them right for scaring you." She turned to see Ken and Betty standing behind them with big grins on their faces.

Sam came up. "Sorry for scaring you ladies. Did you get enough sleep to get to the farm?"

Rebecca looked at Sam and said, "After the stunt you just pulled, I'll be awake for several days."

"Okay then. Let's get this show on the road. Rebecca, you lead off, and we will follow."

"Not until I go into the woods for a minute," Rebecca replied.

"I'm going with you," Ruth chimed in. "Then we will leave."

***

After a restless night and not getting much sleep, Farhad Hafeez gave up on trying to sleep and was sitting in the kitchen, drinking a cup of tea, when Farook walked into the kitchen.

"You're up early," Farook said.

"Yes," Farhad replied. "It's just that I couldn't sleep knowing that my team failed and that the whole plan failed."

"You didn't fail," Farook said, trying to reassure the young fighter. "Your plan was good and sound, but the problem that we now know is it relied on too many players. Some were bound to get caught by the authorities, and some . . . well, some didn't have the commitment for their mission. It's still too early to know how well your plan worked but, we have other resources available to us to bring the Great Satan to its knees. The Americans are so smug that they feel they are safe in their country, isolated and far away, but we are here, and we are almost large enough to teach them all about Allah's will."

***

The Situation Room was crowded with the joint chiefs of staff, along with the directors of Homeland Security, the FBI, and the CIA, the vice president, the Senate president, and the leader of the House. Many of them were talking to one another when the president walked in. They all stopped talking and came to their feet.

"Sit down," Pres. Matthew Roberts said.

There was a scraping of chairs as everyone sat down and adjusted their position at the table.

The president opened the meeting. "Gentlemen and women, yesterday the United States was attacked in a loosely coordinated effort to shut down our infrastructure, communications, electrical grid, and Interstate highway system. Homeland, what information can you give us?"

Howard Farnsworth stood up. "Mr. President, from what we know, an effort to cripple America was enacted last night and early this morning. One railroad bridge over the Mississippi River was destroyed, but rail traffic can be rerouted to other bridges. An Interstate bridge over the Mississippi was destroyed, and boat and barge traffic will be back to somewhat normal after a channel has been cleared. We estimate this should take one but or two weeks, maybe four weeks at most. The electrical grid has been severely damaged in several locations. The worst, for some reason, was in Idaho. We can get some of it cleaned up, but many of the transformers that were damaged could take up to a year to manufacture and replace. Unfortunately, there could be some areas without electrical power for several months until we can reroute power." He then sat down.

The president looked over to the FBI director. "Howard, what information do you have for me?"

Howard Trent, the FBI director, stood up. "Mr. President, so far, we have identified over fifty teams of saboteurs consisting of between five and twelve operatives on each team. To date, they are all Muslims. Some are U.S. citizens, some are here on either work, student, or tourist visas, and some came across the Southern border illegally. We suspect that there are more cells here that we don't know about yet. We are working on this issue vigorously. We should know more in a day or two. We have several terrorists in our custody and are interrogating them as we speak."

***

Sam woke up to the smell of fresh coffee being brewed and bacon frying. It took him a few seconds to clear his head, but he scrambled out of bed and hurried to the bathroom. Sam walked down the hallway of their new ranch-style home, thinking it even smelled new. As he entered the kitchen, he saw Deputy Barns sitting at the kitchen table with a cup of coffee.

Shirley came over with a cup of coffee. "Morning, sleepyhead," she said as she gave him a kiss on the cheek. "Sleep well?"

"Yeah, it was a long time since I'd gotten some good sack time. I needed it. Deputy, to what do we have the honors?"

Taking a sip of coffee, Jesse looked up. "I don't believe it has only been two days since the attack."

"Yes, two busy days. How are things going?" Sam asked.

"I received word that two more people died from their wounds, but the rest will eventually recover. Dr. Smith said it was because of you and your people that we didn't have more casualties, and your people pitching in to help treat the wounded really helped save more lives. This is the good news—if anything from this can be called good. The electrical issue will be a problem for about a month, maybe more, but some areas will be online in about a week. Fire Chief Manley and I feel that we will not need any security at the fire departments fuel point. The communication lines these days are mostly fiber optic, and to get everything back to normal should take about two weeks, maybe quicker."

"Why are you telling me all this?" Sam asked.

"Well, the sheriff and I talked, and we feel we need a larger police presence in this area. He wants me to deputize you and some of your people. It will be an unpaid position, and officially, in the books, you will be carried as auxiliary officers."

"Deputy, I feel honored and also cautious. We have an operation here that we must get up and running before winter. We need hay, straw, and feed for our animals plus food for all the people here. Also, we must be able to protect what we have here if things get worse, and trust me, I feel they will get worse." "I understand," Deputy Barns replied, "but, I think the sheriff wants a small force here like a citizen militia to call on if something like this happens again." "How soon do you need this commitment from us," Sam asked?

"Well, I could put him off for two days. Why do you ask?"

"I want to finish getting things settled here and then have a meeting with all the people," Sam replied.

Just then, Shirley came in with two plates stacked with pancakes and bacon.

"Help yourself, Deputy," Shirley said. "I have more on the stove for me."

***

It was a nondescript ship sitting at anchor just off the Port of Az Zawiyah, Libya. It was riding high out of the water since there was no cargo on it. She was 230 feet from bow to stern, and workmen with torches were working on her. Two round holes about four feet in diameter were being cut on each side about twenty feet from each other, and hydraulically operated doors were being installed to cover these holes, and when they were in place, they could not be seen as holes in the sides of the ship. Titanium ducting was being attached to these holes and connected to a large chamber. A hydraulic cradle was being mounted just below the deck of the ship that could be made to go vertical.

After all of the changes to the ship were completed, it sailed into port and started loading shipping containers onto its deck. The containers were stacked in such a way as to leave a hollow area in the center of the cargo deck. After being loaded, the ship then set sail for North Korea.

***

Shirley, Deputy Barns, and Sam were sitting at the kitchen table, drinking coffee, when there was a knocking at the side kitchen door. Sam looked up and saw Joe Wolfman and James Monroe at the door. Joe and his wife were cattle ranchers who had lost their ranch to border gangs. Before leaving their farm, they were able to load most of their cattle and horses into two cattle trailers, but in their escape, the horses were killed by gunfire by the gangs. James Monroe and his wife had lost their farm, leaving ahead of city gangs. They were able to load their animals into trailers and hay and feed onto trucks with labor provided by the people camping at Peter White's campground. Before leaving their farm, knowing that they would not be back and to keep the city gangs from having anything of value, they burned their barn and house. Sam waved them in, and Shirley got up from the table and got two more coffee cups from a rack on the wall in the kitchen.

"Come in and sit down," Sam said. "You guys know Deputy Barns. Deputy, this is Joe Wolfman and James Monroe. They are our designated animal handlers."

Joe and James shook Deputy Barns' hand and sat down as Shirley put a cup of coffee in front of both of them.

"Gentlemen," Sam said, "Deputy Barns is here to ask us a favor. The county sheriff asked Deputy Barns to set up a sheriff's posse in this area. We would be sworn in as unpaid deputies to be called on if there is a problem."

"The sheriff and I came up with this because of how your group acted during the attack on the Fourth of July," Deputy Barns said. "The sheriff and I hope to be able to rely on support from this group."

"I was telling Deputy Barns," Sam replied, "that we would be honored to do this, but our first consideration is to the support and defense of our group."

"This is why James and I are here," Joe said. "James and I have walked around the property, and there are some good hayfields here, but even with the tractor that we have, there is no way that we can harvest it, and we will need all of the hay we can get for this winter plus some silage for our milk cow. And speaking of the cow, it's soon time to get her breed, so we have to either find a bull or a veterinarian to artificially inseminate her. Then we should think about security. Ken was talking to us, and he would like to start taking people out, one or two at a time, to teach them patrolling and how to set an ambush. The bunker we built was hurriedly done and needs some more work to blend in with its surroundings."

At this point, Deputy Barns chimed in, "This is exactly what I told the sheriff, that you guys are squared away but might need some logistical help to get your operation here running. After all, you guys have been here about a week and have a lot to do."

Sam looked at Joe and James. "I told Deputy Barns to give us a few days so we can have a meeting of the group, and then he would know our decision."

Joe and James nodded, and James chimed in. "We will still have to address the feed situation for the animals. While we brought some grain feed and hay with us and we bought some more two days ago, we are still far from having enough for the winter."

Joe looked at James and then at Sam and said, "I have four steers, two range cows with calves, and three milk goats." "We brought a milk cow and some pigs and chickens from our farm," James replied.

Deputy Barns coughed, and everyone looked at him. "Folks, you have things to consider, and I have some patrolling I must do, but one other thing tomorrow. There will be some funerals for those who lost their lives at the picnic, and it would be nice if some of you came into town for this. I know you don't know any of them, but the townsfolk would appreciate it if some of you showed up. After all, it was mostly your actions that limited the carnage that befell us."

Sam looked at Joe and James, and they both agreed that they felt it would be a good thing if they sent some people into town for this.

"Okay," Sam said as he escorted Deputy Barns to the side door. "Let us know where and when, and we will be there." He waved as Deputy Barns left. Sam went back to the table and, sitting down, looked at Joe and James. "What I understand is we have a problem of not enough feed for our animals. There are three solutions—grow more feed, buy more feed, or butcher some of our animals." At the last remark, Sam saw Joe and James look shocked. "If I had my way," Sam said, "we would have more cattle, so I want you two to come up with what would be needed for thirteen months of feed for all the animals and what it would take to grow and harvest it. I would like to add five more range cows to our heard if possible. So come up with the list—land, equipment, storage, or whatever. Can you guys have it ready in about an hour? Also, what do we need to fence in a pasture for the animals?"

Sam, Joe, and James sat at the table, drinking coffee and discussing mundane things for a few more minutes, finishing their coffee, and then Joe and James left. Shirley came to the table with a cup of coffee and a pot for Sam and sat across from Sam.

"How are things going? From what I was able to hear, it doesn't sound too good."

"Well, honey, a great general once said, 'Don't take council with your fears.'"

"What does that mean?" Shirley asked.

"Just what it says—don't let your fears rule your life. I want to go to Coeur D. I feel that we are in a good position and in a little more time we will be in a great position. Do you want to come with me?"

"I would like to, but we are going to town tomorrow for the funerals. Couldn't your trip wait until after then to do what you want to do?"

"No, we need some supplies for the animals and to make fences for the cattle. Before we go, I want to talk to some people here and tell them to spread the word for a group meeting at five o'clock this evening. I'll tell them of the funerals tomorrow and see how many would like to attend. Then I will get hold of Joe and get the list I asked them to make."

***

It was a nondescript ship that sailed toward North Korea. There were spots of rust forming on the sides, and it looked like a Tramp interisland steamer, an independent ship and captain not affiliated with any major shipping company but one that took on cargo wherever it could and sometimes of questionable nature.

The ship was flying a Panamanian flag since that was the country of registration. Instead of taking the quicker route through the Suez Canal, the captain charted a course through the straits of Gibraltar and then around the tip of Africa, past the many islands of Indonesia, and then on to North Korea. Unlike those of many cargo ships, the captain was not in a hurry to get to his destination and sometimes sailing at half speed and, when possible, being well out to sea. He timed his trip to enter the port in North Korea just as the sun set.

Once the ship was tied up at the dock, there was a flurry of activity both on the dock and on the ship. The top layer of the empty cargo containers were removed, and the doors to the hidden special bay that was constructed were opened to prepare for their special cargo. A cradle with hydraulic rams to lift the cradle into a vertical position was installed. Several hours before dawn, all work stopped, and the doors were closed and containers loaded back onto the ship. All day long, some containers were either added or removed until darkness once again came to the dock.

***

Shirley came out of their home, looking for Sam. She found him in the barn talking to Joe and James. When there was a break in their conversation, Shirley broke in. "Sam, I decided to stay here today and get some women and work on the garden. Since you are getting supplies for the farm, why don't you take Joe and James with you?"

Sam looked at Joe and James. "You guys up to it?" he asked.

"Sure," Joe chimed in. "All of the barn chores will be finished until around four or five tonight, so we can go, right, James?"

"Yep," James replied. "Let me tell Ruth where I'm going, and I'll be ready."

Joe said that he wanted to tell Rebecca and that he would also be ready.

Sam was making good time going North on U.S. Route 95 toward Coeur d'Alene when Joe yelled, "Stop!"

Sam hit the brakes, and fortunately, there was no one behind them.

"Sam, back up if you can."

"What is it, Joe? Someone in trouble?"

"No. Just back up if you can."

Sam backed up, and Joe said, "Stop again."

"What is it?" Sam asked.

"Look," Joe said.

"What is it we are looking for?" James asked.

"Look there. There is a sign on a tree."

"What, a board with squiggly lines?"

"Yes," Joe said. "That is Arabic writing."

Sam put the truck back into gear and continued North. "That must be the Muslim training camp that Deputy Barns told me about," Sam said. "It's about forty-five minutes from the Potlatch cutoff or about thirty miles. On our way back, we will measure the distance with the truck's odometer and then make plans about this camp."

All the way North on U.S. 95, traffic was very light until they got closer to Coeur D. Then traffic started to get heavier. With the normal year-round residents and the summer people there for the holiday week, the streets were busy. Sam went straight to the Lowe's store, and he, Joe, and James looked for the fencing area in the store. They looked at different types and decided on a mix of wooden and barbed wire and hog fencing. They then had to decide on how much they needed. This took almost an hour to do. Once they decided on what they wanted, they searched for and found a sales person. The salesperson assured them that they could, for a slight fee, deliver what they wanted in two days.

"Wait a minute," Joe said. "We will need some other things."

"Like what?" Sam asked.

"Well, we need tools, nails, fence staples—and an electric fence would be nice."

"Okay. You, James, and I will go shopping." Sam looked at the salesman. "Can you come with us, or should we meet you and settle up all at once, and can you ship what we collect with the other supplies we ordered?"

The clerk looked a little stunned. "Yes, I'll be either in my office there or on the floor in this area."

So, for the next hour, they went around the store, loading their carts with all sorts of tools and supplies, and when they were finished, they went back to the contractor's area and found the salesman. They ran their items that they had pulled and the invoice for the other supplies through a cashier. It took almost fifteen minutes to do this since they were buying all at once tools and supplies most farms or ranches gathered over years. When the cashier was finished, Sam showed her his veteran's card for the discount Lowe's gave to military veterans. Sam felt self-conscious as he pulled his wallet out and gave the salesman his credit card for payment. Sam saw Joe and James look at each other with a surprised look. As they were walking out, Sam could feel a little tension between him and Joe and James. They were hanging back and whispering to themselves.

When the truck doors were closed, Sam said, "Okay, out with it."

"What do you mean, boss?" James asked.

Sam half-turned and gave them a stern look. "Okay, first off, I'm not your boss, all of us are in this together, kind of like a co-op. Second, yes, Shirley and I have some money, but it won't last long, We do not want this to be common knowledge, so keep quiet about it. Promise me this."

Joe and James both mumbled that they would.

"I put our purchase on my credit card since Shirley and I think there may soon be a problem and electronic sales will be a problem in the near future. I was told there is a Tractor Supply store here in town. Let's go swing by there and quickly see what they have."

As they were heading South to their farm—or compound, as they started to call it—Joe and James were discussing the high price of cattle feed at the Tractor Supply store. There had to be a cheaper way to get feed for the livestock that they had. Sam said that they would have to talk to some of the farmers and ranchers in the area and see what they did for livestock feed. Traffic was still light, and they made it back to the compound just in time for the five o'clock meeting. Sam was surprised to see a long table set up with camp chairs around it and all kinds of food on it. Everyone found a place around it, and they said grace and then started to eat.

Sam stood up. "Folks," he started, "we have a lot to think about, but first, I want to ask Shirley for a report on our garden."

Shirley got up. "The women, some children and I spent most of the day in the garden area. It wasn't too bad as far as animal damage goes, but the weeds were plentiful. We will need more hoes, rakes, hoses, sprinklers, and other garden equipment. Rebecca would like to build some raised bed gardens to grow herbs, so we will need some two-by-twelve boards and seeds. It would be nice if we could put a fence around it to keep the rabbits and maybe the deer out of it. This brings up another situation. We are running low on meat, so maybe someone could shoot a deer or two. There is enough time to plant a few more items, but we won't have enough to keep ourselves fed through the winter, so we will need to make another Costco run. It was also brought up that we should start moving out of the campers and into the house and have community meals to start having a cohesive group, and it would help to save food."

Shirley sat down, and Sam stood up.

"First thing, Deputy Barns was by, and tomorrow there will be several funerals in town. He feels that as many of us as can be spared from here should come into town. He and many of the townspeople feel it was because of us that the death toll at the Fourth of July picnic was as low as it was. He also feels that it would help us be integrated into the community. So those of you who have suits, wear them. If you do not have a suit, a shirt and tie would do. If you need a tie, I have some extras. I would like to leave here around 9:00 a.m. As you all know, Joe and James went with me to Coeur today. We went to the Lowe's store there and to Tractor Supply. The day after tomorrow, a truck from Lowe's will be here with a load of supplies that we bought. I do not know when it will be here, but it has, I hope, enough to build corrals and fences for a pasture. When it gets here, we will have to sort the tools from the fencing."

The next day most of the group went to the funerals in town. Ken and Betty Bachman, Peter White, and James and Ruth Monroe stayed behind. After the funeral, many people, some of them with bandages on them, came up to members of the group, thanking them for what they had done. Geraldine pulled Sam aside and told him that there was nothing in writing yet, but she was sure there would be an auction or two in the near future since two of the people buried were a husband and wife who owned a farm and their children lived in Wyoming and Texas. She said that she didn't expect them to come back to live here. Sam thanked her and told her to keep him informed if there would be any auctions in the area.

Around 9:00 a.m. the following day, Deputy Barns showed up leading a Lowe's flatbed truck loaded with the supplies they had bought in Coeur D. It had a Moffett forklift attached to the back of it, which made unloading very easy. Deputy Barns told Sam that there was a local farmer wanting to come by and cut the hayfields and would bale it for them. Sam thanked Deputy Barns and told him to have him come by tomorrow. The group then got busy building fences, finishing setting up the solar system for the house, and generally getting their place squared away and ready for haying season. In doing all this, they let their defense training slide.

CPSIA information can be obtained
at www.ICGtesting.com
Printed in the USA
BVHW072205040719
552614BV00006B/82/P

9 781796 041415